ChangelingPress.com

Taken by the Sorcerer/
Taken by The Lady of the Lake Duet

Paranormal Women's Fiction

Megan Slayer

I0834465

Megan Slayer Taken by the Sorcerer/
Taken by The Lady of the Lake Duet
Paranormal Women's Fiction
Megan Slayer

All rights reserved.
Copyright ©2026 Megan Slayer

ISBN: 978-1-60521-963-9

Publisher:
Changeling Press LLC
315 N. Centre St.
Martinsburg, WV 25404
ChangelingPress.com

Printed in the U.S.A.

Editor: Jean Cooper
Cover Artist: Angela Knight

The individual stories in this anthology have been previously released in E-Book format.

No part of this publication may be reproduced or shared by any electronic or mechanical means, including but not limited to reprinting, photocopying, or digital reproduction, without prior written permission from Changeling Press LLC.

This book contains sexually explicit scenes and adult language which some may find offensive and which is not appropriate for a young audience. Changeling Press books are for sale to adults, only, as defined by the laws of the country in which you made your purchase.

Table of Contents

Taken by the Sorcerer (Taken 11)
A Paranormal Women's Fiction Novel
Megan Slayer

She's never been taken seriously. He's seen as a geek. Together, they could be unstoppable.

Skylar Graves is a synth -- she can shift into anything. She's also known all around the world as a billionaire playgirl fool. Parties? She's had them. Money? Bucketloads. Brains... Well, there's the rub. No one's ever believed she had the brains to make the money. No one's ever believed in her at all.

Enter Brody -- and a reason to use those brains.

Brody isn't the best sorcerer. He knows his spells and how to create them, but he's still learning to control his magic. When he finds his perfect mate, he'll be set. But is she out there? The trouble is, he's been tasked with helping other paras find Eerie and he can't do that alone.

The moment he meets Skylar, he knows he's found his match, but the problem lies in convincing her she's more than she ever believed.

Not impossible... *right*?

Chapter One

"I *am* getting into this party." Brody Teague drove up the winding road to the gravel area at the base of the Skylar Graves property. The music blared and vibrated the ground, even this far out. He hated loud noise and didn't really want to be here, but he needed to speak to Skylar.

He just knew she was a para and could help him. He *knew* it.

Still, he couldn't hide his irritation. How did one woman have so much ridiculous wealth? This wasn't just opulence, but obnoxious opulence. He'd bet the people attending this party spent more on one pair of shoes than he did on his rent for the month.

Right now, he needed to speak to her. What would she say if she knew she was meeting a true sorcerer who wanted her help? She'd probably laugh. If she helped him, he could develop his potion to allow paras to move in regular society and also concoct the signal to help paras who didn't even know they were para to find refuge in Eerie. He knew there were more people out there who could come to the town and find a place to exist and understand their abilities, if they had the signal to get there.

He left his car and trudged the last few hundred yards up the road to the main gate. The number of cars parked every which way in his path amazed him. How were these people going to leave? They'd need choreography or a cop to help them.

Didn't matter to him. He wasn't going to be there when they left. He'd get in, give his pitch, hope for the best, and get the hell out. He walked up to the gate and admired the wrought iron. The doors swung loose, allowing him onto the property. He'd bet this gate was locked up tight any other time. He touched the iron and the chill settled in his bones. The gate was spooky, really. It looked like a cartoony alien in the middle.

Aliens… He knew they existed, but they didn't look like the Roswellian versions. They were much more like humans than the actual humans believed. But aliens were good at morphing and shifting to fit their environment.

As he walked among the people having conversations and dancing, he realized he shouldn't be there. He wasn't dressed for the occasion. He'd never seen so much purple in his life. People danced by the pool, swaying and gyrating. The men tended to be dressed in suits and tuxedos. The women wore evening gowns. The plethora of sequins caught the light. Glasses clinked and laughter rang out. The music blared even louder, and the water seemed to thrum with the beat.

Would anyone notice him? Somehow, he doubted it.

He spied the buffet of food. Every fruit and veggie possible for a tray were spread out on the table, along with a chocolate fountain and a stack of glasses, no doubt filled with champagne. He'd bet it was the most expensive bubbly, at that.

There were people at the side table with powder that might or might not be drugs. He forced himself away from that area. He'd never had a problem with drugs or wanted to try them, but didn't judge anyone who did.

He fought the urge to cover his ears. The noise bothered him. He was a scientist and sorcerer. He needed to concentrate. This place didn't allow him to do that. He could barely focus.

He scanned the various people at the party and

shook his head. She wasn't there. He'd know Skylar in a heartbeat. Then again, she was about the most beautiful woman he'd ever seen. Silky blonde hair, willowy and tall, a few curves, and kissable lips. He wanted to look into her brown eyes and get lost.

He balled his hand and gritted his teeth. Damn it. He wasn't there to drool over her. He was there to ask a question.

Brody focused on the money spent to not only throw the party, but to have this house and lifestyle. The paintings weren't photos or pictures printed on canvas, but actual works of art. Was that a Picasso? Nah. He tipped his head. Well, maybe. She had the money to buy whatever she wanted, so it was plausible.

He couldn't imagine having that much cash. He'd barely scraped by all his life. But by being poor, he'd learned how to use what he had and make it stretch to work for his needs. It taught him to be humble, too.

A woman in a blood red body-hugging gown grabbed him. "Look at you. Are you one of the dancers?" She yanked him close and kissed him right on the mouth. "You sure taste good."

He wriggled in her grasp. "I'm not a dancer." He had two left feet. "Sorry."

"Then stay with me." She tugged him across the expanse of lawn toward the pool. "She brought a few newbs. This one's right off the farm."

He managed to disengage himself from her and darted back to the safety of the bigger crowd on the veranda. Why anyone thought they had the right to force themselves on someone else was beyond him. She'd touched him without his permission. Gross.

He didn't know that woman and was sure she

wasn't a para. Hell, she'd probably slash his ass if she found out he was one. Would they turn on Skylar when they found out she was one? *If* she was one...

He rested his hands on his hips and surveyed the crowd again. If she'd used some of her money to help paras and not buy another sports car, she'd be a folk hero. There were plenty of paras who needed a hand in getting to Eerie and more who could use help in figuring out what their magic might be.

But she'd chosen to be decadent.

He moved through the people again, looking for her. Nope, she wasn't there. He'd never forget her hair or smile.

A woman with bright red hair bumped into him, but he doubted she knew he was there.

"I hear she's a para," the woman said. "I don't know how. She's so normal."

What a repulsive thing to say. He kept his back to her but continued to listen.

"Doesn't surprise me," the woman with her said. "She's a freak. I mean, how else could she have this kind of money and do absolutely nothing? It's supposed to be her father's money, but has anyone ever seen him? No. He doesn't exist. I bet she stole it or it's created money."

Judgmental much? He rolled his eyes, then resumed looking through the crowd.

"Think she really is manufacturing the money?" the first woman said.

"Nah," the other woman replied. "It's just a way for her to get attention. She's probably got a dead husband or ex that she bled dry financially."

"She is an attention-grabber."

He hated that these people who'd been invited to the party -- or maybe they'd crashed it like he had -- so openly dismissed their hostess. Like she didn't have feelings or didn't matter and wasn't a person. So rude.

Still, he wasn't so thrilled with Skylar. He wished she'd donate her money or time back to Eerie to help the para community. Paras were dying from harm coming to them via the human and outside world. Vampires were staked for being different. Faeries slaughtered for making magic. Trolls and gnomes killed for being perceived as ugly. It wasn't right.

A golden eagle soared into the space and flew right past him. The bird seemed to keep circling him.

"Go," he muttered. "I'm not dinner. Shoo." Why was this eagle focusing on him? He wobbled. Shit. Was it trained to find the crashers? Could be. He wanted to use a spell to get the fuck out of there, but he'd have to return to get his car. Goddamn it.

The bird flew around him again, then soared across the expanse and landed on the upright next to the DJ stand.

The DJ stopped the music. "And there is Skylar Graves' famous pet eagle. Who else but Skylar would have an eagle as a pet? So majestic and graceful. But watch out. She has a nasty bite! Let's give it up for Audra, her eagle!"

The crowd cheered and the eagle soared out of the way, behind the second floor of the mansion.

He groaned. What a ridiculous show of extravagance. It displayed her wealth, sure, but it was a waste of money. The bird should be in the wild or a zoo, where it could be appreciated and admired. Not stuck in a damn mansion with a woman who had more money than brains.

He snorted to himself. Good God, he was being harsh and judgmental.

"Is she here?" someone asked.

"She's having a party and doesn't care to show up," another said. "She's probably out of the country. She's never here."

"I bet we could rob this place blind and she'd never know," a third person said.

"Except she's got the best security system. This place is protected better than government vaults," another voice said. "Don't try it. This joint will scream and lock down in seconds."

Brody gritted his teeth again. She had to be there. He had no choice. People were discussing robbing her and belittling her… just like he had. Damn it.

He bowed his head. He had to think about her as a person and para, not a source of money. That's how they all saw her -- a reflection of her disposable income. She lived her life like nothing mattered. It was all a big party. She didn't command respect.

Then again, he didn't exactly command it, either. He did better behind the scenes. Let him stay in his lab with his medicines and potions. There he was fine. All he wanted to do was help his fellow paras.

"Excuse me." A woman tugged his arm and yanked him out of the main space and behind a curtain.

"What the?" He stared at her. He'd never seen anyone with golden brown eyes. They were transfixing. But she'd grabbed him. "What do you want?"

"You."

He couldn't look away from her. Most of her face was concealed behind a black, feathery mask. He could swear he knew her, but he couldn't place her.

"I need to speak to you." She held onto him. "Do you know Skylar?"

"No." He hadn't met her yet, face-to-face. "Is she

in trouble? Or do you want to hurt her?" He wasn't sure why he'd asked that. "I'm sorry." No, he wasn't. He didn't want anyone to be hurt. He didn't know her, but he didn't want anything to happen to Skylar. "Who are you?"

"A friend."

"Of whom?"

"Both of you," she said. "You want to speak to Skylar, don't you?"

"Yes." She'd figured that part out, not that he knew how.

"Do *you* want to hurt her?" she asked. "Why do you want to find her? Are you her friend?"

"I haven't been introduced, but I'd like to meet her. I'd like to be her friend."

"I see. You're trying to sell something?" she asked.

"No."

"Trying to con her into giving you something?"

"Maybe?" He frowned. "If you know her, then this is what I'm trying to do. I know she's para. I am, too. I want her to come to Eerie and help me make a potion to help other paras understand who they are, and create a means to get the paras who are out in the larger world to Eerie to be safe, or feel safe to be in the wider world." He'd said too much, but he had to. He wanted everyone to understand that the paras weren't bad, and it wasn't a terrible thing to have them around. Not all paras wanted to hurt humans.

"You've got quite a job ahead of you." She cocked her head. "Are you sure she wants to be used that way?"

"I don't want to use her. I want to collaborate with her. I can't explain why, but I have a gut feeling she knows how to help. She's the missing piece."

She nodded slowly and held her cloak tighter around her body. “Good, then. I’ll hook you up with her. She’s eager to meet you, but I don’t see why. You don’t appear to be anyone spectacular.”

Ouch. He thought he was boring, but to hear her say he wasn’t exciting kind of hurt. He paused a moment before he spoke. “Wait. She knows who I am?” That seemed odd. He’d never met her, but she knew him?

“She does.”

“Do I know her?” He must, right? “Have I met her without realizing it?”

“No, you haven’t seen her, but she’s seen you.” She dipped her head once. “Bet you didn’t know that.”

Well, boogers. “No, I didn’t know that, but I would like to meet her.”

“You need to see her, then.”

“Yes.” It wasn’t a terrible reason, but was she going to convey it to Skylar? “Will you help me?”

“Yes. Be sure to be back at this tent in half an hour,” she said. She disappeared without another word or giving him a chance to reply.

He stared at the void where she’d been, and words escaped him. He didn’t have anyone to speak to, but still. She’d taken his thoughts and left him confused. Skylar was going to meet with him, but he wasn’t sure what to look for. He knew what she looked like. How could he forget her? She was gorgeous. But he felt suddenly unworthy.

He remained behind the curtain. He should be shocked that she knew him or at least she’d seen him, but he wasn’t. She was probably a lot smarter and savvier than she’d been given credit for. She had to be more than she portrayed. It just took the right person to understand her. To give her recognition for what she'd accomplished.

He looked forward to meeting the famous Skylar Graves.

She could be brilliant or playing him for a fool. He massaged the spot between his eyebrows. For all he knew, she wasn't ready to see him for a good reason. She might be about to tease him or out him for being a para. He'd said too much to the mystery woman with the mask.

He'd also outed Skylar as a para. Fuck. He could've gotten her into trouble, and she might want retribution. His stomach flip-flopped. He had no idea what he'd done, but it didn't feel quite right.

He could be at the threshold of his future. Or at the beginning of a nightmare.

He wanted to melt into the space between the boards making up the deck where he stood. One day, he wanted a woman to see him for who he was -- a fallible but earnest man who just wanted to be accepted.

Maybe that's what she wanted, too -- to be accepted.

Chapter Two

Skylar left Brody alone in the tent and ducked into the house. She loved being able to shift into whatever form she wished. She could hide in a crowd or be the center of attention. She could be a snake, a leopard or her favorite, an eagle. She could see everything from the vantage point of the bird -- like Brody crashing her party.

Jesus's balls, it was so refreshing to meet someone who wasn't afraid to go after what he wanted, even if he was afraid of most everything else. The moment she'd seen him, she knew she had to speak to him. The bird was attracted to him -- and the rest of her wanted him, too.

She hoped Brody would stay in the tent. No one would bother him there, since he didn't look like he belonged in the crowd. He wasn't dressed to kill or like he was worth a million bucks. He was just... Brody. The other partygoers would see him and give him shit. At least in the tent, he could exist and be himself without being bothered. He was dorky and sweet. He was the kind of man she liked and was drawn to, even if he didn't think she should be.

That's what she liked about him. He was honest. The other people at the party were there to curry her favor or demand money. They wanted to ride her coattails. They were decked out in their finest sequins and silk, their best jewelry, and wore it all like a badge of honor.

He didn't do that. She'd bet he paid a fair price for his clothes, but probably at a thrift store or at a discount. His jeans were frayed and his shoes scuffed, but he had a scruffy aura about him that added to his adorableness.

He still looked nice, just not in the league of everyone else there. He stuck out. She couldn't believe no one had made a big deal about him or called him out for crashing the party.

He might have used magic, though. Glamoured them all so they didn't see him? Nah, she would've sensed that. She would've detected a potion or spell, too, but she didn't. She'd sensed another para in the crowd, and when she'd flown over him, she'd spotted him right away. It'd been so long since she'd come across another para, it almost seemed impossible that he'd found her.

Now that she'd met him, she liked him because he had pluck.

Was he there to be a troublemaker? Didn't seem like it. He'd come right out and told her what he wanted from her. Other than pushing his plea to have her assistance, she got the impression he didn't even want to be there.

It was so nice. He hadn't fawned over her or given a load of fake praise to win her over. Not that he knew she was the one he wanted to speak to. He'd simply let her know what he wanted and why he'd sought her out -- he'd sensed the para within her and wanted to collaborate with her.

She liked that. He was more of a kindred spirit with her. A fighter. He didn't seem to be a showboat, and she appreciated that. She wanted to be taken seriously. Working with him had the potential to do that.

But what would he do if he found out she was a synth? That she could shift into anything? Her fans and the sycophants around her thought the eagle was her pet. They had no idea.

But before she could talk to him, she had to

pander to her audience and play up her dumb blonde persona.

She shrugged out of her cloak and fluffed her hair. No one had ever asked her to use her brains. Her money wasn't from her father. She'd figured out how to invest the dollars she'd created to make even more in a legitimate way. Someone had created the story that she'd inherited her money from her father, and she hadn't bothered to correct them.

She'd always been in charge of her own destiny, just not the narrative.

She checked her makeup in the mirror, then smoothed her dress. If she'd been given a preference, she might have rocked a T-shirt and sport coat with jeans and loafers. The dress and blowout were too much. She wasn't comfortable in her own skin. No one saw her for her brains -- just her curves and her tits.

She smoothed the dress again and her assistant, Prince, joined her in the smaller room.

"You look fantastic," he said. "Simply gorgeous, but you're always on point."

She clicked her tongue. He didn't know she was a para and could make herself as pretty or scary as she liked. "What would you say to me if you saw me and I wasn't rich? If I wasn't dressed like I'm wealthy and I wasn't done up in all this makeup."

"What?" Prince shook his head. "I don't get what you mean."

"If I weren't obscenely wealthy, would you still talk to me?" she asked. It was a simple question.

"Did you go broke?" He paled. "Do you need help?"

"What if I did go broke?" She hadn't, but the way he reacted told her everything she wanted to know.

"I'd have to find another job, first of all. I need a paycheck," Prince said. "No offense, but I have student loans to pay and a car that needs a new muffler."

"I noticed." She swore everyone heard him when he drove up to the property. "Is it still leaking oil?"

"No." He blushed. "Okay, maybe a little, but I've been putting that drying stuff down to mop it up."

"You mean the little piles of faux cat litter that are all over?" She'd grown tired of them being in her driveway.

"Sorry. I'll ensure they're cleaned up tomorrow." He pulled out his phone and made a note.

"Would you kiss my ass if I wasn't rich and paying you?" she asked.

"First, I need that paycheck, but second, I don't know if we'd be in the same social circles if you weren't. We run in a very specific crowd, honey." He stared at her for a moment. "You're testing me, aren't you?"

She wanted to roll her eyes but refrained.

"I would so talk to you, and we'd be best friends."

And there was the answer she'd expected. He was just as much of an ass-kisser as the rest of them. "You'd pander to me? I hate when people do that." She narrowed her eyes. "What if you found out I have a brain?"

"You're not just a body." He shrugged. "Everyone knows that."

"I'm not, but I'm also not a piggy bank, either."

"Ouch." He grasped his chest and whimpered. "I'm hit. I'm hurt. Do you doubt my devotion?"

"Yes." She wasn't mincing words any longer. "I believe you say what you think will curry my favor. It's not always the truth."

"I..." Prince's eyes widened. "At least you're smart. You could be one of those freaks. You've got money and brains, but you're not one of those..."

Her frown deepened and she narrowed her eyes. "A what? What freaks?" He'd piqued her curiosity and anger. If he was saying what she thought he was, she wasn't a freak and didn't appreciate being referred to as such.

"The paranormals that are rumored to exist," Prince said, spitting out the words. "They're dangerous. You can't trust them."

"Why?"

"They want to kill the rest of us, and they're delusional. They think they're something they're not. One guy thought he was a bird and could fly, then jumped off a building and became street pizza. Another one claimed to be a vampire and killed unsuspecting women who wanted a walk on the wild side. I'm sorry, but that guy was a serial killer pretending to be something else. And the rest of them... They're under the misguided notion they've got abilities. They don't. They're no better than the rest of us, and they're dangerous."

"Us?" She didn't like his tone or description.

"Humans." Prince fluffed her hair. "We know the score. We're not trying to be something we're not. We're just ourselves and that's important. You're a beautiful woman who throws the best, most lavish parties. I'm your loyal assistant who helps to make you look even better. We're adjusted and smart. We're not crazy. By the way, where did you put your eagle? Isn't it time to feed her? I checked the cage and she's not there."

What a great way to change the subject. He'd stepped into it up to his eyeballs. "She's upstairs in my private suite. She was overly stressed and needed the calm, quiet, mellow space up there. She'll be fine."

No, you fool. You're staring at her. She's one of the freaks you just insulted. No wonder Brody wanted to help the paras. If they were treated the way she just had been, then they had to be scared. Prince couldn't be the only one calling them names and believing they were less than everyone else. What a load of horseshit.

"One day, you'll let me in that suite," Prince said. "You'll finally really trust me, and it'll make my heart happy."

Yeah, no. She'd allowed Prince to handle her schedule, her appointments, and drive her around, as well as dress her from time to time, but he never touched her money or her private suite. The only way to make money and keep it was to keep it to herself. Sure, she could spend it on whomever she wanted, but she always had the checkbook firmly in her own hand. Her suite and bedroom were her inner sanctum, and no one went in there. Not boyfriends, not lovers, not even her best friends. She'd learned long ago not to trust anyone. Prince proved why her mentality was spot on.

"But you're not broke, right?" Prince asked. "Not having financial hardship?"

"No. Quite the contrary. The money's doing very well." She flipped a lock of her hair over her shoulder. "I need to meet my audience. It's time to make some magic -- real, not the para bullshit as you referenced. Everything here is completely real."

"And dazzling." He yanked the curtain aside. "Showtime."

She forced a smile. Until she got to talk to Brody, she'd have to put on her facade. It was her armor. A way to protect her money, but more so her heart. If no one got close to her, then no one could hurt or exploit her. No one would know she was a synth and part alien. No one could make fun of her for being different in all her iterations.

They saw the money and glamour. They wanted to be like her, be friends with her… or better yet, be one of her hangers-on so they could have what she had, by extension. It was all so tiring.

Just once, she wanted to be applauded for her brains. She'd been the one to make the money. If she'd told everyone that instead of letting the lie grow, then she wouldn't have one of her problems, but the rest? It wasn't time to let anyone else in on her secret.

Except Brody.

He'd figured her out. He'd known right away, and that bugged her. Was she that obvious to those who weren't human? Did she give off a vibe? Or was it something simpler? Had he felt the presence of magic and was drawn to it? She wished she knew.

Could he want her for what she could do with her mind and wits? Or just her body? He seemed genuine, but she'd been fooled before. Good thing she hadn't revealed her secret that time.

But Brody revealed it for her, yet he kept it private. She couldn't put her finger on why that both bothered and intrigued her.

She waved to the crowd, then stepped into the middle of the dancers and moved with them. This was part of the facade. Pretend to be like them so they didn't see her differences. She allowed a tall man in a burgundy tuxedo to capture her in a box step before twirling away to another man in a black suit. Neither of them drew out any animalistic desire to be with them. Sure, they were handsome, but almost too perfect. She didn't want the uber-polished look. She needed reality.

The music played and she moved along with it, but a sense of emptiness hit. It always did at about this time of night. These people didn't care if she showed up. All they wanted were the freebies -- free food, drinks, place to party, and ability to score illegal things. She wasn't into drugs and didn't appreciate them in action around her, but she'd built up this image of a woman who did as she pleased and didn't care who she hurt in the process. She could be as bold as she liked. They didn't like it? Tough shit.

She spied Brody by the tent. He'd strayed outside, but not far from the safety of the structure. Good. She didn't want him to be tainted by the over-the-top displays of wealth and grandiosity. She liked him simple and sweet.

"There's my girl." Derrence Tule captured her in his arms. "Is tonight the night I get to be with the beautiful Skylar? To feel her coltish legs wrapped around me and hear her cry out when I make love to her?"

She'd been rumored in the papers to be having an affair with Derrence, not that she'd ever sleep with him. She was barely friends with him, let alone had allowed him into her bed. Seeing them together was good for the papers and kept up the overall story that she was untouchable. She held onto his shoulders and kept space between his body and hers.

"Come on," he said and yanked her close. "You know you want me. Everyone knows you want me. You're trying so hard to resist because it's keeping the chase alive, but we both know where this ends -- you naked with me and riding my cock until you scream my name."

She admired his total focus on himself. His cock,

his name, her on him, him in charge… It was all so tiring.

"So? What do you say?" he asked. He patted her ass. "Coming home with me?"

"Why would I do that?" She removed his hand from her backside. "I love the chase. It keeps things fresh and entanglements non-existent. Can't lust after what you've already had, and you don't have me."

"I will."

She glanced over at Brody. "Not so fast."

Not if she had the opportunity to find a connection with someone else first.

And Brody could just be that one.

Chapter Three

Brody watched the dancers and felt his nerves fray. He wasn't big on dancing or mingling, especially with people he didn't know. It required him to be too social.

He couldn't look away from Skylar, though, once she'd made her grand entrance. She had a presence. A definite something that required his attention. He tried not to gawk at her, but she quietly demanded his focus. He watched her interact with various men and women in the crowd. She moved about with them with ease. Like she'd always been in this world. Maybe she had. He didn't know her life story. It wasn't his business. But she certainly knew how to talk to them, always with a smile and a few moments of her time. She made them feel important, even if only for a minute or two.

A man with dashing good looks and a certain aura about him swept her into his arms. Brody wasn't the type to step in on a couple and be brash, but something about the way she struggled and how the man had practically captured Skylar bothered Brody.

Was it jealousy? He should be the man with her.

No. He watched her for another moment and understood exactly why he was bothered. This man was a predator. She might be able to hold her own, but she shouldn't have to do that against this man. She should be able to walk away if she chose.

Brody darted through the crowd and slipped his hand across her back. "There you are, my love."

She stared at Brody for a split second, then melted into his one-armed embrace. "I knew you'd find me." She cuddled up to him. "Where were you?"

"On a food delivery run," the suave man broke in. "I hope you got a decent tip to buy yourself some better clothes," he continued. "You look awful. Didn't you realize this was a ball? You don't show up to a gala event in a damn pair of jeans."

"Uncool." She crinkled her nose at the man, then turned her attention to Brody. "I'm just glad you're here. Since you've saved my ass, this is Derrence Tule. Derrence, this is Brody. We've been together for years, which is why I won't date you. Sorry."

"No, you're not." Derrence curled his lip in a sneer. "You'll get tired of him and come looking for me. When you do, I'll be waiting."

"Right." She didn't look at Derrence, but rather kept her focus on Brody, sending a shiver up Brody's spine. "I'm glad you're here."

"Me, too." Brody rubbed her shoulder. He had no hold over her, but he had to sell the lie that they were together. "Do you want to dance?"

"Yes." She kept her back to Derrence and embraced Brody.

He swayed with her and moved away from the predator.

She didn't speak for a long moment and held onto him. She caressed Brody's shoulder and a lazy smile curled on her lips.

He couldn't read her expression. Was she happy or pretending and annoyed? She'd done a good job of faking it before. He didn't want to be the latest victim of her facade.

"Thank you." She danced with him toward the tent. "Derrence is a terrible man."

"You know him, I see. You've dated him?" It wasn't his to know, but he believed she deserved someone better than Derrence.

"Unfortunately, I know him. Never dated him. He wants nothing more than us to be a couple, but I can't do it." She shook her head. "He makes me queasy."

"I see why." He kept dancing with her. "I'm sorry he keeps pushing you, though. I assume, then, it was a good thing I stepped in so you didn't have to be with him any longer."

"Yes, you're a lifesaver." She grinned. "He chases me, and I do my best to dodge him. He pushes and wants his name to be dropped in the tabloids so people notice him. That's all he wants. To ride my coattails and get press so he can be given credibility."

"Whoever is with you gets attention, I see. I don't like it. It's not fair, but I understand." He groaned. "It's not natural. You should be able to choose who you want to be with, not have him pushed onto you."

"You're very astute." She toyed with the hairs at the base of his skull. "But *you* want my attention, and you *did* just push right in. Are you looking for press, or something else?"

"I don't want press." He shook his head. Good God. "I'd prefer as little attention as possible. I live in the --"

"Shadows?" she asked, interrupting him "Gonna use that line? It's been used a lot."

"No." The tips of his ears burned. "I was going to say the lab."

She tensed. "Lab?"

"Yes."

"Are you going to do experiments on me?" She stopped and held her ground. "I'm not going to be anyone's fucking experiment."

"No." He shook his head again and fought to find the right words. "I don't want to experiment on anyone."

"You're in medicine?" she asked, relaxing just a

bit. "Or testing?" Her brows furrowed.

"Testing, but not on animals or beings." How could he explain this in a way she could understand, but without outing them? "I want to help people and could use someone to partner with... To put our heads together to make the problem better. To fix it."

She brightened and resumed toying with his hair. "Good to know."

It wasn't the right time to discuss the rest. "I strive to be ethical."

She laughed. "We should go somewhere to talk. Sounds like you've got a lot to say."

"Not here?" He'd prefer to get the hell out of the pressure cooker of the party.

"Nah, there are too many ears here." She guided him to the tent. "I did ask you to meet me here in half an hour."

"Has it been that long?"

"I don't know, but we've found each other, so it's fine." She let go of him and yanked aside the curtains shielding them from the rest of the party.

"Is this better?" He would've preferred to keep holding her. She felt good in his arms. Sure, this had to be a result of him not having a date in what seemed like forever, but he felt like there was a connection between them. Right now, he needed to show her that he didn't want anything from her outside of her help.

"Not really." She nodded to the other side of the tent. "There are still listening ears all over. So... we're getting out of here."

"Why would we leave? This is your house." Wouldn't she want to go to a quieter part of the property? Maybe an underground room or a balcony spot? There had to be places to have some peace. "We could go upstairs? Or somewhere else in the house?"

He didn't understand.

"Hold up." She waved her fingers. "Technically, this is my house, yes, but it's staged. All that stuff inside and out there is fake. You don't think I'd actually have a real Picasso where anyone could touch it, do you? They're props."

That made so much more sense. "If a rowdy partygoer decides to do something foolish, like spilling champagne on the painting, then it's not actually being ruined."

"Exactly. I've had three of the statues knocked over and the Picasso drawn on. Yeah, they put moustaches on the figures. I replace the art and they think I've got so much money I can just buy another. You can't buy another Picasso. You can't just make this shit up, but that's what I've done. It's all fucking fake."

"Sounds like you're smarter than they realize. That's the safest way to prevent the stuff from getting trashed -- not having the real thing here."

She touched the end of her nose. "You catch on pretty quick. All the real pieces are locked up and vaulted where they can't be touched."

"Seems a waste, though. You should be able to admire what you have." At least it seemed that way to him.

"I can see them when I want, but this way they aren't at risk." She snapped her fingers. "Did you drive? Or were you dropped off?"

"Drove. I'm down the hill on the gravel plateau." He marveled at her intelligence and ingenuity.

"Then you and I need to go over there." She snapped her fingers again, then waved her hand. As she did, she opened a portal right to his car. "Go."

She had some serious magic if she could do such a thing. "Yes, ma'am."

"I'm not that freaking old." She shoved him through the opening, then hurried after him and closed the portal "Now we can actually talk."

"I thought we were." He stood in the dark with her. "No one will interrupt us out here?"

"Nope." She stared at him in the blossoming moonlight. "I know what's going on up there, but down here, there's no one for miles."

"Yards, but sure." He hesitated a moment. "Do you want to go for a drive?"

"I'd love to." She smiled and the growing moonbeams glinted off her hair. Her eyes sparkled and heat radiated from her.

He jumped into action and opened the passenger door for her. "It's a shabby car, but it's clean. Just old."

"That's okay." She caressed his jaw as she inched past him. "Thank you."

"You're welcome." He couldn't move. Not because she'd used magic on him; he was dumbstruck from the electricity that had come from her fingertips.

"Do you mind if I change?" she asked. "I hate wearing dresses like this. Too constricting."

He stood in front of the car and frowned. "Here?" She didn't have a bag with her. What was she going to change into? Besides, he should give her privacy. "Uh… Do you need to go back and get something to wear?"

"Nope." She shivered, then stretched and shifted from the dazzling blonde in the black sequined evening gown to more of a college co-ed look in a pair of jeans, loafers, a T-shirt, and sportscoat with her hair in a ponytail. The thick evening-wear-appropriate makeup was replaced with something more natural. "That's better."

He hurried around the car and sank behind the

wheel. He stared at her. The fresh-faced appearance was better. It showcased more of her beauty -- if that was even her true form. He understood exactly what she was and admired her skill. "Now I get it. You're a synth. That's how you have the magic."

"Is that bad?" she asked, her words clipped.

"Nope," he said, parroting her. Not bad at all. Quite fascinating and beautiful, really.

"Is this what you needed to see? Is it what you needed to know to exploit me?" Her words were harsh and guarded.

No wonder. She'd probably been used by others. "No." He admired her. "I don't play that way."

"You don't?"

"Nope."

"You're not shocked by the change?" she asked. She continued to narrow her eyes. "You're not seeing all these possibilities to make yourself a mint on my back?"

"No." He shook his head and swept his gaze over her. "I could sense the magic in you." If he had to be honest, he appreciated her ability. Her synth powers gave her the unique perspective from being able to go anywhere and be anyone, but only if she wanted. If she chose to. She could move about in public as a hundred different people, if she desired, and collect all sorts of information. She could be a powerful spy -- if she wasn't captured.

He rested his forehead on the steering wheel as realization hit hard. Now it all made sense.

"What?" She tensed. "What are you thinking? I know damn well this is a leap of faith to be out here with you. I don't know you other than what I observed when I spoke to you earlier. I've put a lot of trust in you that you, a fellow para, won't do me dirty. Tell me what you're thinking," she demanded.

"You're afraid."

"What?" Her voice cracked. "Excuse me?"

He had to salvage the situation. He'd unintentionally stepped in it up to his eyeballs. "You've created this whole charade, pretending to be a ditz and a social climber because once people find out who and what you are, what you can do, they'll exploit you," he said. "You're brilliant and calculated, but running scared. Once you're discovered, you'll be expected to do what they want. Dance for them. This act lets you run the show and control them."

She stared at him and her lips parted. She said nothing but paled.

"I wasn't supposed to figure that out, was I?" he asked. "I'm one of you. I'm not a synth and don't have a special power -- I can't shift into anything or drink blood or anything like that. I have magic. I create potions and medicines. I weave spells to help other paras. I want the paras to have safe spaces. I want them to feel empowered to be themselves, not killed for their differences or used for their abilities in ways they can't handle."

She balled her hands on her lap but still hadn't spoken.

"I don't want to use you. I'd like to collaborate with you, though, but not as a form of control. I need your brains and insight on how to help paras get to Eerie and save them from the outside world." He offered his hand. "It's a huge leap and probably frightening. I get that. I don't like to leave the lab because the world around me can be scary as fuck. I risk being killed every time I leave Eerie. Is someone going to think I'm a vampire? Something else? Will they kill me to have the bounty and glory of hurting a para? I don't understand the fame for doing so. We're individuals and should be allowed to live."

She nodded slowly. "How old are you?"

"Me?" He hadn't been asked that in forever. "Forty in human years, but my spirit has existed for centuries." He'd been in multiple bodies throughout his existence but had always had his magical abilities.

"You've seen stuff." She shifted in her seat to face him and laced her fingers together. "No wonder you're guarded. Was this a huge step, getting here? You crashed my party, although I don't know that anyone noticed."

"They noticed." He tensed. He'd been seen by plenty of people, but they probably thought he was a homeless man or delivery person, like Derrence believed.

"You stepped out of your comfort zone," she said. "Impressive."

He wouldn't have said that. "I'm just a sorcerer who is trying to make the world better for other paras." He paused. "I know it's terrifying to step outside the comfort zone, but will you assist me? Be a partner? Work with me?"

He let the words linger in the air. He hadn't even turned on the car. The future was in her hands, and he'd live with the ramifications of her choice -- he hoped.

If she answered.

Better yet, *how* she answered.

Chapter Four

Skylar stared at him and processed what he'd said. He'd seen her down to her core. He'd understood her desire to stay hidden in plain sight. He knew her act was just that -- an act. He saw the real person and hadn't blinked.

No one else had done that for her. She hadn't been honest with anyone, though, either. He'd figured her out.

He was like her.

"Is it hard to stay behind the wall for this long?" he asked. "Is it easier the more you do it?"

She chuckled, happy he'd unintentionally lessened the tension. She could talk about the charade. It was like a coat she kept right on the chair to grab at any time to get by. "It's not easier. It's just… it is. I can't really explain it. You boiled it down pretty well, though. It's a big mask I wear so I don't have to be me. I don't like being me."

"Why?" He offered his hand. "You're amazing."

"Because I'm rich?" If he said yes, she'd get right out of the car.

"No, because you're damn strong. You've figured out how to control your world and be how you want," he said. "I can't do that. I feel like I'm in the middle of a storm and being kicked around."

"Why?"

"Because I can't always make sense of the world around me." He massaged his temple. "I see people who have abilities being hurt and I can't figure out how to help them. It's a storm."

"I suppose." She accepted his hand. "You're like all the rest of us -- trying to find a place and make sense of what's going on while making it a bit better."

He caressed her hand. Whether he knew he was doing it or not, the gesture offered her much needed comfort.

"Why don't we go to Eerie?" she asked. "I've never been there and should've, but I'd suspected I'd be followed, so I stayed away." She'd heard of the town but never tried to venture there in case she'd expose it.

"The town isn't visible to those who don't have para blood." He let go of her hand and engaged the engine. "You'd have seemed to have disappeared. The town would be visible to you, but whoever followed you wouldn't see it. It'd seem to disappear around you until you vanished too."

She had to think about that one for a moment. Crazy. The town would poof. It almost made no sense. She settled in for the ride. "Wow."

"It's pretty neat," he said. "But I bet you disappearing in front of someone's eyes would make a better story."

She laughed. "Nah, they'd think it was one of my many quirks to gain attention."

"You could, if you wanted." He shrugged. "It'd be something."

"Not something the town would want." She stretched her legs. "Do you know I have no family here?"

"In the area? Or in Eerie?" He turned onto the main road. "You're truly alien, aren't you? I'm not trying to be a dick. I'm fascinated."

She didn't mind talking about herself this way with him because he wasn't going to laugh at her. She also appreciated finally getting away from the nightmare she'd created for herself.

"I'm made of stardust," she said. "I've never told

anyone about my origins before."

"No? You should… in a safe space," he said and picked up speed. "How did you get here? I mean, couldn't you go anywhere? Why here? Why Ohio?"

"In theory, I could, but I decided to come to Earth because my heart led me here." She hadn't understood why this place demanded she come here. She hadn't met any men or other beings she couldn't live without. Her heart hadn't pulled her toward anyone. Yet here she was. "I arrived and adapted. I figured out how to make money and how to get it to grow. Then I blended in and learned how to grow that cash even faster. But you can't make a few bucks without someone noticing."

"And people thinking you're smart."

"Oh no." She chortled. "They think I got it from my parents. It's not logical that I would've made it on my own. A journalist who contacted me about the instant riches said I must've inherited the money from my father. I don't know who fabricated the story -- or if they simply assumed. I did put the name Peter Graves on the initial paperwork. It was silly to lie, but no one checked." She'd never told anyone about her financial origins, either. She'd tried to keep it so quiet, but Brody was easy to talk to about such things.

He shrugged. "All paras have to adapt to the human world. How would anyone believe you could pay with gnome currency?"

"I hadn't considered that." She'd never heard of that type of currency, either. "What do you get for… gnome currency?"

"Slugs." He chuckled. "No, it buys stuff, but only among the gnomes."

She had so much to learn about the paras. "I'm glad you crashed my party."

"You are?"

"Uh-huh. I'm learning so much." She folded her hands on her lap. "It's so fascinating."

"Yeah? Wait until you meet a few of them."

"I don't know if I can hold out that long." It sounded like a great adventure. "How long until we get there?"

"About four hours. It took me most of the day to get here."

She flexed her toes in her shoes and settled in. She didn't drive much these days and tended to ride in the back of luxury cars. "Usually when I go places, my assistant drives."

"Fancy. Where we're going, there's a princess who has that unique right."

"A real one?" she asked. She'd never met royalty. Not actual royalty.

"She is."

"That's exciting." She applauded, giddy from what she'd learned so far. She didn't want to shift here or get out of the situation.

"A princess, a gargoyle, a siren, cyclops, faeries, gorgons, gnomes, trolls and all sorts of beings. Vampires, shifters who change into animals, ghost, nymphs…"

"Any synths?"

"You're it as far as I know."

"Oh."

"Doesn't mean you have to advertise. Just tell the princess or, if you visit the hall of records, you just have to speak to the historian. You can stay on the down-low if you wish. The princess likes to know what's going on and she'd want to meet you, but she's known for discretion."

"Makes sense." She crossed her ankles. Her

phone, which she'd forgotten in her coat pocket, vibrated. Part of her wished she'd left the device at the party, but the rest of her capitulated to the need to have it. She should answer the vibrating. At least see who wanted her.

"What's wrong?" Brody asked. "Everything okay?"

"My phone is buzzing." She debated getting the device out. "I don't want to answer."

"Then don't. Will someone freak out if they can't get a hold of you?"

"Maybe." She checked the phone and groaned. "It's Prince."

"Who?"

"My assistant."

"Do you need to answer? I'll be quiet."

"I'll check the thousand texts first." She swiped to retrieve the messages.

"A thousand?"

"Not really, but a bunch." She pulled up the first text.

Where R U?

Can't find U.

Did U leave?

She sighed. She should answer these, but he didn't have to be so aggravating. What if she'd met a man and gone off for a tryst? Or was in the middle of hot sex? He was too damn nosy.

She sent a reply. *Do you need me*?

She held onto the phone while she waited for the answer she knew was coming.

"Everything okay?" Brody asked, repeating himself. "I shouldn't have whisked you off like this, should I?"

"You didn't. I went voluntarily. I could've said

no, and I didn't because I wanted to come along." Her phone buzzed. There was the annoyance.

"I didn't put too much thought into this part because I didn't think you'd come along," Brody said.

"I wouldn't right away."

"I figured I'd have to plead my case."

"And you didn't. I like to do things my way." She checked the reply.

U need 2 tell me when U go. Ur fans asking about U.

The only one asking about where she'd gone was Derrence because he wanted to get into her pants and the tabloids.

Who?

"He'll drive me crazy." She put the phone down. "I hired Prince to iron my clothes and keep my shoes in order. He drives me places and keeps my appointments straight. He has no access to my wallet or security codes. I have magic protecting my safe and financial documents. If he tries something, he'll be burned alive."

"Vicious." He flexed his hands on the wheel. "Do you need to call him?"

"Maybe."

The reply arrived. *Derrence said Ur w/ a BF. Since when?*

She needed to call Prince and settle this. "Just a moment." She tapped the icon to call Prince. After four rings, he answered.

"Where are you?" Prince demanded. "You were supposed to be here. Are you hiding?"

"Yes," she said, finally getting the chance to speak. "It was too full and busy at the party, and I wasn't feeling it. I needed some peace. Is that bad?"

"No, but you need to tell me," Prince said. "I'm your assistant and I should know."

"You should, but I needed to get away. I'm fine."

Brody continued to drive and didn't look over at her. Was he trying to be polite? She appreciated it if he was.

"Derrence said you had a boyfriend. Since when?" Prince snapped. "You don't date."

"I told him those things to get away from him," she said. "He only wants my money and notoriety."

"And a reputation."

"Yes." She refused to give him anything. "I lied to get away, and bounced."

"Where to?" Prince asked. "You should have an itinerary and plan. You should have me on hand wherever you are so I can get you out of trouble because you know something will happen. Why don't you give me your coordinates and the code to the safe, and I'll come get you. We can get the hell out of there and you'll be safe."

"We?" She scoffed. "Um, I'm not giving anyone that code and my coordinates aren't your business. That's why I ran away with him."

"Who?"

"Someone I met at the party." It wasn't a lie, but it wasn't the entire truth.

"Who did you meet?"

"No one you know, but he's sweet and cute." That wasn't a lie, either.

Prince growled. "You need to be smart. The cute and sweet ones tend to be liars."

"You don't know that."

Prince tended to paint everyone with the same broad brush, and it wasn't pleasant. What if he were wrong about Brody? What if her gut, which hadn't been wrong so far, was right about Brody? Then what would Prince say?

"I do know that. You tend to attract a lot of wolves in sheep's clothing. Why? Because you're beautiful and they want something," Prince said. "You need someone who can keep them away and have your best interests at heart, especially when you're not capable of handling them."

Her blood boiled. "Not capable of… What exactly are you saying?" He'd pissed her off. He'd believed the charade, fine, but assumed he knew better. "You might be a man and might think you're smarter than I am, but you're my assistant. You should be helping me, not trying to order me around."

"No one's trying to do that," Prince said. "But you're emotional."

"And you're being sexist." She wanted to toss the damn phone out the window.

Brody continued to drive and wait patiently.

Her magic and stardust stirred within her. Her stomach lurched. The dust in her body only stirred when she was under duress or aroused. Prince hadn't turned her on, but he'd pissed her off. He'd belittled her. Would Brody do that, too?

He might be awkward in his delivery, but he hadn't been outright mean to her.

"Are you listening to me?" Prince demanded.

She laughed. "No, I'm not." She'd allowed her mind to wander and regretted it not one bit. "What did you say?"

"You move on emotions and not common sense. You need me to help you and keep you in line. Tell me where you are and I'll rescue you."

She bit back a snort. "So you can be handsomely rewarded, I gather?"

"For a woman who likes to portray herself as a wounded, sweet, lamb-like soul, who is naive and using her father's money to make her way in the world, you're being quite vicious."

"Am I?" He'd grated on her last nerve. "I made my own money. Yes, I had a startup, but I built my own empire," she snapped.

"You never told me that," Prince replied.

"You never asked."

"Well, the men you attract tend to want something and I bet the man of the hour wants something from you. Now let me know where you are so I can rescue you. I don't expect anything in return, just your friendship," Prince said. "I worry about you."

She'd come to figure out who wanted her cash or her name on a project because she'd grown good at weeding those beggars out within five minutes of meeting them. "I'm fine."

"You're not. You've been kidnapped."

"No, I haven't."

"Kidnapped and dragged away from your own party. I'm shutting this down now. I'll find you."

"No." She didn't want to be found. She wanted to stay in the shadows for a while longer.

"Sky, listen to me. I know what's best for you."

"No, thank you," she said. She glanced over at Brody. "I know what I'm doing. I'll be fine." She hung up on him and tossed the phone into the back seat of the car. She'd worried enough about everyone else. She should take care of herself. She could do this all on her own.

Except he said he'd find her.

She reached back for the phone, then powered it off and snapped the device in half.

Brody jerked. "Holy shit."

"Sorry, but I needed to do that." She tossed one half of the phone out the window. "I shouldn't litter, but I have a good reason." She waited a few miles, then chucked the rest of the phone away.

"I don't know what it was, but I'm sure you do."

She settled in her seat and flexed the muscle in her jaw. Throwing the phone away was the first step in making a change. Finding her heart, going to Eerie and doing something worthwhile.

It was about time. She wanted to do something respectable. Something noble. Something the other synths would be proud of -- finally. She could do this. She centered herself. Yeah, she could. Her heart needed the chance to beat for someone else.

Chapter Five

Brody drove the four hours to Eerie and enjoyed the conversation with Skylar. She'd turned out to be so much more than he'd expected. A great conversationalist, funny and smart. She wasn't easily dismissed -- not that he wanted to -- and hadn't backed down. He admired her ability to make money, sure, but her sheer will to survive was sexier.

Holy fuck. He saw her as sexy. He was so screwed.

"What is Eerie really like?" she asked. "I've never been there… obviously."

"It's magical," he said, glad to have the interruption from where his thoughts had gone. "And yes, I know that sounds odd considering it's an actual magical place. All sorts of paranormal creatures, like I said, and it looks like magic."

"That's so cool."

"You'll get to see it soon. We're about five minutes out." He flexed his hands on the wheel again. "I know this will sound silly, but I'm kind of glad you tossed your phone."

"Oh?" She faced him. "Why's that?"

"In case we were being followed -- I heard the conversation because he's loud -- and I don't want him to follow us to Eerie. Not because I think he could get in, but you sound like you need a break."

"I do." She folded her arms. "I disabled the tracking a long time ago, but I didn't trust he hadn't done one of those 'locate my phone' things. He's sneaky that way. If he tries to find the phone, it's poofed and in pieces."

"There we go." He pulled off at the gravel lot outside of town. "To anyone who doesn't know Eerie is here this is a strange dumping spot for gravel for the state. An otherwise boring place. It's also the last chance to turn around if you've changed your mind."

"I haven't." She smiled, seeming to sweep her gaze over him.

"Anyone who isn't para will think they've driven by a huge lake and around some woods, but there aren't any pull-offs to visit it and there are posted signs every so often saying it's someone's property. So far, no one's tried to push in."

"Well, they haven't until I go there. The attention I bring might draw someone," she said. "I always do. People see my money, the charade, and think they can swindle me. I've been okay so far, but I don't trust anyone."

"Probably smart," he said. Synths could take any form, and he'd love to see it. "You probably do draw too much as Skylar Graves, but you could just be yourself."

"You mean not this skin slipcover?" She blushed. "I'm not sure I could go back and not sure I could handle the stares if I can't shift back."

"Why? You're stared at as Skylar." He wanted to see her true form. "What would be the change? At least here you'd fit in by being different." He might find that the synth form was just as attractive. She might even be more popular by being herself.

"I'm magenta."

"So?" Some of the faeries were in bright colors and he didn't care.

"That doesn't bother you?"

"Nope." She was probably beautiful. "I want to see the Skylar you are when no one is looking. The special one you hide."

"You do?"

"Yes. That's the you who is most authentic. I want to celebrate her. You're appreciated in Eerie -- by me and everyone else because we like and have all sorts."

"Yeah?" She glanced at him. "You're different from Prince. He hates paras. He doesn't believe they exist and are really just people who are messed up in the head."

The jerk. "If he's not para, then he won't get into Eerie." Not that it was that easy anyhow. "He won't find you, if you're worried about it. There are spells and portals to get through, but you have to know a para to get the spell and if he hates them, then he won't ask."

"I'm afraid, though. It's a huge invasion of my privacy that he's trying to find me. I don't want anyone to track me." She met his gaze. "What if I decided to go back home? What if I wanted to leave this planet for good?"

"Go to space?" He'd like her to stick around.

"Yes. How would that be explained?" she asked. "Billionaire floats off through the atmosphere without a space suit."

"Are you wanting to leave?" He didn't want her to. "I'd like you to stick around. I'd like to get to know you."

"I'm happy to be a woman of mystery, but I can do that in Eerie. With you."

"You can," he replied. "Will Prince really come looking for you? Because he's concerned? Or because he's trying to get something for himself?"

She shrugged and laced her fingers together. "He'd pretend to be concerned, but I don't know. I do know I like looking this way, but you asked to see my actual form."

"I did." He remained parked in the gravel area. "If you're going to shift, I'd suggest you might want to wait until we're fully in Eerie. You'll be safer that way." She might want to be away from the prying eyes of everyone else. If the rest of the world saw the famous Skylar Graves switch forms, it'd be a sensation and scandal.

"You're right." She sighed. "I should wait."

"*Do* you want to go to Eerie?" This was her last chance before they crossed the boundary into town. "We can head back." He wanted her to be sure.

"I tossed my phone a couple hours back and psyched myself up to see this place, plus pissed off my assistant. Yeah, I want to go. I need to see this place for myself." She reached across the console. "I've been on lots of adventures, but this is one I won't miss."

"Well, okay." He grinned. He couldn't wait to show her his world. "I hope you like it."

"I know I will." She squeezed his fingers. "I'm excited."

"So am I." He wanted to see her in her true form when they were safe, but he also delighted in being with the prettiest woman in this form. "Here we go." He pulled onto the road and drove the short way into town.

"There's a sign." She clutched his hand. "I didn't see it before now. That's so cool."

"Like I said, it only happens for those who are para, and appears to them alone." He kept driving, crossing into town. Where the rest of the world was drab, beyond the city limits the town became colorful and vibrant, even at night. He wished he could see Eerie through her eyes -- like it was brand-new.

"There's so much color." She let go and leaned into the window. "It's like a candy-colored… I don't know. I've never seen anything like it."

"These are the faerie lands. They do love color. When we get to the troll and gnome neighborhoods, it's all dark. There's a deep woods area which is dark and damp."

"Brody." She practically giggled. "This is fantastic. It's like a movie set."

"It could be." He'd never seen a movie set, but the town was truly fantastical. "Have you been to many sets?"

"A few." She grinned. Was it sheepishness? He couldn't tell. She half-shrugged. "I do a lot of stuff."

"You don't have to get my approval. I don't have a say in what you do."

"I have a lot of friends who've invited me to visit their sets," she said. "It's pretty cool, but also boring. They wanted me there to give the films credibility. If they could say they partied with me on the set, then it made them sound better than they might be. Maybe it did, maybe it didn't."

"It probably did." How would he know?

"Are we going to your lair?" she asked. "Or castle?"

"I don't have a castle. It's more like a loft than lair. I don't live in the dark, either." She made him sound like a comic book villain. "I have a loft in my lab."

"Sounds cool to me." She shrugged again. "I want to get all pushy, though, don't I?"

"It's okay."

"I've got a thousand questions and concerns," she said. "I mean, I'm bankrolling this, and I have some thoughts."

"I didn't want you to bankroll it. Never said I did." He drove to his apartment building. He parked in the underground lot and turned off the engine. "We should go upstairs."

"When can we tour the town?" She left the car and clasped her hands together. "I want to see everything."

"We will." He'd take her wherever she wanted to go, but it was four in the morning and no one was awake. They'd need to wait a few hours. "But it's too early to go out."

"Oh." She covered her face with her hands. "I forgot that. I tend to be up all night and sleep all day. Normally, I'd be drunk by now."

"I don't care if you drink or whatever, but you're not living if you're partying all the time." He winced, then bowed his head in discomfort. That sounded so terrible. "And your assistant cleans up after you? You're hiding from life." Good God, he couldn't get out of his own damn way.

She stayed by the hood of the car. "Yeah? So?"

"You deserve better than that." He needed to keep his mouth shut. It wasn't his place to say something. "Sorry."

"You started this." She folded her arms and closed herself off from him. "You think you know."

"I…" He could get defensive and frustrated, or he could take a moment and think. He exhaled and focused. "You're brilliant. I've seen it. You know how to work people and get out of situations. You play the ditzy role to keep people at bay, but it's not you. Not the real you that I've seen over the last few hours. You don't want anyone to get close to you and see that real person in case they see it and hurt you. The being inside you is beautiful and should shine."

She twitched and opened and closed her mouth but didn't speak.

"Yeah, it's true. You want to be shielded. You're very smart and I want you to use it."

She averted her gaze. "Brody."

"Tell me I'm wrong. Tell me." He wasn't going to let this die. He'd get her to embrace her intelligence and power. "Tell me you like the charade."

"I hate it."

"Then don't use it here." That seemed easy enough. "I'm not whoever hurt you. I'm not the person who made you believe you had to be someone else to be accepted. I like the you I've gotten to know. The one I've talked to."

"You're being difficult."

"And?"

"You do this to all the aliens you're hitting on?"

She wounded him. "I've never hit on one."

"Until me."

He gathered his patience. He hated being tried, but this was her defense mechanism. Keep people back. "I won't hurt you."

"No?"

"No. I respect you." He held up both hands. "I do, and I want you to be happy."

"Even if it's not with you?"

"Yes." She kept wounding him. He swallowed hard and his stomach lurched. This wasn't the easiest conversation to have. "I'm not them."

"No." She exhaled and closed her eyes. "My true form." She lowered her arms. As she did, her body turned magenta and translucent. Her hair faded away and she sparkled. Not like glitter, but like her body was comprised of a thousand stars. She still had her human face and general form, but she seemed to float.

It was like looking at a star.

"Wow." He reached for her. "Amazing."

"You like it?" Her voice came out like she spoke through water. "I'm not a perky, stereotypical woman."

"No, and it's beautiful. May I touch you or will you burn me?" He wasn't sure why he'd asked her that. "Sorry."

"I might. Nobody's ever touched me when I'm this way." She allowed him closer. "I apologize in advance if something happens."

"I'll take the risk." He almost had to. He was drawn to her like a moth to a flame. He held his hand out to her.

She slipped the glowing form of a hand, her fingers not delineated, into his.

He groaned at the deep chill. Touching her was like putting his hand into a bucket of water -- no, into a glacier. It wasn't painful, but different. He whimpered. Not only was she cold, but he swore there was a current running between them. "Are you charged?"

"Huh?" She recoiled and shifted back into her hipster college girl form. "No."

He didn't move. He wanted to replay the moment he'd touched her in his mind. Seeing and touching her righted something in him. It made him feel something. He couldn't explain it.

"Brody?"

"You zapped me."

She rolled her eyes. "Right."

"No, when I touched you, electricity went through me. It was brilliant." He didn't know how to explain the sensation. "It didn't hurt."

"Stop."

"Why?"

"You're being silly."

"How?" He'd loved the experience. "It was

magic." He wished he understood what had happened.

"Just stop." She folded her arms again. "So, I'm here and you've seen me."

"Don't shut me out," he said. "You're tired. I'll give you my bed and sleep on the sofa. Why don't you get some rest?"

"You'd give me your bed?"

He sighed and bowed his head. "I know it's hard to fathom because you've got a lot of people around you that are fake, but there are real gentlemen out there who do have a heart and don't want something from you. Take my bed and get some sleep. The town will still be here in the morning."

She eyed him, then nodded once -- slightly. "Okay." She inched by him.

"I did enjoy touching you. You're beautiful in your alien form. Thank you for sharing it with me, because it's stunning." He'd screwed up everything he'd wanted to say, but Jesus. She stole his breath. "The electricity I felt is because I'm drawn to you. Not the form or shell, but whoever is in your heart."

She eyed him again, then ducked into the bedroom without another word.

He sank onto the sofa and rested his head in his hands. He knew where he'd gone wrong. Talking to women freaked him out because it was difficult. If it was possible to screw it up, he would.

He'd spoken words from his heart, but when the words came out, they'd been wrong and upset her. Why was this so hard?

Because he didn't have the same magic as everyone else. He didn't have a spell or potion to make him suave. One of these days, he'd be the sophisticated man he wished he could be -- a man worthy of Skylar.

One day.

Chapter Six

A blue sparkle lit up the room and he sat up straighter. He knew that sparkle. "My Princess." He bowed his head. Royal protocols hadn't been written that he knew of, but he respected Piper and averted his gaze. "Welcome."

"Oh, Brody." The light got brighter, then dimmed. She must've used a portal. "Have you forgotten to pay the electric bill?" she asked.

"No, I haven't." He kept his gaze low as he reached over and turned on the lamp. "Sorry."

"You can look at me and don't have to apologize." Piper sat next to him. "So I heard you've been working on the challenge I gave you. The potion or pill or something for the paras?"

"Yes." He finally looked up. Piper was indeed a beautiful woman, but not as pretty as Skylar. "I'm not sold on either, and know there has to be a better way. We can't market a spell or potion or give out a pill without drawing attention. Marketing is attention."

"I agree." Piper nodded. "You've really thought about this."

"I have."

"And you brought in help?" Piper asked. "I haven't met her."

"I know. She'd like to meet you." He wasn't sure how to ask Skylar to join them.

"So?"

"I messed up," he blurted. He hadn't wanted to say that, but the words tumbled out.

Piper frowned. "What do you mean?"

He fought for words. "I met Skylar Graves. It took me a lot of courage that I don't have to find her and even more that I didn't have, to meet her. She's amazing. She's a synth and can shift into whatever she wants."

"A synth?" Piper laced her fingers together around her knee and focused on him. "Tell me more."

"She's sweet and pretty and a great conversationalist. When she's in her true form, she's stunning. We had a great chat on the way to Eerie and it's been… I don't have the words. I just… she's wow." Nothing seemed to be enough.

"Sounds like you like her," Piper said.

Did he? He might, but it was too soon to tell. He was drawn to her; he'd agree with that. "She turned into a bird!"

"So she's a shifter?"

"A synth. She can shift, yes, but she's an alien. She's not of our planet," he said. "She's amazing."

"You've said that." Piper unlaced her fingers, then crossed her ankles and narrowed her eyes. "And yeah, you do like her. I need to meet her."

"I'll get her if she's awake." He turned, but Skylar stood in the doorway. He jerked. "Skylar."

"You bring me here and you've got a girlfriend? You talk about me like I'm not here and spill my secret?" She shook her head. "You were supposed to be different. You're just another sleaze."

"Stop." Piper remained seated but held out her hand. "May I speak?"

He sure wished she would. He did like Skylar, it was true, but he didn't appreciate her sharp tongue. Besides, right now, he had no words. Skylar had no idea who she'd spoken to, and it killed him. He hated confrontation and being insulted, especially when he hadn't done anything wrong. Not this time. If she wanted him to say something to get him into trouble, he could do that.

"I'm tired of men like you who think they can use me, can be jerks and I'm just supposed to take it. I'm supposed to let you do what you do because you're a man and I'm a silly little woman. I have feelings and they're pricked right now," Skylar said. "I can't believe you'd do this."

He hadn't done anything. He'd wanted to introduce her to the Princess and treat her like… royalty. Why couldn't she see it?

"And now you're mute," Skylar said. "Typical."

Piper stood and snapped her fingers. "I don't like doing this, but if you won't listen to what I have to say, then I won't let you speak. I'll explain this because you've got the wrong impression."

Skylar opened her mouth, but no sound came out. She glared and pointed at Brody.

If looks could kill, he'd be dead. He had to say something. "Skylar, you're about to meet the Princess."

She would, if they weren't reprimanded first.

* * *

Skylar hated not being able to speak, but it forced her to listen to him. This person she'd just insulted wasn't his girlfriend but the Princess? The actual Princess?

Well, shit. She'd really screwed up then. She'd assumed this gorgeous woman was his girlfriend. Damn it. He hadn't been the man she'd expected. She kept looking for the worst in him, but he hadn't done what she thought he would. He wasn't perfect, but she'd jumped to the wrong conclusions.

Brody managed to stand. "You wanted to see Eerie. This is the person who can make that happen. Skylar Graves, this is Princess Piper. My Princess, this is the famous Skylar Graves, millionaire and synth."

Piper crooked her brow. "Millionaire, eh?"

Billionaire was more like it, but still. She wanted to run and hide. She'd stuck her foot firmly in her mouth. No wonder they'd sentenced her to silence. She deserved it.

"I will give you back your ability to speak, but first you must listen," Piper said. "Will you listen?"

She nodded. When she could speak, she'd apologize profusely.

"Very good." Piper snapped her fingers. "You're free to speak, but listen. I'd tasked Brody with the herculean task of helping the paras. He's been working hard to help and has hit a wall. He must've thought you could help. He brought you here, but it's a privilege. Yes, you're welcome to be here because you're para, but don't waste the opportunity. There's one thing about paras -- they can sniff out bullshit very easily and won't put up with it. If you're going to march around here thinking you're special in a world of special people, you won't like the reaction. If you're willing to help the greater good, then we're happy to have you."

"Yes, ma'am," she said. "I'm sorry." She'd been put in her place many times before, but not with so much conviction or true concern for her well-being. Her money and status wouldn't help her here, and that was fine. She could use her brains and make an impact that way. Hell, she welcomed that challenge.

Piper folded her arms. "I'm challenging the both of you to solve this problem. We have plenty of paras in the whole of the bigger world. I should know because I was one of them out there. I've seen them and they're struggling. They want to fit in and find a place to belong. But how will they get here if they don't know how to or even that Eerie exists?"

It was a real problem, she had to agree.

"Do you need to hide yourself?" Piper asked. "Are you out to the rest of the world?"

She hesitated a moment. "No, I'm not." If the rest of the world knew she was magenta in her real form, let alone an alien, they'd freak out. "It's too dangerous."

"Because *you're* dangerous?"

"No." She should be insulted, but she understood. Piper wanted to protect the people of Eerie. "It's because the rest of the world doesn't understand paras or aliens. They're a joke or not real. They're those ridiculous-looking Roswellian things. We're not. Paras are real and they're not always dangerous, just as not all humans are dangerous."

"You're right."

"And we could help them, too." She liked the idea of being useful. "I don't know how just yet, but the answer is within reach."

Piper frowned. "I'm not disagreeing with you, but I'm not sure how this works." She nodded to Brody. "Poor guy. He's out."

She swept her gaze over him. "I feel terrible, but he is tired."

"Why do you feel bad?"

"I blamed him. Most men who revolve in my orbit and that I've dealt with in the past think they can treat me like I'm a silly woman." She swept her hands over her curves. "It's like they think that if you have boobs, you don't have brains. I did what he told me not to do -- I painted him with the same broad brush I'd painted everyone else with. It's not fair."

"No, it's not," Piper replied. "It's cruel."

"Agreed." She sagged in her seat. "He's been very kind to me. He did tease me into coming with him, but it didn't take much."

"I see it worked."

"It did because he's good at convincing. I do this thing where I shift into an eagle. What's absolutely insane is that someone could own an eagle. I have too much money and want or have ridiculous things, so to keep up that image, I pretend to have an eagle."

Piper stared at her for the longest time. "Huh. And the eagle is you, isn't it?"

"Yes." She smiled, proud of her ability and her choice of animal. "It's pretty impressive. But I'm expected to have something that far out there. No one realizes I made that money for myself and most of the stuff I appear to own is just props. It's not real. Why would I have that much junk? The money is in various accounts and untouchable. As for the eagle, she's me, so she's just as smart."

"I'm sure she is." Piper crossed her legs and sat back in her seat. "You've seen how being different can be a problem. A rich woman who shouldn't have brains. A woman who isn't from this world. A woman who can switch forms. That's a lot to deal with."

"You're not wrong. If the greater world knew I could shift… it'd be bad," she said. "But when I was in the eagle form, I homed in on him. I couldn't look away. The animal knew where he was and that he was special. He even shooed me away. The others want to tame the animal."

"They want to tame all of you, I'm sure. Get in on your money and run your life so it's really for them? And he's not like that."

"Exactly. I'm drawn to him because he isn't, and doesn't. He kept asking me if I still wanted to go. He gave me so many outs."

Piper watched her and said nothing.

Should she keep talking? "I don't know. He's

nothing like anyone I know and it's refreshing. He wasn't shocked by my synth, and he encouraged me to use my abilities."

"I'm not impressed that he wasn't surprised, but I'm impressed you were."

"Guys tend to dismiss me. I have one who wants to be seen with me for his own advancement." Come to think of it, Prince wanted her for the same reason. He wanted the credibility. If she paid for a few things, then even better. Good fucking God. The only ones who didn't want to use her for her piggy banks were the ones in Eerie.

"This isn't a perfect place. There are characters here and an entire underbelly you don't want to get involved with, but it's relatively safe," Piper said. "I'd love to understand your abilities, but not through testing or attacking you. By talking. By getting to know you. That's more important, and it's how I'd want someone to treat me."

She appreciated Piper's viewpoint. "What do you want to know?"

"Mostly, I'd like to see how you'd handle the issue of bringing paras here and how to make them feel safe about coming here. A potion or pill? I don't know."

She nodded, immediately trying to figure the problem out. She liked this kind of challenge.

"With Brody."

"Sure." She saw no issue with that. "Two minds are better than one."

"They are." Piper stood. "I believe it's time you come with me."

"I should." She hopped to her feet. "What about Brody?" She felt guilty leaving him behind.

"He'll be fine, but I need him to rest."

"He won't be upset? I don't want to let him down. If I'm not here when he wakes, he'll be hurt."

"I'll make sure he knows and understands. We'll let him rest and I'll give you the grand tour of Eerie."

She would've liked for Brody to come along, but he did need to sleep. Plus, Piper was the Princess and should be trusted. "Okay."

"I have some thoughts about the problem, and I'd like to discuss them while we tour Eerie," Piper said. "That and I need to tell Diesel where I'll be." She opened a portal into a white-on-white room.

"Diesel?" She followed Piper through the portal, though she had no clue where she was. "Who's that?"

"My partner and Prince Consort," Piper said. "He's a cyclops and he's here in the castle."

In the castle? Sweet. "That's fantastic." She'd never seen a real castle. But being in Eerie, she'd see lots of things for the first time, she had to admit.

"There's a lot to experience here," Piper said. "How did the eagle know to go to Brody?"

What an odd question, but she didn't mind answering it. "The eagle is very observant. When I shift, I assume the abilities of the animal or being. The eagle is perceptive and so am I. It was drawn to him. Why? Because he was different. He didn't fawn, he didn't get ridiculous, didn't mention money from the start, and didn't expect me to do something for him. He was innocent and unassuming. How do you turn that down?"

"I don't know." Piper walked with her along a corridor. More white-on-white. "I knew I'd portal to the wrong hall. I tried to outthink Diesel and he's probably in our private quarters."

"He hides?" She couldn't argue with that desire.

"He's shy," Piper said over her shoulder. "Like

Brody. He's very shy."

"I gathered that. I pulled him in to talk without telling him who I was. He was dressed so shabbily compared to the others at the party. Maybe that's what I liked. He's different." But she believed to her core that something in her was drawn to him. Like he was meant to be the one she'd find.

"Then accept it and work with him." Piper stopped outside a door. "This is your chance to change your mind. I can portal you back. If you don't want to be here or you're scared, then say so. I won't fault you."

She did have doubts. Who wouldn't? She was about to step into a world she barely understood, but what was so different in coming to Eerie compared to coming to Earth? She hadn't known anything about Earth when she'd arrived. She'd like to be with Brody on this part of the journey, but they'd have time after the tour. She and Brody had a challenge to conquer, and she wasn't about to let the population of paras and Eerie down.

Challenge accepted.

Chapter Seven

Brody woke up with a start. As soon as he did, he knew he was alone. He sat up and scrubbed both hands over his face. A sickening feeling washed over him. He should've known she'd leave. He wasn't the kind of man or para that women stuck around with -- not when they could find someone better. There were vampires and shifters and so many other sexier paras in Eerie.

He could hear Jeni's voice in his head. He'd only dated one woman, and she'd lied to him. She'd told him he could do anything when they both knew better. When she finally stopped lying, the truth came out and his heart had been broken. She'd only wanted him to help her capitalize on her being a singer and a para. Jeni wanted to be famous and if he could get her there with a spell or potion, then even better. But she didn't have the innate talent of a singer, and no magic would help her.

The day she left, she'd slapped him. *"You're a washed-up sorcerer who can't help anyone."*

Maybe Skylar had figured that out already, too. Probably.

He left the couch and wandered down to his lab. He stared at the various tubes and books. If he was going to help paras get to Eerie, it would help to have a network. If there were paras in Eerie who were willing to go out to the greater world, then they could be that network. That'd be one way to get the paras to Eerie or at least to help them.

He sank onto his stool. If they had a system, then they could have a portal to get the paras to town faster. But what about anyone volunteering to be part of the arrangement who didn't have the ability to create portals?

He needed to talk to Piper and Skylar -- if either would speak to him. His stomach grumbled, not from hunger but from frustration.

He toyed with one of the spell scrolls. He needed something, not that he knew what.

A portal opened and Skylar stepped through. She waved at Piper. "I had a fantastic time, and I will. Thanks. Talk soon."

Weren't they chummy? He felt a bit left out. "Hi."

Skylar grinned. Her cheeks flushed as the portal closed, and she tucked loose locks of her hair behind her ears. Her eyes shimmered. "Hi."

"Have fun?"

"I did," she said. "Did you sleep?"

"Kind of." He remained on the stool. He had no right to be angry. She had no ties to him, yet he wanted her attention.

"We left you to rest," she said.

"Well, good."

"You're upset."

He shrugged, trying to keep his emotions in check. "No."

"Liar."

"What should I be upset about?" He had to stop this. He was being mean, and he knew it.

"I went to visit Eerie without you."

"You did."

"So why are you upset? Because I did that?"

He should leave it alone and stop being angry. This wasn't worth the argument. Wasn't kind of him to be irked.

"Stop stalling." She stood before him and cocked her head. "Are you angry we didn't include you?

Because you wanted to be seen with me? You wanted my attention and to be part of the entourage?"

"No." He shook his head. "I'm not angry. I'm just… I feel left out. Not because I wanted to ride your coattails or be an entourage. It's not unusual for me to be left behind. I have that happen a lot, but I thought… never mind." She was different and he needed to stop.

"Why are you left behind? I don't understand?" She dragged one of the stools over. "Talk to me."

"I'm not exactly popular. I'm happier here in my lab because I can't get shot down. I'm what the rest of the world refers to as a nerd. A magic nerd."

"Because you're smart?"

"Because I know what's in all of those magic books in the town library. I know the spells and incantations and can rattle them off, but talking to women is impossible." God, this was embarrassing. He wanted to melt into the floor. "You're good at mingling. I'm not."

"Someone hurt you badly." She grasped his hand. "I'm sorry."

He fought the urge to recoil. He didn't do well when he couldn't fall back on magic. Going to see her and convince her to come to Eerie had been one of the most difficult things he'd ever done in his life. "It's fine."

"Like it was for me?" She sighed. "I was hurtful to you when we first got here and I'm sorry. I wasn't kind because I'd been hurt and was on my guard. Doesn't make up for it, but it's the explanation."

"It happens." She'd apologized? He hadn't thought she would.

"Who hurt you? Besides me?" Skylar asked. "Someone destroyed your heart and self-esteem. I don't know why that was done, but it sucks. I've been hurt like you and I'm here, so I understand and I want to know what's going on."

"You do?" She had him speechless.

"When I first started making insane money, I dated a man who came off as being so sweet and kind. My heart knew there was something wrong, but I fell hard for him. I knew it was an act, but I trusted him. What he wanted was to get into my circle and exploit my money for his own ends. I thought he was so nice and handsome, but he was ugly on the inside. He tried to burn through my money, what I earned, because he wanted it. He deserved none of that money and when I rebuked him, he had the nerve to tell everyone I was cheating on him!"

"That's cruel. Why do people do that?"

"Because he wanted something for nothing." She toyed with his hand. "If he hurt me, then it covered for his own shortcomings. Why should he take responsibility and look back when he could change the narrative, and look better because he wasn't responsible?"

He mulled over what she'd said and allowed himself to truly understand. "He sounds like a real treat," he said. There wasn't any advantage in trashing the man, though. He switched points. "What did you want to do? Since he wanted to spend your money, if you could be anything and follow your ultimate goal or dream, what would you do?"

"Funny you asked me that," she replied. She left the stool and walked around the lab. "No one sees my brain."

"They could." She still had time.

She faced him and grinned. "May I shift?"

"Please." He loved her alien form.

"Thank you." She shifted into her true body, the

glowing magenta figure with stars and vibrancy. She lit up the room.

He'd never seen anything so beautiful and majestic in his life.

"If I could do whatever I wanted, I'd be in this body all the time and using my intelligence. The money is great and has opened doors, but it only does so much. I'd be taken seriously if I was using my mind, not cash. What can I do to make things better while using my intelligence? I want to be that and find excitement in my life."

"Yeah." He understood to his core. "I want to help without being seen."

"I want to help without being seen as one thing."

They were so much alike.

"Which is why I'm sorry I blamed you. I didn't give you what I expected of you. So can we start over?" she asked.

"Don't need to," he replied. "We keep going. This was a moment of learning."

She smiled and radiated with light. "Thank you."

"No problem." He sighed and glanced over at the table. "Did you experience Eerie?"

"A quick tour. Piper wanted me to see the town and get a feel for who and what's here. I never realized there are so many paras and how it's so segregated."

He'd never really considered that, but she was right.

"The paras need to see themselves in our communities. We should be able to show them as a town that we can live together."

"Most of the royal court is that way," he said. "None of the members are with anyone else of their… type?" Kind? He wasn't sure how to explain it. "Some groups tend to keep to themselves."

"I get it. Safety in numbers."

"That and the trolls have a bit of a mafia thing going." He'd learned the hard way not to piss them off. "You tread lightly with them. I made a terrible pass at one of their women and nearly lost my hands because I spoke out of turn. I don't go to that part of town now, so I don't end up dead."

She shook her head. "Oh my."

"It's the same everywhere, though."

She floated over to him. "So the idea we need to work on… What are your thoughts?"

She'd changed the subject, but for some reason his mind turned to his past. Maybe it was the discussion of the trolls or his bone-deep desire to get the words out. "Her name was Jeni," he blurted. Shit. He hadn't wanted to share that, even if a part of him did.

"Jeni?"

"Yes." He tried to keep the words to himself, but it was impossible. "She was my only girlfriend. I'm shy and she spoke to me. I fell in love with her right away, but she didn't love me. She wanted me to make her famous."

"And you couldn't."

"Nope."

"She's para?"

"She has faerie blood and wanted to be a famous singer. Her ability to create pyro was her strongest power, but when you can't stay on key it makes being a singer difficult." He winced as he remembered the day she left. "She decided I wasn't enough, but it wasn't my fault. She had all flash and no substance, but instead of taking the responsibility for working on her voice, she blamed me."

She placed her hand over his heart. His chest

tingled and he swore the air left the room. His head swam. He met her gaze and for a second, it was like he was underwater.

"That's just a taste." She smiled. "Now you see how it feels to be me, too. You see now how I don't always feel comfortable in my skin or respected for what I am, not what I do."

"I do." He blinked. "It's trippy."

"Can be." She let go, then shifted back into her college girl form. "I wanted you to experience what it's like to be me."

He nodded, still feeling floaty. "Have you done that to anyone else?"

"No. You're the first." She remained close to him. "I like my form because it's original, but this one has certain advantages, too." She eased her arms around his shoulders. "It allows me to do this."

She tilted her head and kissed him.

The second her mouth touched his, the same floaty, tingly feeling hit. He eased his hands onto her waist. He'd never felt like this before. Not even when she'd touched him a moment ago. He loved the softness of her lips, the tiny whimper in her throat, the way she opened to him, and when she did, the way she tasted.

He shouldn't be kissing her. It was unprofessional, but he couldn't help himself. She intrigued and delighted him. She drew him in. He never wanted this moment to end.

He patted her hip. When he did, she broke the connection. "What's wrong?" she asked. "Did I make a mistake?"

"No." He didn't realize his grasp on her. He'd pulled her right to his chest. "You were fine."

"Then what?"

"I don't want to take advantage. Do you truly want to kiss me?" Or was this research?

"Yes, I do," she said, her voice low, like a purr.

"Skylar."

"Yes, I want you to experience what I feel, but I also want to kiss you. I realized when I was out in town that you're special. I'm attracted to you and your spirit."

"You are?" She'd shocked him. He wasn't sure how to process this.

She nodded. "You're unlike so many others I deal with every day and it's interesting. It's refreshing. You fascinate me."

"I do?" He needed to stop asking so many questions.

"Yes." She toyed with the hairs at the back of his head. "I'm not sure how I could sleep with you when I'm in my alien form, but I know how to in this body and I want to. I want to share that connection with you."

"I do, too." He encircled her waist with his arms. "But we need to wait."

"Why?"

"I don't want to be your regret." It'd kill him to wait, but it felt right. "I don't want you to move on and realize that you never should've been with me. That I was the one you wished had gotten away."

"Never." She brushed her nose along his. "But I respect your fear. It's natural because this is a new thing we don't know about. We have no idea how this will play out."

"Yes." He craved her. God, it'd be so hard to wait, but if they climbed in bed right now, it'd destroy all future work.

"I get it." She smiled and situated herself

between his legs. “I wanted you to see how it is to be me so we can understand what we need to do.”

“Yes.” But having her this close would be difficult. “What do you think will help others in our position?”

“Sex.”

She made him horny and uncomfortable, but he loved her frankness. “Besides that? Sex won’t cure everything.”

“But it’s a start.” She winked. “We need to be pushed out of our comfort zones.”

He couldn’t agree more. “You have to show your brain, and I have to accept help.”

She nodded. “But if you need to kiss me or we happen to fall into bed, I won’t argue. Sex could be the best stress relief and the means to take our mind off the problem so we can come back fresh.”

He groaned, wanting to strip her right now and make love to her, but knowing he needed to be patient. “I won’t argue, either.” He kept his arms around her. “You’re confusing my thoughts, but I do have some ideas about the problem.”

“Good.” She wriggled, getting closer. Her breath warmed his cheeks and her breasts rubbed against his chest. “What did you come up with?”

“What if we created agents and sent them out to seek out paras? Like a special force that’s for good. Not one to arrest them or anything like that. Not find and haul back, but brave souls who might want to be envoys. A pill or spell won’t be enough to bring them back but maybe give them the ability to create portals.”

She continued to play with the hairs at the back of his head. “Yes. Empower the envoys with the ability to open portals and send them when needed.”

“But they should be vetted so they don’t use the

ability for the negative."

She met his gaze. "Might be good to use people who have already been out there."

"Because we sense each other -- paras do."

"My eagle found you."

"I thought that might be you." He kissed her. "It was brilliant."

"You think so?"

"I know so."

She stared at him. "Why?"

"Because you showed me who you are and that you were a para. I saw how you're special and I felt a connection when you flew past me," he said. He should keep this to himself, because it was too early, but the words came anyway. "I was drawn to you in a way I couldn't explain. A magnetic pull. I don't want your money or status. I want the sweet alien who's magenta. I like her mind, adventurousness, determination to survive, and intelligence." He should stop talking, even if the words were all true.

She caressed his shoulders. "It's funny you said that. The eagle helped me decide. It knew."

He couldn't be this lucky, but it sure seemed like he was. "I want to see where this goes, but we need to solve this first. Will you go with me on this ride and explore whatever this is bubbling between us?"

She threw her arms around his neck and flashed magenta, then squealed. "Yes. Absolutely yes. Let's solve this problem and have the best time because we're together."

How could he say no?

Chapter Eight

Skylar couldn't wait to solve this issue. She stayed in his arms, thrilled to have him in her life. She'd been waiting for an eternity to find him. Now that she had, she refused to let go.

"I've tried to figure out a pill, but there's the issue of distribution," he said.

She agreed. "How do you get it into the hands of the masses and not into the hands of the humans?"

"And what happens if humans get it?" he asked. "What might be their reaction? Or will there be a reaction? There are so many possible outcomes. I've got a journal where I've written some of them down, but I don't have evidence. We need to prove all this all before we can release it -- which is why I was going toward envoys, versus potions or pills."

"I get it." She considered what he'd said and let go of him to pace the room. She thought better when she could move. "They could find it as a means to get high or something like that."

"It's possible, and I don't want to be responsible for that. They don't understand it and will explore it -- if it even gives them a reaction."

She agreed. "We need to speak to Piper about creating a special force of sorts. She'll have a good idea as to whom to approach and might want to do the recruiting or that sort of thing."

"She will." He left his seat and paced with her. "Piper will know how to imbue those individuals with the ability to create portals, too. We need to train them on who to look for and how not to scare them."

"True. Some might not even know they're para." She'd bet quite a few didn't know. She faced him. "I haven't been tired until now, but we need to write these all down, so then I can crash."

"How long have you been awake?"

She wasn't even sure. "Over twenty-four hours? No, I took a short nap earlier. I don't know, but I've used my powers twice for you and shifted into the eagle, so I'm tapped out." She needed to sit. She dragged over the stool and settled on the wooden seat.

"Do you require anything special to recharge? Like light or something? I'll help you get what you need."

She appreciated his concern. He was the first being to want to help her because he cared, not because of financial gain or benefits for him. "I need sleep. Darkness would be good."

"Really?" He rubbed his chin. "I'd think you'd need light. You're made up of stars."

"But stars shimmer in the darkness of space. I'm one who shimmers in the dark. That's why I spend most nights awake and days asleep."

"You're basically nocturnal." He nodded. "Fascinating."

"Am I becoming a specimen?" She wasn't worried about it. If he wanted to learn, then she'd tell him. Now that she'd entered a world where she could be herself and her quirks weren't questioned, she could stretch and relax.

"No, I'm truly fascinated by you. I expected one thing and you're more. That's why it's so interesting. You keep showing me you're so much more than everyone expects. That's not just exciting, but sexy."

She cocked her head. "Oh?" He'd intrigued her.

"Yes, because it shows who you really are. That's sexy."

He knew how to say the right things. She appreciated it because he was honest. He wasn't trying to get her attention and on her good side or use her. He'd spoken from his heart. She hadn't slept with him, yet somewhere in her heart she knew he was the one she should find. She'd come to Earth for a reason -- to locate her soulmate and make a difference.

"What?" He left his spot across the room. "You look odd, like you're deep in thought or about to pass out."

"I'm thinking." She smiled. "Not to the point of passing out."

"Thinking about the problem?"

"Yes." One of them anyway. She'd get him to see he was important and worthy as well. She'd convince him they belonged together. "Will you rest with me?"

"I will."

"Will you wait until I'm rested to speak to Piper? A united front will work best." She didn't want to miss out. This was the biggest and most important thing she'd ever done.

"I can't speak to her on my own. I need my partner to be there. I didn't come up with the idea alone. You're integral to this solution and if it works, then we'll help so many beings. You need to be there."

"Brody." She rushed up to him and embraced him. Tears sprang to her eyes. He had no idea what he'd said, but he'd touched her to her center. He made her heart fly. She clung to him. "Thank you."

"For what?" He rubbed her back and petted her hair. "You deserve to be there. You've done half the work and made me a better man. I needed to be one and you helped me. That's priceless."

"Better?"

"Yes." He cupped the back of her head. "I can't think of anywhere else I want to be but beside you."

She rested her forehead on his and closed her

eyes. “That’s where I want to be, too.”

“Then come with me and we’ll rest. I need to get some sleep, too.”

“Yes.” She opened her eyes and grasped his hand. She walked with him from the lab, through the living room to the bedroom. She’d hardly paid it much attention. Now she did. He had no imagery on the walls and no real personality with the space, either. Very utilitarian and bland. She didn’t get a sense of him at all. “I don’t see much of you in here.”

“In my room?” He flipped on the lamp and closed the blinds. “Is this enough darkness? I don’t know how much darker I can make it.”

“It’s fine.” She stepped into his path. “You’re stalling.”

“I am?” He blushed. “I’m not trying to.”

“Oh?” She shrugged out of her jacket, then kicked out of her loafers. She unzipped her jeans but left them in place as she took off her socks. “Want to tell me why there’s no personality in here?”

“I don’t spend much time here.” His blush deepened. “I sleep in my lab most of the time.”

“Why?”

“I get wrapped up in my work.” He wrestled free from his shirt. His hair stuck out at odd angles. His nipples beaded. The fine trail of dark hair leading from his navel to below his belt glistened in the soft light.

She drank in the image of him. He was so much more than he believed. Her energy craved him. Her body cried for him. Her magic needed his touch for renewal. “Do you sleep in the nude?”

“Wow.” He stumbled and shoved his jeans to his ankles. “No. I have sleep shorts. You?”

“Why?”

He fumbled again. “In case someone comes in

here in the middle of the night or whatever. Then they don't find me naked."

"Oh." That made sense. She removed her jeans and wore only her bra, shirt and panties. "I usually sleep in an oversized T-shirt. May I borrow one?"

"Yes." He clumsily removed his jeans, then hurried to his bureau. He offered her a blue shirt. "Will this do?"

"Yes." She switched the shirt she wore for the one he offered. She left her bra on for now. Every speck of starlight within her needed to be naked beside him and to tempt him. She didn't want him to keep her at bay, even if it made perfect sense. She wanted to do something wild. Impulsive. To lose herself in his touch and drown in his kiss.

But they needed to wait. She didn't want to burn out with him.

She stretched out on his bed. The sheets smelled like him and the bedding conformed to her -- like being held. She needed his stability.

He joined her in bed. "Much nicer than the sofa."

"You sort of collapsed, though." She snuggled in the sheets. "I felt bad for leaving you."

"Did you? I thought you might." He turned off the lamp, bathing them in darkness. "I needed to sleep, but I was worried about you."

"Why?" She cuddled up to him. She twined her legs with his and draped her arm across his belly. "I wasn't in trouble."

"No, but I worried that you'd decide I was too boring."

"No." She pressed her mouth to his shoulder. "You're more than you think." Which seemed like a theme for them. They had so much more potential than they believed. Once they harnessed it, they'd be unstoppable. "I couldn't wait to get back to you. It was nice to see the town, but I'd like to do that with you, too. Let you show me what's so great about Eerie. I know you have special places you visit."

"I might." He chuckled. "Not many, but I have a couple."

"Good." She couldn't wait to see them. "When I'm with you, I'm safe."

"You are."

"I feel valued." She didn't feel that often.

"You are. You have so much within you."

"You, too." And when they embraced it, they'd find heaven. "I haven't felt valued in a long time."

"Because of the money?"

"Yes, and because I'm not taken seriously. I'm seen as a piggy bank and means to a social end," she said. "When I first arrived on Earth, I didn't have any experience with men."

"With other synths?"

"No." She wished she had. "I didn't know any others." Still didn't.

"There must be more."

"Maybe." Somewhere, but she wasn't interested in finding them right now. "But I didn't have any experience. My first time wasn't of my choosing, either." She wasn't sure why she was telling him this, but the words came anyway.

"What?" He tensed. Even in the near full dark, she could feel his upset. He growled. "What happened -- if you don't want to tell me, that's okay, but damn. I want to find this person and rip his heart out."

She marveled at his protective streak. She wished she'd have had him then. Then again, she would've had experience with him and not the bastard. "I want to tell you," she said. She needed to get the words out.

"He was older and told me I was pretty. I wasn't interested in him, but he assured me I needed to let him have a few moments of time. I didn't need him for anything. What he wanted was to say he'd deflowered me. I fought him off, but he insisted."

She remembered the moment like it'd happened yesterday. The stench of his breath, the clamminess of his hands, the grunt as he touched her and the odor of his cologne. His ego practically choked her. He believed she owed him her virginity, but she didn't owe anyone anything.

"You fought him off and won?"

"No." She trembled. "I tried and he forced me. I hated it."

"I bet." He held her tight. "He took something precious from you."

"He did." She clung to him. "For a long time, I believed love and sex weren't one and the same. You could fuck without love. No one cared."

"You can, but it's not fulfilling."

"No, it's not." She held onto his hand. They might be in the dark, but he offered her a ray of light and warmth. He offered her a lifeline. "I didn't believe I could be loved after that."

"Not even by that man you loved?"

"I knew he didn't and that reinforced my belief. Not anyone until you came along. Now, I see love can be part of sex and make it better."

"We haven't made love yet."

He'd called it making love… She wasn't sure she could love him even more, but he kept proving why she was right in her faith in him. "We will." She kissed his shoulder. "When the time is right and we both need it, then it'll happen. It'll be beautiful."

"And perfect -- even if it's awkward and we

laugh because we're together," he said.

"Yes." He knew her so well. He was the one person who understood everything. He could take away the terrible memories and replace them with better ones. She could rest, knowing she was respected and loved. She belonged.

"Sleep," he said. "I might not be the biggest or baddest guy, might not be perfect or even always do the right thing, but I'm putting my heart into your hands. I'll take care of you and let you fly. I'll be a partner, not a dominant."

"I know you will." She closed her eyes and allowed the darkness to rejuvenate her. She welcomed the power resurgence. He helped her to find the piece of her to make her new.

Finally, she could be whole.

* * *

Skylar woke in the sheer darkness with a delicious man beside her. For the first time since she'd come to Earth, she felt valued and complete. She'd recharged and could shift a hundred times right now.

Not that she needed to shift. She'd rather simply enjoy being with him. Brody had no idea how sexy he was because he wasn't trying to be. He was his own dorky self, and she loved it. Loved him.

He stirred in his sleep. "No, I won't. I need to get you. Come with me."

She doubted he was talking to her. He was dreaming -- had to be. About her?

"No, you need to come with me. I need to save you. Please," he said. "You're not safe." He reached out, touching nothing, but still trying.

She jostled him. He wasn't talking to her, but she worried about him. "Brody?" She nudged him again. "Brody, wake up."

He tensed. "No, Sarah. It's not safe here. Why won't you listen to me? Please." He punched out again, then seemed to gather Skylar in his arms. He wasn't trying to hold her. This was more like grabbing in an attempt to protect.

Sarah? She shook her head. This wasn't the time to be jealous, but she wondered who he was talking to. "Brody?" She straddled him. "I'm here with you. Skylar."

Brody stopped moving and opened his eyes. "Fuck me. Skylar."

"I'm here." She stayed on his lap. "Who are you trying to save? Who is Sarah?"

"Fuck." He scrubbed both hands over his face. Stalling again? She didn't mind. He groaned and rested his hands on her thighs. He shook his head. "Sarah is my sister, and I failed her."

"It's okay." She wasn't sure how, but part of her made sense of this. He'd felt like a screw-up because he hadn't done what he believed he should've for his sister.

"She left Eerie and tried to make it in the larger world, but she couldn't get back home. I tried to save her and I failed because she didn't want to come with me."

"Not at all?"

"No. She couldn't," he said. "She died."

Oh God. "Brody." She wasn't sure what to say. "I'm sorry. Was it quick?"

"No. She was murdered and I failed her. I should've been more persistent. Should've grabbed her and made her come back. I should've done more."

"Stop." She smoothed her hands over his. "You tried, but some people just aren't meant to be saved. They need to do what they do because it's their fate.

That sounds shitty because we want to save them all, but some can't be saved so we learn to value them and learn from the experience."

"Yeah."

That's why he needed to save the paras in the larger world -- it was his penance for not saving his sister when he believed he should've.

"We'll save as many as we can," she replied. "I promise." And she'd do her best to keep that promise because he mattered. He was important, not lost. Not geeky or dorky.

He was special and loved.

Chapter Nine

Brody scrubbed both hands over his face again. Fuck. He hadn't wanted to dream about Sarah because it was more like a damn nightmare. He couldn't hide his embarrassment or hurt and anger. The memory of his sister floating in a pool, surrounded by red water, her own blood, haunted him.

"What did she want to do? Once she was out of Eerie?" Skylar asked. "Something big?"

"She wanted to act." He blinked back tears. "She loved doing plays."

"Yeah?" She caressed his bare chest. Her touch relaxed him.

"She wanted to do commercials and eventually get into movies."

"That's difficult."

"I know," he replied. "Also difficult when you get in with the wrong people."

"And she did?"

"She got into drugs to hide her magic and fit in," he said. "If she'd have just listened to me, she might still be here. She hid her powers and got hooked on cocaine. She loved the high and the men who supplied her more than anyone else."

She stretched out on top of him and held him. "I don't know what to say. I wish I could help you bring her back, but we can't. What we can do is help all the others and hook them up with chances. If they don't take them, then we can't accept responsibility for their choices. They'll do what they feel they need to. It's not our fault -- just like it wasn't your fault that she didn't do what you wanted. I don't like that it happened, but it did so you'd learn a lesson and be better. You're going to do something big because she pushed you."

He held onto her and let the words wash over him. She was right and her patience offered him comfort. He appreciated her help. "You're right."

"She's like a little faerie on your shoulder," she said. "And you use her guidance. She's making you better."

He blinked back a fresh wave of tears and held her. "Yes." His sister pushed him forward. He'd help others where he'd failed her.

"Are you ready to write up our plan? And contact Piper?" she asked. "I know we've got a strong plan."

"We do." He gathered his wits. "Let's do it."

"Good." She lifted her head and kissed him. "I'm proud of you. You're going to make her proud, too. You already are."

"I hope so."

She crawled off him but didn't get dressed. She remained in her T-shirt and bare legs. "Let's work. Come on. The change of topic will do you good."

"It will." He left the bed and followed her to the lab. He'd forgotten about magic or trying to be better. All he could do was focus on her. He trotted after her. "I thought a spell would help. Like to glamour them, but I realized it was like caging them and forcing them to come back."

"Don't want to do that." She grabbed one of his notebooks. "Pen?"

"I'll get one, but here, I'll get you a fresh sheet of paper." He opened a new notebook, then offered up a pen. "Here."

"Thanks." She settled on the stool. "Our plan is… a special group of agents?"

"Yes. I like the way that sounds." He began to pace. "It sounds more professional. This group of special agents will be dispatched around the globe to assist paras in reaching Eerie and help them if they're in trouble."

"Good." She wrote quickly. "How long would they be in service?"

"Up to Piper, but they'd have to be able to blend in and be able to portal."

"Yes," she replied and kept writing. "They need to have contact with Eerie. Should they have a central reporting place? Piper can't monitor this alone."

"No, she can't." He kept pacing. "There should be a central reporting staff. Somewhere to report to and get guidance from when needed." He tried to think of other things they'd need, but nothing came to him. He snapped his fingers and sparks shot from his fingertips.

"You can do that?" She stopped writing. "Brody?"

"Yeah." He rested his hands on his hips, unimpressed with his magic. "I do it when I'm stressed."

"Because you're a sorcerer." She nodded. "Makes sense."

"Yeah. I have some magic and I know as many spells as I can possibly remember." He resumed walking. "There's a reporting place and pipeline to get them where they need to go. There should be a program for helping them when they get here."

"Oh. Right." She resumed writing. "It's not such a shock that way. Smart. Not like a holding pen, but a way to ease their way into society here. Help with drugs, or someone to talk to for adjustments."

"Yes, and places to eventually live." He stopped again. "But we don't need to have this part sorted out. We should have a guide, yes, but not a full plan."

"Because there has to be wiggle room. It's a fluid plan."

"Right." He joined her at the desk. He rubbed her back as she wrote everything out. "We might be ready to speak to Piper soon."

She finished scrawling the words, then tossed the pen down. "I think we are, and it's time to celebrate."

"Oh?" He turned her around in her seat. She faced him and her eyes sparkled. He liked that sparkle. "I've got a few ideas for how we could do that."

"You do?" He eased her off the stool. He embraced her as they swayed together. He wanted this moment to last forever. He feathered his mouth over hers.

She pressed against him in his arms and kissed him back with vigor. He loved her sense of excitement and adventure.

She took control of the moment and dragged him into the bedroom. A giggle bubbled in her throat. The sheer delight on her face pleased him. When she reached the bedroom, she whipped his shirt off, then crawled onto the bed. She knelt before him in her bra and panties. Her nipples beaded beneath the delicate lace.

"Want me?" He crawled onto the bed with her and eased her onto her back. Her hair spread out and she opened her legs to him. He kissed her again.

She draped her arms around his neck, holding him to her. "Make love to me."

"Yes." He couldn't tell her no. Not when he wanted her more than his next breath. He eased one hand between her legs and caressed her pussy through the silk of her panties.

She broke the kiss and groaned. "Yes. More."

He nibbled along her mouth to her cheek, then

her jaw. "Crave you."

"You've got me." She unhooked the front of her bra, letting the lingerie fall away from her chest.

His mouth watered. Christ on a cracker, she had great breasts. He continued to kiss her. He made his way to her chest. He palmed one breast while he flicked his tongue across her other nipple.

She wriggled beneath him, then threaded her fingers into his hair. "Brody."

He sucked hard on her nipple, then pinched the other one before switching.

She panted. Her muscles twitched. "Brody? You're scrambling my brains."

"Yeah?" Blood rushed to his dick. His senses reeled. Magic swirled within him. He needed to be inside her. "Want to make love to you." It was too fast, but he couldn't help himself. The need was too great.

"Yes." She let go and shoved her panties down her legs. She stretched out before him, deliciously nude and inviting.

A groan rumbled in his throat. He struggled out of his shorts and nearly tripped. "Sorry."

"When the need is this strong, it's okay to be a little clumsy." She caressed her breasts and parted her thighs. "It's sexy when you're so real."

He'd never expected to hear that. He joined her on the bed and crawled between her legs again. He rubbed his cock across the silken perfection of her pussy lips. Her liquid heat seared him to his core. He wouldn't last.

"Make love to me." She wrapped her arms and legs around him, pulling him to her.

How could he resist her? He situated himself, lining up his cock with her cunt.

"Please?" She lifted her hips to encourage him to

fill her. "Brody."

He loved hearing her call his name. It sounded so sweet on her lips. He kissed her. As he braced himself on his hands and knees, he pushed into her.

She held him tight to her body, so snug -- like she was created just for him. His magic swirled within him and manifested in sparkles around them. He worked slowly into a steady rhythm. He pushed in and pulled nearly out.

She met him thrust for thrust, arching her back into each push. She tipped her head back and whimpered. "Feels so good," she said. "I need more."

"Yes." He poured his heart, soul and magic into this moment. Everything he had belonged to her for a few moments. He lost himself in the act, needing to be one body and soul moving together. Everything seemed to slow around him to half-speed. His world seemed to blur and everything centered on her. The orgasm started low in his belly and manifested through his limbs. "So close."

"Yes." She trembled. Her skin tinged with magenta, and her body seemed to vacillate between both forms. He didn't mind. Hell's bells, he loved it. He increased his speed. He lost himself in being with her. The orgasm filled his brain. "Fuck. Skylar."

"You are." She giggled, then trembled and tensed. "Coming." She squeezed her legs around him. Her pussy seemed to flutter. She turned magenta, but in her human form. She cried out, then sagged beneath him.

"Oh my God." Seeing, hearing, and feeling her come sent him right over the edge. He growled as he slammed into her and grunted when he came. She pulled everything out of him, zapping his energy but renewing his mind. She helped settle his thoughts and his world made sense.

He added a couple more thrusts, then stilled. He curled his back and rested his head on her shoulder. "Hot fuck."

"Yes, it was," she replied and laughed. "Felt awesome. I want to do it again."

"I'll need a minute," he puffed. Not that he minded. She was a balm to his soul. His mistakes weren't so glaring.

"Brody?"

"Yeah?" He pulled out and flopped beside her onto the bed. "Right here." He needed a few moments to catch his breath.

"Do you always sparkle during sex?" she asked. "It's pretty."

He'd noticed and thought nothing of it. "I guess so."

"You've never paid attention before?" She rolled onto her side and met his gaze. "Wore me out, though, watching and experiencing you."

"Yeah?" She'd done the same to him.

"I like the sparkles and if that's part of you, then I love it." She slid her foot along his calf. "You should do it again."

He kissed the tip of her nose. "You flashed magenta."

Her eyes widened. "What?"

"It was beautiful." He smoothed his hand over her hip, trying to offer her comfort without caging her in. "Like my sparkles, I think it was your magic and stardust surging because of us being together."

Her smile faded and she stared at him. "No."

"I know you're self-conscious, but I loved every second. I got to see the real you. Maybe I even brought out that real you. Either way, you stole my breath and it was gorgeous." Was he helping the situation? Or making it worse?

She stared at him a moment longer. "Am I still magenta?"

"Not really. Why?" He didn't mind her being the brilliant hue. "It's pretty when you are."

"Maybe, but I want to be able to control the switch. Not having control bothers me," she said. She shook her head and dug her nails into his shoulders. "I hate not having control. I hate when I can't be in charge of what's happening to me and can't say no."

"I get it. I'm sure there have been plenty of times in your life when you haven't." He embraced her, remembering her story about her first time. "I can't take away your pain, but I can help right now be better because I understand."

"You do?" She seemed to brighten. "Brody? You remembered."

"I did and I do. You've had certain things pulled out of your control and whenever you can have a piece of it or claw it back, then you'll do it because this is your life, and you should have control. It takes steely resolve to do what you're doing, and I admire it." He kissed the tip of her nose again. "I don't want to control you or anything like that. I'm your fan. I'm right here behind and beside you." He'd give her whatever she needed to have peace.

She grinned and seemed to relax. The magenta tinge to her skin disappeared and she relaxed completely. "You're too good to me."

"It's not difficult. You're wonderful." He held her. She made his life complete.

"You're too sweet and kind. I bet you're like this to everyone, but you need someone to pull you out of yourself. I'm intrigued by you and am so glad I went along with you." She continued to smile. The spark within her increased. "You're a great stress reliever, too."

"Oh?" What a stinker. He liked her teasing because she kept him grounded. "You're not too bad at it, either."

"Aren't we a pair?" She laughed and clung to him. "I'd been looking for you and guess I've found you."

"Right here? In bed? I didn't go far." He joked with her, but the sentiment wasn't lost on him. "I've been looking for you, too." He'd been trying to find someone who understood him and wanted him to shine as brightly as he'd help her to sparkle.

She sobered and stared at him a long moment before she spoke. "This is usually the part where I'm asked for money."

"Have you turned magenta for anyone else?" he asked.

"Weirdo." She nudged him but still smiled. "No."

"Then I don't want money or whatever the others did. I want you."

"I want you, too." She rested her forehead on his. "We should go social media official."

"Could." He held her. He didn't want anything to do with social media. He'd rather stay holed up in his quiet lab and work on his spells with her beside him. Social media could wait until another day, a long time in the future. "Let's sort out the special forces situation first. We have time."

She laughed. "I'm normally trying to hide from social media, and I've suggested it. I am losing it."

"Or you're truly happy." He'd like to believe that.

She beamed. "I am -- because of you."

His heart swelled and he thanked whatever force had sent her into his life. She made him happy. Made him fly and sparked his creativity. He couldn't imagine life without her.

Maybe he'd never have to find out how that felt.

Chapter Ten

Skylar snoozed beside Brody, happy and safe. She'd found her person. Her heart rested. She didn't need social media or the eye of the public to approve of her new relationship.

But she shouldn't forget what he'd said. She'd turned magenta during sex. She'd never done that before, but she knew why. When a synth met their destined partner, they were able to switch freely between forms and show their true selves. She'd been able to come into her own because of him. She was so lucky.

Brody stirred. "I believe someone is here." He sat up. "Oh fuck."

"What? Who?" She scrambled to sit up. "Brody?"

"The Princess is here." He covered her with his blanket. "Fuck me. I didn't think she'd come back this fast."

"Are you sure?" She pulled the sheets to her chest. "Shit."

"It'll be fine. Get dressed or whatever you need to do and I'll buy time."

"I'm okay." She shrugged and shifted into a simple T-shirt and jeans. She left the bed and stood barefoot next to him. "Doesn't hurt to be able to shift. You get yourself together, and I'll stall for you."

He shook his head. "Okay. I give."

"I'll wait for you until you're ready to join me." She kissed his cheek. "It's okay."

"Thanks." He dipped his head and held out his hand. "Won't be a minute."

"Take your time." She left the bedroom space and walked out to the living room area, then lab. "Princess."

"Hello," Piper toyed with one of the beakers. "I forget how much work he does. He's very smart, but not seen as intelligent because he's quiet and keeps to himself."

"He does." She hooked her fingers into the belt loops of her jeans. "Are you here for the update? We have one and I'm waiting for Brody to join me before we present it, but I think you'll like it." She hoped Piper would.

"Yeah. I'm glad to hear it." Piper didn't look at her. Instead, she seemed distracted.

"Princess?" She wanted to get her attention. "What's wrong?"

"Well, I'm here to protect my town and keep the inhabitants safe. I can't do that when there is a target on it."

She paused. "What?" What target?

"I'll cut the bullshit." Piper sighed. "I try to put a positive spin on everything because it's better to be upbeat than negative, but I can't spin this." She created a bubble in her fingers.

"What's this?" She held the bubble and tried to make out the images. "I don't understand."

"That person is your assistant and some individual named Derrence. They're out looking for you because their favorite playgirl is missing. I don't know how they got the idea to look for Eerie, but they're trying to get in," Piper said. "They want to burn the place to the ground to find you, and I won't have it."

She noted the change in Piper's voice and couldn't mistake the problems. "I'll handle it."

"You will." Piper snapped the bubble. "They haven't found the town, but if they find the right para, they'll get in. I don't want them here."

"I don't either." She nodded, trying to decide how to handle the situation. She had to intercept them before they caused real problems. "How close are they? I've got this once I know."

"They've asked questions, but haven't come within sixty miles." Piper shoved her hands into her pockets. "Skylar, I don't dislike you. I'm quite glad you've found Eerie and have helped Brody. I like the two of you together. I believe you have a spot here in town, but you bring baggage."

"I do."

"And that baggage could jeopardize everything you've worked for."

"I know." She glanced over her shoulder as Brody rushed up to them. She'd risked him and that wouldn't do. She liked him too much for him to be hurt.

"What'd I miss?" Brody buttoned his shirt, then bowed his head. "My Princess."

"Brody." Piper's voice softened. "I hear you have a plan."

"We do. So, we formulated an idea to have emissaries or envoys who are trained to spot paras and know how to spirit them here, through a portal. It's not just that, but a network of envoys out in the wild, so to speak. The ones in the greater world would help those back in Eerie who will help the new paras to acclimate to town," Brody said. "It's a simple framework, but it seems viable."

"I agree," Piper replied. "And we'll try it."

"Wonderful." He beamed, then sobered. "I'm missing something. Did I make a mistake?"

"No." Skylar fortified herself. She needed to be the one to tell Brody. "Remember how I said Prince would want something?"

"He's trying to find you," Brody said. "And won't stop?"

"Nope." Piper folded her arms. "He could get into town with the right help."

"I don't think he'd try that because he's very anti-para, but we need to quell him before he gets the notion," Skylar said.

"Agreed." Piper shifted her gaze between him and Skylar. "What are you going to do?"

Skylar tapped into her intelligence and street smarts. "We go to the mansion."

Fear filled Brody's eyes. "We do?"

"If you believe it's right, then do it," Piper said. "I'll give you whatever you need to aid your situation."

"Good." She formulated a plan right away. "This is what we do. We portal to the mansion."

"To somewhere he won't look," Brody said.

"My private quarters, where I keep the eagle. We make them think we've been there for the last three days having sex and being silly. A three-day binge. When they get into my bedroom, when I let them in -- they can't get in there otherwise -- then we'll look disheveled and filthy," she said.

"Like we've been in bed the whole time," Brody replied. "Messed up and a little strung out. But your phone…"

"We took a drive and I lost it." She'd have to lie, but didn't care. "He's probably checked on me and tried to get into my bedroom. Wouldn't be surprised if he's not tried to get into my vaults, too. He's my assistant, not my handler."

"Sounds like you've got a good plan. If you need me, let me know, but I'll leave you to this," Piper said. "And I like the envoy idea. It's smart and if the envoys blend in, that's even better. You'll save lots of paras. I'll start screening people right away." She left them in the loft.

Once Piper exited, Skylar exhaled. "Fuck me sideways."

"What? Now?" Brody paled. "I mean, I will, but it's an odd time."

"No." She embraced him. "I'm frustrated. Prince isn't trying to find me because he's worried. He's doing it because he wants money."

"And Derrence? He's in on it."

"For money."

"You think so?" Brody asked. "From what I heard of your conversation, they're both being bold and it pisses me off. They want to use you."

"They do." She shook her head. "But we're going to be smart and beat them at this game. He thinks he's so much greater than me. Derrence isn't any better."

"They're not."

"They're both greedy." She waved her fingers, finishing her look. "Let's portal to my bedroom. He can't get in there."

"Do you have a special closet or something where they can't get into… just in case?" Brody asked. "I'm worried he managed to break into your room and would know we haven't been there."

"Impossible. They need my eyeball to get into the room. If they use a photo, it won't recognize it. If, somehow, they do manage to get it to work, then they need blood."

"Blood?"

"It's one thing they don't have on hand. I've never bled around them." And made damn sure to clean up and burn whatever she lost any time she had.

"Okay, then." He picked up one of the tubes and

dumped the contents onto his fingers, then blew. A bubble formed and a vision of her room filled the bubble.

"Wow." She stared at the image. "That's my inner sanctum, and it looks like I left it."

"This is real time, so there's that." He moved the bubble on his fingers. "Does it look like he's been in there or the door's been corrupted?" He moved the view, giving her a clear shot of her door. It didn't look disturbed.

"I'm not sure."

"I can zoom in." He moved his fingers a third time. "It won't last much longer, though."

She noticed the door handle jiggling. "Can we hear anything?"

"Only if we portal in." He met her gaze. "Want to?"

"Yes." Without question. "I'll change us to help the story. Go."

He snapped the bubble, then created a portal.

She stepped first through it, then shifted into a sloppy T-shirt and nothing else. She smudged her makeup and tangled her hair. She nodded to the bed as he joined her. He closed the portal. When he turned, she tossed stardust on him to shift him. He changed in an instant into wrinkled boxers, his hair a mess and scratches on his back. He jumped into bed with her and tangled in the sheets.

Time for the performance of her life.

A giggle bubbled in her throat as she threw herself into the act of pretending to be in the midst of sex. She and Brody were partners in crime. She couldn't think of a better partner.

The door rattled again. "I can't tell if she's in there. She's never let me in the room."

She knew that voice. Prince. It figured. She listened closely, trying to sort out the instigators.

"You're sure? Her phone was ditched over an hour away," the second voice said.

"She probably bought something illegal and lost the damn phone. She's pretty, but irresponsible," Prince said. "I can't get it to open."

She gritted her teeth. She knew both voices. Derrence and Prince. The jerks were working together against her. She sat up and Brody stopped her.

"I can do it." He sent magic to the door. "It'll let them in once without a key or blood."

"An illusion?" She loved it. She flopped onto the bed with him and kissed Brody. "You're wonderful."

"Only if we get out of this unscathed." He nibbled on her neck.

The door jiggled, then opened. "It worked," Prince said. "Yes!"

"Good." Derrence pushed in first. "Wake up, sleepyhead." He crossed the room to the bed and swatted her foot.

"Are you high?" Prince asked. "What a terrible look, love."

She brushed her hair from her face and eyes. Time for the charade. "Hey, guys." She giggled and wobbled into Brody, whom she batted at. "Hey. Hi."

Brody grunted and nuzzled the pillows. "Go away."

She laughed and feigned a groggy head. "You're here." She reached out to Derrence. "Are you real?"

"Christ. What did you take?" Derrence slapped her hand away. "If you had half the brains you should have, rather than all that money, you'd be dangerous."

"You mean if she had brains instead of money," Prince said. "But you're right. She's foolish."

She laughed again. They were such assholes. "I didn't take anything. Why?"

"No?" Derrence sat on the edge of the bed and curled his fingers under her chin. "You look like hell."

"When you have a good fuck, you might as well be high," she proclaimed. She wasn't totally wrong. She flopped back onto the bed. "How long have we been up here?"

"A couple days," Prince said. "You ran off with that man you claimed you're seeing."

"With him." Derrence clicked his tongue. "The geeky one."

"At least he's not one of those para freaks," Prince said. "We got word one of them was at the party. No one saw who it was, though. It's believed they were pretending to be invisible."

"Someone can really be invisible?" She sat up again and focused on him. "Amazing."

"What?" Prince asked.

"I think he's behind you." She pointed. "There's an invisible man." She broke into a fit of giggles. "Made you look."

Brody didn't move, but groaned beside her. "I told you they weren't real."

"We need to dry her out," Derrence said. "Right now."

"I have a better idea." Prince opened one of the blinds. Sunlight poured into the room. "Now, we've had enough of this."

She frowned. "Yes, enough of this goofiness." She giggled and clapped her hands. "Lighten up. We had fun. Parties are for *fun*. Let's go back to having fun. Come on now."

"Oh, we'll have fun." Derrence pulled out a pistol. "You're going to sober up, you worthless cunt, and sign over a big, fat check to Prince, then agree to marry me. We're tired of this game."

"Oh?" She sat up and dropped the act. "I need to give him money and my ass goes to you? Uh... why? Because you feel entitled?"

"I've put up with your bullshit all this time," Prince said. "Cleaned up your messes, and I deserve payment."

"I'm tired of getting the runaround from you," Derrence said. "You owe me."

Brody sat up. "Wow. You're full of shit. Both of you. Complete and utter bullshit."

"Fuck off." Derrence aimed at Brody. "You're her dick of the minute. You're replaceable. Get dressed and get out."

She snorted. Other than Brody, they hadn't figured out her game. They'd underestimated her... again.

"Oh, no." Prince whipped a knife from his pocket. "I say we castrate him -- unless she does what we say."

She rolled her eyes. She'd had enough. "If you want this fight, then you've got one on your hands."

"What?" Prince asked. "You're cooked. You're high as a fucking kite."

"Am I?" She stared at him. "You've just proved my point. I'm just here as a piggy bank for *you* and a piece of ass for *you*. You only ever wanted to work for me so you could get a fat paycheck. Now you're demanding it. I don't have that money any longer. I invested it, and it's gone." She turned to Derrence. "As for you, I wouldn't sleep with you if you were the last man on Earth and I needed to for the planet to continue."

"Invested it?" Prince swiped the knife at her.

"You probably dumped it all into blow because you don't think. Never have."

She shrugged, shifting from her slovenly appearance into a bodysuit and boots. She flicked her hand, producing her own knife. "You've never had an original thought in your life. You're both pieces of shit."

"You really want to have this argument?" Derrence asked. He cocked the gun and aimed at Brody. "You're one of those fucking freaks."

"I knew she was. There's no way she made all that money on her own. Probably stole it," Prince said. "I feel so dirty. Bitch." He swiped the knife at her again.

"Yes, I am a bitch. I'm the bitch that's going to fuck you up." She opened her hand, magnetically forcing the knife from his fingers. She sent the weapon sailing into the ceiling and out of his reach. "I'm a freak, and your worst nightmare."

"I've had enough of this." Derrence pressed the gun to Brody's chest. "Any last words?"

"This is ridiculous." Brody grasped the barrel of the pistol, disintegrating it. "Fuck off."

"What the hell?" Derrence pulled the trigger, but nothing happened. "What did you do?"

"Protected my mate," Brody said. He pushed Derrence from the bed.

His *mate*? She couldn't focus on that, but she'd remember it. "Boys? This room is mine and it's monitored. The video feed goes to a server in D.C. All I have to do is release it and you're both in trouble. No one will believe you and will think my money bought the editing to make me look good. Do you want to take your chances?"

"You're lying," Prince snarled.

"Maybe, but do you want to roll those dice?" She grasped both men by the fronts of their shirts. She summoned the strength she'd hidden all this time and pulled them close. "Prince, you're fired. Leave my property and never *ever* use my name. You're a lying sack of greedy shit."

Prince paled. "With severance pay?"

"Fuck you." She flicked her hand, sending him flying across the room. "And you." She glared at Derrence. "You fucked with the wrong woman. I'm not just a pretty face or even an obscenely wealthy person. I'm a fucking synth and I'm tired of your greasy hands. You're never going to hurt another woman ever." She sent him flying into the opposite wall.

"She's fucking crazy," Prince managed. "We're screwed."

Derrence simply groaned.

"She might not be crazy, but I am." Brody stood. He shrugged back into his regular form and pinned both men to the wall with the sheer force of his magic. "And you've fucked with the wrong paras."

Chapter Eleven

Brody grinned as he snapped his fingers. "Good night." He smashed Derrence and Prince into their respective walls once more, knocking both men out. "Jesus, they're obnoxious." He hated bullies and they'd pissed him off royally. Who did they think they were to demand money from Skylar? Demand her cooperation? She didn't have to cooperate with anyone unless it was her decision.

"Are they dead?" she asked. She crept up to Prince and waved her hand in front of his face. "They look dead. I want to kill them, but we can't. It's not right."

"They're not dead. Just silenced for a while so we can figure out what to do next." He sagged onto the bed. "I used a lot of magic, though, and I'll need a recharge. Is that talk of filming real? Is this all being recorded?"

"No. I don't have any cameras in here. I lied to redirect their attention." She faced him. "You're quite a man when pushed to act."

"I am?" He debated what to do next. Open a portal? Call the Princess? When Skylar eased up to him, he slipped his arm around her. He'd never really considered himself brave, but he had to protect her.

"It was sexy." She cuddled against him. "You let me handle them and backed me up. No one's ever done that."

"You had it under control." He held her. "I can't stand to watch bullies be bullies. You're stronger than they think and smarter, too. It's time you realized it for yourself."

She pressed her face to his shoulder. "You've seen all the different sides of me and haven't backed down. You called me your mate, too. We need more time for this to develop, but we've each found our person."

"You're probably right." He knew she was. He tipped her head back to look her in the eye. Prince and Derrence wouldn't stay knocked out forever. "I had to protect you, and it helped me to be stronger than I ever thought I could be. Right now, though, I'm worried the magic won't hold and they'll wake. I can't wipe their memories. Only Piper can do that."

She nodded. "We should alert her."

"We will." He opened a portal. There was only one place to go. "Shove them through here."

"Where are we going?" she asked and gave both men a shove into the darkness.

"The castle dungeon."

She gasped. "The what?"

"This is the best way to alert Piper on safe terms." He closed the portal. "Princess? You know we're here. Might as well help us." He bowed his head, awaiting her.

"Brody?" She'd never heard him quite this commanding. Then again, she barely knew him. "The dungeon?" She hadn't expected Eerie to have one.

"We're letting Piper have her proper say in this." He nudged them. "If they think we're freaks and want to kill us, then they'll want to kill others. Let them experience a few of the so-called freaks. Don't call us names without knowing who we are."

"Vengeful much?" she asked.

"Nope. Just enlightening them." He backed up as Piper and Diesel, her Prince Consort, entered the darkened space.

"So these are the two," Piper said. "Pretty boys."

"I used magic on them to get them here," Brody

said. "You can reverse it."

Piper nodded to Diesel, who lightly kicked Prince's foot. "Wakey-wakey," Diesel said.

Skylar didn't like Prince or Derrence, but worried about what would be done to them. She stood tall next to Brody. Did she want to intervene? No, but she didn't want them to be cruel.

Prince roused first. "Where? Who?" He spotted Skylar and snarled. "You."

"Me." So much for not wanting cruelty. She didn't know the look in his eyes and didn't deserve it. This wasn't her assistant any longer -- or who she'd thought she knew. He'd become a stranger. One she feared. "Does that bother you?"

"Yes." Prince fumbled to sit up. "What'd you do to me? And who are these fools?"

Derrence groaned. He clutched his head and sat up. "My head."

Prince elbowed him hard. "She's abducted us."

Skylar rolled her eyes. They were too dramatic. "I did not."

"Who or what are you?" Derrence asked. He shook his head, as if to clear it. "You owe us. You lied to us."

"About?" She refused to back down now. "What did I lie about?"

"Your money, identity -- whatever the fuck you are," Derrence said. "You lied and misled me. It's all bullshit."

"Oh stop." Screw them. "Even if I had lots of money, I wouldn't share it with you."

Derrence struggled to his feet. "Who are you people? This is a fucked-up party and I'm leaving."

"Are you?" Diesel asked. He widened his stance and stood over both Prince and Derrence. "You're the guests of honor."

Skylar stood beside them. "You've insulted me for a long time. You consider me brainless, just a body to fuck and a piggy bank. I should be discounted because I'm a woman. You have no idea."

"You're crazy," Prince spat. "I expect a huge severance for this, and I *might* forget what I've seen when I get the paycheck. I might not. It's your call as to how generous you'd like to be."

"You won't forget." Piper strode up to him. "You threatened my town."

"I can be bought off," Prince snapped. "What town? This looks like a dump."

"Eerie. You seemed to think you could come to my town and cause trouble," Piper challenged. "You threatened it all over television."

"We wanted her back. She's our nest egg," Derrence said. "What is this? The mob? You can't abduct us."

"They might be kinder." Skyler helped box Prince and Derrence in. "All these people are the ones you've been calling freaks and fools. They live here. *I* live here. We're not freaks or fools." She considered Eerie her home now. Wherever she could be with Brody, that was her home -- if he'd still have her.

"I researched you. I've seen your interviews and conferences as well as the way you speak at parties," Piper said. "You've both insulted paras. Called us names and treated those you've known terribly. Because you knew they were para? I doubt it. Because you're just shits."

"You're not para," Derrence said. He stood and stepped into Piper's personal space. "You're too beautiful to be a para. Him? He's a freak." He pointed to Diesel. "Should be a wrestler. He'd be good entertainment."

"Don't push me." Diesel barely moved. "Wrestle your own ass."

"You're clowns. Too bad, really." Derrence reached for Piper. "I could do so much with you."

"Really?" Piper asked, feigning interest.

"Strip you down, force you to your knees to worship me and delight in that spicy mouth of yours. You'd beg for my dick and to be on my arm at every party. We could have it all if you'd give in."

"I have to give in?"

"That's all you're good for," Derrence said. "Sucking cock and being pretty."

"Then is this pretty?" She touched his hand, burning him. His fingers smoked. "Fire is pretty."

"Fucker!" Derrence yanked his hand back. "What kind of freakshow is this?"

"The best kind." Piper flicked her hand, sending him backward onto his ass. "I don't take your shit."

Prince screamed. "What did you do?"

"Easy," Piper replied. "Magic."

"Paras aren't freaks." Diesel grabbed Prince by the scruff of his shirt. He held him six inches from the floor, enough to make him squirm. "We could work together. Could be assets for each other."

"Could," Skylar said. She walked over to Prince. "But you won't. You wanted my money because it made you feel important. When you found out I wasn't rich -- which I am, and have been fucking with you about -- you showed your ass. You only wanted me for that money. Nothing more. You wanted a payoff. I don't pay people off."

Derrence held his injured hand. "You lied to us."

"I did," Skylar said, embracing her power. It felt good to be herself. She didn't shift, but the stardust rushed through her body and her skin tinged with magenta.

"What the hell is wrong with you?" Derrence screamed. "My God, you're pink! When did that happen? What's wrong with you?"

"Nothing. I'm being my authentic self." She flexed her hands. "I've been hiding my true self all this time. I made that money. I didn't need anyone to help me. I did it, but you wouldn't have believed me. I'm from space and you don't want that. Don't want me to be a freak. I'm not. I'm magic, rich, powerful, and smart as hell. I'm not to be discounted. Not by you or anyone else. I'm like they are. I'm magic, para, and worthy."

"You're a freak," Derrence spat.

Diesel grabbed Derrence by the scruff of his shirt and held him like he was already doing with Prince. "Don't insult her."

"Put me down," Derrence said, struggling. "I don't have to put up with this. I can have you sued and killed. I will have you murdered in your sleep."

Skylar rolled her eyes again. "You wish."

Piper stood in front of them both. "You want to get rid of paras because we're different. Tough. We aren't going anywhere."

"You can't scam me," Skylar said. "I told you I'd never date you. Don't like you. I can't be myself with you, nor do I want to. I can't stand you."

"You wanted me," Derrence said.

"Nope. And I didn't want you, either," she said, poking Prince in the chest. "You thought I'd collapse on you when he turned me down. No, thank you."

Prince tensed and paled. "What are you going to do to me?"

"Have you thrown out, warn everyone I know

that you're trouble, and fire your ass." After they had their memories wiped. "I demand respect and an apology. You've both treated me like shit because *you* thought I deserved it. Joke's on you."

Derrence struggled again. "Apologize for what?"

"She spoke plainly," Diesel said. "Apologize to her for treating her like shit."

"For being a cash box? A freak?" Derrence asked. "No. She had it coming."

"I'm sorry," Prince screamed. "I wanted your money and fame by extension. I wanted to belong. I'm sorry, I'm sorry, I'm sorry."

"Think he is?" Piper asked. "I'm not convinced."

He'd said more than she expected, even if it was all in fear. "Let him go." She waved her hand. "Whatever, Prince."

Piper touched the middle of Prince's forehead. "Paras are good and worthy. You won't treat them poorly again. Won't scam anyone, either. You've never heard the name Skylar Graves. Never heard of Eerie. Goodbye." She tapped his head, then sparkles filled the air. He disappeared, leaving Derrence with them.

"And you." Piper frowned. "I hate empty flattery as much as I dislike you. Now, what do you need to do?"

"Nothing," Derrence snarled. "You both should kneel before me. I'm your god."

Skylar snorted. "I'm sorry? I swear I heard you say something about being a god."

Brody, who'd been in the shadows until now, finally made his presence known. "You're full of shit. You've been trying to bed her for years and she's said no. Either you'll get the hint or you won't, but that doesn't matter to me. You will never hurt or insult her or any other paras ever again."

Piper met Skylar's gaze as if to ask, *well*? Skylar didn't disagree with Brody. "Your choice," Skylar said. "Which do you want?" she asked Derrence.

Derrence spat at her, sending a wad of goo flying in her direction. "You're worthless. I'm glad I never fucked you. Would've gotten your disease."

Disease? She sighed. He'd made his decision. "Fine."

Piper turned to Brody. "Should we castrate him?"

"He's not worth it." Brody sent a shot of fire at Derrence, singeing his hair. "He's too full of hate. He's yours, Princess."

"Done." Piper grinned. "You will never hurt or bother another para. Won't ever remember Skylar and every time you hear her name, you'll develop a rash. You won't understand it, won't find relief, and will beg for help. You've done enough damage and won't hurt anyone else." She poked Derrence in the chest, making him disappear just as she had with Prince.

Diesel snorted. "Finally got rid of the trash."

"We did." Piper hugged him. "I bet your arms are tired. Thank you."

"Nah. I was just starting to flex." Diesel laughed and nuzzled her hair.

Skylar paused. "We didn't really solve anything, did we? They're not cured. All we did was scare them and wipe their memories."

"Sort of," Piper said. "Yes, I've wiped their memories. I've got the power to change their minds, and I did. But you also had the chance to speak your piece."

"They know. They might not realize it because the magic has taken their memories, but they know," Brody said. "They'll never treat another para like they did you. You stood up for yourself and they got the message."

He might be right. They both might be.

"They know and will change," Piper said. "I'm tired of being sweet and nice. Some people, like them, needed a rough answer to change."

"Can't always have sparkles," Diesel said. "Let's go. I hate the dungeon." He walked away, leaving Piper behind.

"It's okay. They'll learn eventually, but you needed to save yourself. You did and I'm proud of you," Piper said. "Now, you two need to talk and I'm due in the throne room. I'll find you." She left them alone in the darkness.

Skylar bowed her head and glanced at her hand. She wanted to shift, but the color didn't go away. Why wouldn't it go away? "I'm still magenta."

"You are." Brody stood before her. "If it's any help, it's pretty. I mean, truly beautiful."

"Thanks." Panic set in. "Will I look like this forever?" She wasn't sure if she wanted to.

"Does that upset you?" Brody asked. "Honey, I like it because it's you. I can't imagine your spirit being anything but brightly colored. You're gorgeous."

She should be reassured, but she wasn't because she was worried. She'd always had her looks and money to fall back on. He didn't care about either. Would he still like her later?

Brody cupped her jaw in both hands and caressed her cheeks. "I don't give a rat's ass if you can shift, are pink, rich, powerful, or whatever. I care about you. I fell for you. I want to keep going on this ride with you and see where it leads because you're you. You're fun, sweet, and exciting. Magic has nothing to do with it. You're the draw. You."

She stared at him. "Brody?"

"Cross my heart." Brody kissed her. "I can't not love you. I've tried to dislike you, tried to tell myself this wasn't happening, but it did. Not because of the things they liked about you. Because of who you are. That's what drew me in. You did."

"You haven't gotten to know me. What if I leave socks on the floor or a ring in the shower? Or glow at night? I might keep you awake because I can't turn my color off. I might show you why you could dislike me again."

"Could," he said. "But you've showed me how to be me. How to embrace my strengths and quirks. We're a good team. If we keep putting our heads together, we'll be unstoppable."

She loved his faith in her. She bit back a whimper as he held her closer. "I'm game to keep trying if you are."

"I am," he said, his voice deep and gravelly.

"Would it be wrong to ask you to shower with me?" She rubbed on him, sending electricity through her body. She yearned for him. Yearned to be nude with him and feel his hands all over her. "We haven't gotten clean since we ran away."

"Only to be dirty?" He grinned and held her in his strong embrace. "Come here, you. We've got a lot of work ahead of us to keep this union strong, but I found my mate and I can't imagine not having you around. Plus, I do want that shower."

Excitement overwhelmed her. She had somewhere to belong and someone who loved her. Someone who was her mate. How could she say no to him? Easy. She couldn't. "I can't wait."

Chapter Twelve

Brody had no clue if Piper would want their help in setting up the special envoy group. Their work might be done now that they'd provided the plan. He wasn't sure. They could be there to formulate the idea, then rely on others to make it happen.

He could ask Piper, but she had other problems right now. He'd bother her later.

Skylar stopped in the living room area. "I should close up that house and sell it. Should get rid of the silly stuff."

"You have time. There's security protecting the house, right?" Had to be.

"Yes."

He frowned and his thoughts raced. "What if it became a base for the envoys?"

She stared at him for a moment, then slowly nodded. "Yes. It would be a good base of operations outside of Eerie. It's private and protected. Unless you know how to get past my spells, it's safe."

"Then how did I get past?"

"I had them open for the party."

"Makes sense. Everyone knew it was there."

"That's why I change the codes frequently. If you've been to a party, then that's your visit to my house, but I see what you mean. We can have it protected by better spells. I'm sure Piper has some."

"I know a few." He had quite a list in his head. "But we can ask her later."

"We can." She averted her gaze and red infused her cheeks. "It's a lot to think about."

"It is." But there was time to sort it all out. "When Piper comes to discuss this with us, we'll offer the house and property. Until then, we'll be here, having a good time and enjoying each other."

She looked at him and grinned. "I still can't believe you're real."

"Me? Why wouldn't I be real?" he asked. "I'm right here." He'd never had to work so hard before, and he liked it.

"Because you seem to care, you say you love me, and you're here, being kind to me. I'm not used to kind people who are genuine."

That was a shame. "I'm very real and I do care. I do love you. Everyone who discounted you lost out because they didn't get the chance to know how wonderful you are. Knowing you is a treasure."

Her pink seemed to vibrate, growing dimmer, then stronger. Like a heartbeat. "You're too kind."

"I'm just me."

She trembled. "You've said a couple times that I'm your mate. How do you know? How are you so certain?"

She asked such easy questions. He'd never tire of reassuring her. "I had no idea until I stood in the bedroom with you and realized they could've killed us both. I couldn't lose you. That's when I knew. I've never felt this strongly about anyone else."

"Have you ever had anyone else?"

She frustrated him, yet he didn't mind. He welcomed her challenges. "Not really." Jeni hadn't fired him up in the same way. Skylar did. True, he didn't have much experience, but he didn't need it. Once he met Skylar, he'd lost his heart. "I'm just fine with the experiences I've had. It's perfectly okay."

"You don't need more time?"

"Sky." He closed his eyes and caressed her cheek. "I need more time, sure."

"I knew it."

"I need that time to fall further in love with you. I'm already there, but we have a whole lifetime to keep it going. That's not a bad thing. It's the best thing we could do because it gives us time. We'll figure it out."

"Brody."

He figured out what she was doing. Trying to argue to find out if he'd truly fallen for her, or if he'd get aggravated and change his mind. "Keep trying. I won't change my mind." He opened his eyes and swept his gaze over her. "I really am convinced."

Hope filled her eyes. The beginning of a smile curled on her lips, but she said nothing.

"When I make up my mind, I don't change it. I'm odd that way."

She balled her hands on his chest. She nodded and a tear slipped down her cheek. "You're either good at lying because you're a fine actor, or you're terribly truthful and hold my heart in your hands."

"May I hold your heart?" he whispered. He didn't have time to play games or lie.

"Yes." She slid her hands to his shoulders and held on tight. "Very much, yes."

He let the moment happen and basked in it. He knew his heart, and it belonged to her alone. He'd known she was his mate, but he wondered if she agreed. He wondered what synth people did when they found their person or being. What did they call their mate?

"What?" She stayed in his arms, but her brow knotted. "You're so far away."

"Just thinking." He had so many questions about synths.

"How to spend my money?"

"No." She'd insulted him by asking him that, but he refused to get angry. "Not your money."

"Then what? I can't go into public like this."

"Pink?"

"Yes. No one will understand."

"They will here in Eerie, but the outside world doesn't need to understand." She should be happy to be so free.

"Then what?"

"There's so much I don't know about synths," he said. "I'm excited to learn about you while we grow old together." He paused. "Do you grow old? I do."

Her eyes widened, then her grin brightened and she sagged into him. "We do grow old. It takes a while, though."

"Does it?" He patted her ass. "Does this mean I've got a cougar?"

"A what?" She laughed. "I'm over two hundred years old according to the universe, but I've been on Earth for about thirty-five years. You?"

"Forty, this time." He felt old, but she vitalized him. "I love being loved by a cougar."

"You do?" She smiled. "But I can shift to match your age. We can grow old together."

"I'd like that." He continued to pat her ass. "Do you have mates or something like that?"

"Destined person or being."

Interesting. "Do you get training or education in knowing that? Or is it intrinsic?"

"Intrinsic."

"Do you believe I'm your destined person? I do understand if I'm not or you have doubts."

She shook her head. "No doubts. Not one." She adjusted the collar of his shirt and caressed his neck. "I want to go home so we can have some peace."

"It's quiet here." But he understood. "I want to go home, too." He'd rather be out of the dirty, dingy, gross darkness. She gave his heart and soul light. He wanted to keep it going and bask in it.

"Open a portal?" She let go and held out her hands. "This place gives me the creeps."

"Yes, my love." He opened a portal and gestured to her to head through first.

She stepped into the lab, then waited for him as he stepped through, then closed the portal. Once the hole between spaces closed, he relaxed.

She threw herself into his arms, nearly toppling him over. "Thank you."

"For?" He braced himself. "What'd I do?"

"Getting me out of the shit with them, for believing in me, and bringing me home. I belong here in Eerie with you." Tears slipped down her cheeks. "I never realized how lost I was until you showed up at the party. I have a purpose."

"Always did. Just had to find your cause." He kissed her. "Now you've got it and you're unstoppable."

She continued to cry but also grinned. "I have a purpose and a partner. I hope she comes back to have us help with the cause."

"Piper?" He couldn't say for sure, but he believed Piper might. "She'll find us."

"I hope so." She exhaled. Her pink deepened, then faded. She shifted, disrobing before him. "I'd like that shower now."

He should have something intelligent to say, but the words escaped him. Seeing her in her naked glory stole his breath. She was beautiful inside and out. He needed -- no, craved -- and worshipped her. Yes, he needed that shower and everything else she could give him. She filled him up, renewing his senses, lifting his soul and making him one again. He offered his hand

and led her to the bathroom.

For once, he wished he had a better place to share with her. This bathroom seemed too bland.

"What?" she asked.

"Nothing." He turned on the water. While she watched him, he took off his shirt. "Just admiring the view."

"Are you?" She remained outside the stall. "I'm impressed by your command of magic. You don't think you have much, but you do."

"I try." He tripped as he removed his jeans. "Damn it. One day I'll look smooth for you."

She shook her head. "Don't need to look smooth. I like you when you're authentic." She offered her hand, giving him a chance to steady himself. "You're sexier when you're not trying so hard to be sexy."

He admired her honesty. He finished removing his jeans and stood tall. Blood rushed to his cock as steam billowed in the bathroom. "Ladies first."

"Thank you." She stepped into the stall, right under the spray. The water sluiced onto her head, plastering down her hair. Water droplets formed on her lashes. She parted her lips. Instead of her pink from her synth side, a deep blush spread down her chest. Her nipples beaded. She reminded him of a goddess.

Maybe among synths, she was. She was to him.

He joined her in the stall. "Hello."

"Hi." She collapsed in his arms and sighed. "Missed you."

"Never got far away." He slid her hair from her face. "Beautiful."

"Am I?" She stood on her toes and kissed him. "You're sexy, too."

"Want you." He kissed her deeply, wanting everything she could give him. He sucked on her tongue, then caressed her breast. She leaned into his hand and whimpered. He'd never get enough of her.

She broke the kiss. "Make love to me."

"Right now?" He barely felt the sting of the hot water on his back. All he could do was see her. She consumed his senses and scattered his thoughts. He scooped her into his arms and pinned her to the tile wall. "I need you."

"Got me." She hooked her legs around his waist and threaded her arms around his neck. She rocked into him. His cock slid along her pussy lips. The electricity shot right through him. Christ. He craved this.

"Want to be inside you," he said, panting. He kissed her again. He needed her to be right on the edge with him.

"Yes." She rocked into him faster. "Please?"

He couldn't resist her. He pinned her between the wall of the tub and his body. He angled her hips, cradling her ass under his hands as he entered her. The second he filled her, she squeezed around him.

Just like before, Skylar fit him like a glove. So perfect. He basked in the ripples and nuances of her body. Being inside her was like coming home. Like finding his other half. She made him better. Made him want to be the best he could.

Skylar squirmed. She whimpered and panted. "Brody. Yes." She dug her nails into his shoulders. "Move. Make me come apart."

"Yes." He held onto her hips. He looked into her eyes as he began to thrust. Each plunge into her pussy nudged him closer to coming. The beginning of the orgasm built in his body. He lost himself in the thrill of making love to her. He didn't just feel the silkiness of her body. Yes, he loved the way she felt. He could have this feeling every day of his life and be happy. He'd be complete.

But this was more than physical attraction. This was almost spiritual. Their souls twined together in a perfect tangle. One he never wanted to unravel. He felt her moving in his soul. She was the one he never saw coming and never expected to find. Now that he had her, he never wanted to let go.

"Brody." She writhed and held on tight. Despite the heat and water around them, her skin tinged pink, then deep magenta.

"Christ." He loved that she could be herself with him. He embraced her uniqueness and pumped his hips. He filled her, pushing to the hilt before nearly pulling out.

The sparkles from the first time returned as the orgasm became stronger in his body. The world around him seemed to melt away. He forgot about being in the shower and the stresses on his mind. The only one who mattered was Skylar.

The glitter increased. It swirled around him and Skylar like a whirlwind. She tipped her head back and cried out. She turned almost translucent, yet magenta. Like she'd become stardust in his arms.

She met him thrust for thrust, bucking into him. "Brody. Oh fuck. More, Brody, please."

Her breasts skimmed his chest. The light touches turned his senses inside out. Nothing else mattered. The orgasm splintered within him and the sparkles and glitter swirled harder. When he glanced down at his arms, he'd become magenta, too.

"Fuck, yes." He'd become one with her in the deepest way possible. He pressed his face to her shoulder and lost himself in fucking her. He couldn't think straight. The orgasm overwhelmed him, and he allowed it to sweep him over the edge. "Skylar!" Welcoming the rush, he surged into her, filling her with his seed.

She cried out. "Fuck. Me." She trembled and tensed around his dick. "Fuck," she said, drawing the word out. In seconds, she slumped in his arms.

Just as quickly as the magenta crept over his skin, it evaporated. The water bit his skin and slid down his face. He looked into her eyes and saw forever. She was his home.

She loosened her grasp on him. "Brody."

"Present." He kissed her, then rested his head on her shoulder. "Worn out, but present."

"Brody?"

"Yeah?" He slipped out of her and sighed as the water washed them clean.

"You're pink, too."

"I am?" Still? He chuckled. "I guess I am." Not that it mattered.

"You're not upset?"

"Nope." The moment he noticed the pink, it faded. So much for being one -- all the time. He didn't mind. They were good together and he trusted their bond. "Oh well. Maybe next time."

"You don't mind being pink?"

"Nope. I like being with you and if you're in me… then I'm good. You make me happy." He lowered her to her feet. "We should get clean."

"We should stay right here." She held onto him. "I'm happy because I'm here with someone who sees my potential and encourages me, which is huge. You're not anyone I saw coming into my orbit, but I'm glad you conned me into going with you. Best decision ever."

"Best decision to go out there." He'd gone out of

his comfort zone and done something that scared him to death… but it was also the best leap of faith he could've taken. Chilly water sluiced down his back. "Holy shit. The hot water's gone. We should get out."

"Then let's." She twisted the knob. "I love you, Brody."

His heart hammered and the silence enveloped him, but she consumed his senses. "I love you, too."

He might be naked with her in the shower and completely vulnerable, but he didn't care. He had nothing to hide from the synth he loved. The synth of his heart.

Chapter Thirteen

Three days later, Skylar stood in the middle of the call room and admired what she and Brody had created. The center was filled with paras answering phones, bubbles, and handling portals. The room was a hub of excitement and action. She admired the smoothness with which the system ran.

"We really did it," Brody said. "This is crazy."

"Yeah." She slipped her arms around his biceps. "So far, it's all working."

"Yeah." Brody eased his arm free, then embraced her. "I feel sort of useless, though. We created this baby and it's time to let it go, but I kind of don't want to."

"I know." She caught sight of Piper in the room. "Piper."

"Princess," Brody corrected. "You should speak to her that way."

She'd forgotten. She'd met Piper and was introduced by her name, so she'd grown used to her being Piper, not the Princess. Piper was her friend. The Princess was something almost impossible to consider. Yes, she knew Piper was the Princess, but she was mostly her friend.

"Hi." Piper joined them. "Everything is humming along well. We've had a couple of rejections and three people trying to scam their way in, but we've been able to catch them before something happened. So there's that."

"Good." She nodded and stuck to Brody's side. "What can we do? I feel a little helpless."

"Ditto." Brody rubbed Skylar's arm. "I don't know what to do."

"Enjoy the fruits of your work," Piper said. "We could use a better location for the greater world center.

The old apartment building is good, but we need something more and probably a couple locations."

Skylar bit back a groan. They didn't have to look too far to find a solution. She had five. She'd had them all along. "I can help even more."

"Oh?" Piper crinkled her brows. "How?"

"I have two homes and will gladly let the people of Eerie use them for this. Except for the personal effects in my suite, feel free to use them and the three apartments I have. I'll get the addresses for you."

"Are you sure?" Piper asked. Her eyes widened. "That would be awesome and so kind of you."

"I'm positive." She leaned into Brody. "Let me get the keys and codes, as well. Won't take long." Mostly, she'd forgotten her various addresses. She'd allowed Prince to keep that straight for her. She spent so little time in the various locations that she hadn't grown too comfortable in any of them.

"I'll get a team ready to convert them. Thanks." Piper hugged her and Brody at the same time. "I knew you'd be able to solve this problem. Brody, you're brilliant. Keep embracing it. Skylar, thank you for everything. We're glad you're here and part of the team. You and Brody together are the best combination."

"We try." She appreciated the compliment. When Piper bounced away, Skylar retrieved her phone. "I've got the info. Hell, we could portal people there right now and get them started."

"Could." Brody let go of her. "How much do you need to move?"

"The contents of my suite." She fiddled with the phone, finding the information. "Won't take long."

"Then I'll tell Piper you've got a plan." Brody left her alone in search of the Princess.

Skylar located the address numbers and last codes. "Here." She chased after Piper and Brody. "I've found it all."

Piper stopped walking. "Oh. Cool."

"Why don't you portal people there? It'll give you more access to the building and help you all get used to it."

"Duh." Piper sighed. "I've got too much going on here. It's crazy. I knew this would take time and take off, but not this much. I'll get a portal going and select the team."

Brody hesitated, then tapped Piper's arm. "I have a suggestion. You can say no and I won't be offended, but I have a thought, and I bet Sky would agree with me."

And she'd thought she'd said a mouthful. "Brody?"

Piper grinned. "I have the feeling I know what you're going to say but say it anyway in case I've got it wrong."

Skylar slipped her hand into his back pocket. "I agree." She had no idea what he was talking about, but she trusted him. "Go for it."

Brody cleared his throat. He fidgeted as he spoke. "What if Sky and I head up the center and give you some help? We could run the place or one of the satellite locations. We could refer the sketchy people, too, and help you handle it. Maybe one of the trolls or gargoyles could be the heavy we need to toss the scammers."

The brightest grin appeared on Piper's face. "I was hoping you'd say that. Skylar? Are you in with it? I'll get Diesel to suggest a team as bouncers, so to speak. I love this idea."

"I think it's a great one, too." Skylar loved that

she had a job in Eerie. "I'd like to move my money to Eerie, too. This is my home."

"It is when you're here." Brody kissed her temple. He embraced her again. "We've got this."

"We'll work together right now until you're up to speed, but yes. This is good." Piper waggled her hands. "I've got to talk to Diesel. Be right back."

Brody snorted and chuckled. "You just saved the day."

"I did? What about you?" She grasped his hand. "I don't need my various homes, and we could use a new purpose. So, if we can help the cause in these ways, then great. As for the money, I'd like it where I can keep an eye on it. I'm still making more, and the accountant knows what's going on. But I don't need every single cent. Some money might help here, so let's let it help."

"Agreed. I wish I could offer something, too, though. I feel so inadequate," Brody said.

"Why? You've done so much for this town. Did a lot for my spirits, too." She hugged him. "Let's go to the mansion."

"Yes, my love." He opened a portal and led her into her bedroom. "I do wish we'd have been able to fuck here. That bed is great."

She had to agree. "Maybe it can come along. I don't know." She did want to take her most prized possessions through the portal to the loft. "Can we shrink things to make them fit better until we get to your place?"

"Could," he said. "Are you officially moving in with me?"

"I assumed I was." She froze. "I should've asked before I assumed." She wished she hadn't acted so quickly.

"I expected you would. I want you to live with me. That's where you belong."

She appreciated his honesty and sweetness. "Then I'm glad I was too bold." She surveyed the room. "I have too much stuff."

"I guess so."

She nodded, thinking through what she wanted to bring. "You know, a lot of my junk could be used for the cause."

"It's not like there's a famine," Brody said.

"No, but the clothes would help someone else. I don't need one hundred and sixty pairs of jeans."

"You have that many?"

"I do." She sighed and rested her hands on her hips. "It was a moment of weakness. I went on a shopping spree and was encouraged by 'friends.'"

"It happens."

She faced him, still deciding what to take with her. "Have you ever been pushed by your friends to do something silly?"

"Not really." He sank onto her bed. "I don't have a lot of friends and most of the people I know don't want to hang out with me because I'm too different."

"You are?" Personally, she disagreed.

"I took a long time to sort out my magic. It was a bit… unpredictable for a while," he said. "No one taught me how to harness it, so I had to figure it out for myself."

"That stinks. I bet you'll have lots of friends by the time we get entrenched in the job."

"Why? To curry favor?" He shook his head. "Nah. No one will care. I'm still a dork."

"You might think so, but people will want to be friends with the new girl. I don't want to be their friends unless they treat you properly and don't try to fawn all over me. I want honest friends for once."

"I can't disagree." He remained on the bed. "Do we start moving stuff?"

"Yes, but let me finish this. I'm on a roll. I want honest friends, not people who are fake. Mark my words. If I get sycophants, I'll be pissed." She handed him her jewelry box. "This needs to go."

"Don't have to shrink it." He held onto the box. "What else?"

"I have another one, but most of my expensive stuff is in the vault. We can portal there next. The rest is just junk." She held the second box. "I'd like someone else to have most of this stuff."

"No photos or personal effects?" he asked. "You don't have that stuff?"

"Don't need to. The papers and websites had plenty for me. For a while, it was like every step I took landed in the papers, and it was so silly. I didn't do anything. I was a playgirl. No one took me seriously. Yet, there I was, with my face plastered all over everywhere." It was a waste of time.

"I guess." He opened the portal and followed her back to the loft. "I don't have a safe."

"No, but you have a lab and that's enough. Who wants to steal stuff from you when there's a good chance whatever's in your lab could explode?" she asked. "I don't want to touch half of it."

"You might be right." He put the box on the table. "Oh, shit." He fumbled as a bubble formed in his hand.

"Brody?" Piper held up both hands. "I wasn't sure where you were. Is Skylar there with you?"

"Yes." He turned the bubble, allowing Skylar and Piper to see each other. "What's wrong?"

"I'm flustered," Piper said.

Skylar stood beside Brody. "How about we come back and I help you? Then you'll get the right places, and we'll get them up and running faster. Good deal?"

"Yes. Come back." Piper sighed and bowed her head. "This is working so well. I don't want to stunt its progress."

"No." Skylar grinned and left her jewelry box on the table with the other box. "We'll be right there." She nudged Brody.

"Let's go." He portaled them back to the command center. Piper paced and seemed to talk to herself.

"No, I need you to follow directions. I'm one person," Piper growled. "Enough."

Skylar touched Piper's arm. When Piper looked up, she smiled.

Piper gestured to her and Brody. "Yes. Just handle it." She put her hand down. "There are times when I'm glad I'm in charge and then there are days like today when I'd rather hide. Fuck, some individuals just don't listen. Okay. I hate to be blunt again, but I need you to get the homes set up a little faster than we'd planned. Like right now. I'm sending a couple of faeries to help you, but you're in charge. You said five residences?"

"Yes." She nodded. "Five."

"No shit?" Piper asked. "I mean, I know you said it, but wow."

"No shit." She pulled her phone from her pocket. "There's one home in Cleveland and one in Arizona. The apartments are in Florida, California, and New York. I had one in the Hamptons, but I don't remember if I still own it. I'll have to check because I've never actually stayed in it."

"What a problem to have," Piper said. "We have

our work cut out for us. Lydia, Sonya? Now." She snapped her fingers.

Two green-haired faeries joined Piper. "These are your faeries. Whatever you need, they can create."

"Very good." Skylar smiled. "Good to be working with you."

"Ladies, you will listen to and respect both Skylar and Brody as if I were there. They're extensions of me. I can see you and we'll be checking on you when you least expect it. If you act like shits, I'll know."

The faeries nodded. "Yes, Princess," they said in unison. "We'll behave."

Piper touched each faerie's chest, creating a locket. "I hate controlling anyone, but you need to prove yourselves."

Both faeries nodded, but neither spoke.

"Okay." Piper brushed an errant lock of hair from her face. "It used to be so easy and sweet. The harsh realities have set in. People don't want to listen, and I can't be kind all the time. I have to be a hard-ass."

"I understand," Skylar said. "There are all sorts of things that seem fun until you have to pay bills and be an adult. That's part of why I checked out. I didn't have a childhood. Synths don't. We just show up, so I pretended to be irresponsible. It was fun for a while, but just as tiring. It's honestly easier to be an adult. You're responsible for yourself and can see the rewards for what you've accomplished."

"I know, but it sucks. I never planned on being this tough of a ruler. I like being kind while in charge. This full-on powerful shit is for the birds."

Diesel joined her in the command room and slipped his arm around Piper.

Skylar admired their connection, but she had one with Brody that was just as strong. If this was what happened when beings came to Eerie, found their match, then even better. At least they were all home.

"He's the best one ever because he keeps me grounded and reminds me we're all going to be fine because we're working together. We're in this together," Piper said. "Trust your team and partners."

Brody shook hands with Diesel. "It's true," Brody said. "You surround yourself with smart people and choose them for a reason."

"Trust that," Diesel said. "What are you questioning?"

"The faeries going with Brody and Skylar to the Graves Mansion. I'm not sure I can trust them, despite warning them and giving them trackers," Piper said. "They've got honesty lockets, but they've been trouble before."

Diesel nodded. "Okay. That's a start and it was a good idea. But I have a suggestion."

Skylar hoped it wasn't something about her. But she had to get that out of her head. She wasn't guilty and hadn't done anything wrong. She wasn't being used for her belongings -- she'd offered them up and used her brains for this situation.

"Send Brody and Skylar along with the faeries, yes. Since it's Skylar's house, make sure she's fine with it, but you mentioned using some of the guards and I'm for that. I'll send Chero and Geral. Those two gargoyles are ready to help and they'll keep the faeries in line. Let Skylar and Brody help you get it going, like you said, and it'll work out. We're all on the same team."

Piper nodded and bumped shoulders with Diesel. "Thanks."

"You had the answer all along, but you had to hear it out loud. Your gut is right," Diesel said. "Yeah?"

"I like it," Skylar replied. "It's a great idea, Piper."

"You have a court and trusted members for a reason," Diesel said. "You want to rule by fairness and order as well as collaboration, Pi. It's okay to use it."

Skylar agreed. She didn't feel she or Brody were part of the internal group, but she could help the overall system. She wanted to. She'd been trying to find a way to do something with her life. This was one way she could. "I'm in."

"Brody?" Piper asked.

"I follow her," Brody said. "I got her into this world, and she's got my back. We're here to help you, so yeah, I'm in."

Skylar hugged Brody. She couldn't have said it better herself. She'd only change one part -- they had mutual trust and she'd follow him anywhere, too.

"Then we'll get this going," Piper said. "Chero can accompany them right now. When Geral is ready, he can follow."

"Smart choice." Diesel patted Piper's shoulder.

"Why don't you round up who you believe could be just as strong as bouncers for the other locations and we'll keep moving," Piper said. She turned to Skylar and Brody. "Deal?"

"Deal." Skylar loved the sense of belonging and collaboration. Everyone had a piece, a place, and reason to work together. It was up to them to make it all work together.

Brody elbowed Skylar. "We should make a plan."

"Yes." She and Brody might as well while they

waited for the others to come to the command center. The plan of attack was ready, and they'd have it running soon. She even knew what she could do to handle the extra stuff back at the mansion. "I suggest we go through the house and get rid of the stuff that's fake."

"Magic?" Brody asked.

"Fine by me. We could bring some back to Eerie if anyone wants it. Then someone who might want it or could use it can have it, rather than it going to waste," Skylar said. She'd rather have the items reused than tossed.

Brody's eyes sparkled and the grin lit up his face. "Remember how you told me you said you wanted to do something of substance and be more than you believed you were?"

"Yeah?" She cuddled up to him. "I wanted to be taken seriously."

"You did and are doing that. You've proven your intelligence and worth. You've proved you're not just a playgirl. You're leaving a legacy and being more than you ever thought. You're brilliant and amazing."

"So are you." She hugged him tighter. He'd seen so much in her, and she loved it. "Are we going to keep on this ride together?"

He kissed her temple. "I love you, Skylar Graves, so yes, I'll follow you anywhere. I'm thrilled to go on this journey beside you."

She held onto him and embraced her power and intelligence. She could be anything she wanted to because he'd showed her what she'd already possessed -- her own smarts. Time to use it and make the world better.

"I love you, too, Brody. My partner." She closed her eyes and breathed him in. She'd never expected she'd be pulled out of her old life by magic, but she had and she loved it. She'd found her purpose, all because she'd been taken by the sorcerer. Sure, he wasn't the bombastic, showy sorcerer that fit the stereotype. He was simple, sweet, and full of magic. To be taken by this sorcerer fit her just fine.

Now, it was time to make magic together.

Taken by The Lady of the Lake (Taken 12)
A Paranormal Women's Fiction Novel
Megan Slayer

She's an urban legend. He's adrift. With a little magic, they'll discover their fates are entwined.

Amanda Fortune never expected to be left in the lake, but after her murder and subsequent dumping, that's exactly where she is. She's become an urban legend, her ghost seen only by a very few. She longs to have a second chance at life, but that's not possible when you're dead. *Is it*?

With the right circumstances, anything is possible.

Sawyer Gibson doesn't know what he's meant to do in life. He has abilities to read the Fates, but his talents aren't needed in the town of Eerie. Everyone here has magic. He's nothing special. But Aunt Chloe is dying, and she knows more than Sawyer ever thought possible. Amanda is -- was -- her best friend. So Aunt Chloe sends Sawyer on a chase to find Amanda's killer.

But Amanda's a myth. A ghost. And ghosts can't be seen. *Right*?

The moment Sawyer lays eyes on Amanda, he's smitten. There's the tiny problem of her being a ghost... but that detail won't stop Sawyer, even if someone else thinks it will.

Chapter One

50 Years Ago...

"You will find love divine upon the right time," Amanda Fortune whispered and cocked her head. She read the words three more times before the letters disappeared into the cauldron. She didn't know what to make of what she'd seen. She had a boyfriend. Was this the Fates' way of telling her she'd found the one? It seemed too ominous for that.

She should call her best friend and have a chat about what she'd learned. Chloe was good at understanding what she didn't. Chloe had the magic of the witches. She could discern what made little sense otherwise, and she knew the languages of the coven. She hadn't spoken to Chloe in days and wished she'd been better about checking in with her.

But her boyfriend hadn't wanted her to leave the house. He claimed there was bad magic in the air. Something that would destroy anyone within it. She'd tried to ask him if he'd been affected by the uneasiness, but he swore it didn't bother him.

Could've fooled me.

She wanted to get away from him, but circumstances prevented her escape. Claude had promised too high a price for her not to marry to Claude. She'd been told she'd saved the family with this joining, but she'd still been hesitant to marry. Hesitant to share her life wholly with Claude.

Her spirit wasn't interested and turned to ice in her veins when the mention of setting a date was uttered. Claude cared little for her, raised his hand to her on many occasions, and left her with bruises she'd had to cover before going out in public. He'd threatened her so many times, she'd lost count. Every cell in her body screamed to run, but it wasn't safe.

She might not be strong enough to get away from him, but she sure as hell didn't want to marry Claude Washington.

"Making your magic?" Claude asked from behind her.

She hadn't heard him come into the room. She swiped her hand, erasing the remainder of the letters and the steam from the cauldron. "I am." She couldn't explain why, but she didn't want him to see what she'd learned. Part of her knew why. She didn't want him to feel pushed to speak the words of love she longed to hear. She wanted them to come from his heart.

Some days, she wondered if anything came from his heart -- even blood. He could be so cold to her. So calculating. Like he didn't care for her much but stayed with her out of duty.

"What are you thinking about?" Claude asked. "I see you got rid of the spell before I saw it."

"I might have." His words prickled along her neck and sent shivers down her spine. "You don't care much for my magic."

"No, not much." Claude circled her with a peculiar smile curled on his lips. "You're so secretive."

"No." She shook her head. Since she was small, she'd been told not to share her magic unless she felt completely comfortable. She'd never wanted to let him in on her abilities. Truth be told, she was more embarrassed by her magic than anything. She didn't have the ability to create spells. Couldn't conjure anything. She simply read the words of the Fates and could steer people in the direction needed. The knowledge was magic in the right hands but otherwise seemed silly -- at least it did to him.

"Then what are you doing?" He folded his arms.

"You can tell me."

But could she? She toyed with her locket. She'd lied to him the entire time they'd been together, claiming the locket contained her magic, but it didn't. She controlled her visions. The locket was simply a bauble from her mother that glowed when the magic came through.

"You never tell me anything. You're guarded." He rounded the cauldron, cornering her between his body and the wall. "It's like you don't trust me."

"Why wouldn't I trust you?" She could think of a hundred reasons, but she'd keep that to herself. "Our families knew we were matched and put us together. They must know something."

"They did, but they expected us to be married and have a family by now. Expected us to be happy together and share everything." He met her gaze, but something odd sparkled in his eyes.

The shiver down her spine increased. The more her concern increased, the more she wanted to guard herself. "I'm not ready to be a mother." Would she ever be? She wasn't sure. It seemed too pushy to demand someone have children. She didn't even like kids. Why would she want one?

"You've said that for years."

They'd only been together for just under two years. She'd been painfully honest with him the entire time. "I know."

He inched closer to her and tipped his head. "You told me you'd consider it." He braced his right hand on the wall behind her.

She collided with the stone and the breath wrenched from her for a second. "I did, and I don't want to." Something within her screamed to duck and run. She stared at him, running through various exit strategies. If she could get under his arm, she could get away. "Claude, you're scaring me."

"Am I?" He tipped his head the other way. "I'm trying to get close to you." His voice was even and almost frightening. He wasn't smiling -- but he wasn't exactly glaring either.

"You've never done anything like this." She balled her hands. The closer he got, the more her chances of escaping went down. "I need some air. Please back up."

"Amanda." He shook his head. "You'd push me away forever if you could."

"No," she said. "You're caging me in, and I don't like it." She trembled. He'd been controlling and pushy the entire time they'd been together. Her father claimed it was Claude demonstrating to the world that she belonged to him. If that was what belonging meant, then she wasn't interested. She'd never believed anyone should belong to anyone else -- especially when dating or in a relationship.

"You don't like anything I do. I'm doing everything for us. For you. Trying to make you into the woman I know you can be. The woman I know you want to be. But you won't allow it. Won't let me get close to you or see your magic. You're hiding from me. You're cold to me and punishing me. For what? Making you into the woman I want?" He grasped her biceps with his left hand and kept her caged in with his right arm.

"I would like you to let me go." She needed to breathe. "I'm not cold. I'm scared."

"Of me?" He pressed his body to hers. "You're supposed to love me."

She'd never actually said she loved him. "Claude."

"If you can't love me, then give me that fucking locket." He moved his hand from the wall to her throat where he clutched the necklace.

"No. I can't share that with you." It'd been a gift. It'd belonged to her mother. Besides, it had no magic. It wasn't worth anything. "Please."

"You don't share your life, your love, or your magic with me. How can I be the husband you need without it? How can I make you into the woman you're meant to be?" He yanked the locket from her throat, then moved his left hand.

She winced, ready for him to strike her. He'd done it so many times before and she'd lied to anyone who asked. No, he wasn't abusing her. Wasn't hitting her. Hadn't spit on her.

He curled his lip in a sneer and his eyes flashed with malice. "You've been a thorn in my side the entire time. You want to embarrass me. I will not have it." His hand swiped through the air.

A dreadful ache started in her head and spread down her body. She saw stars and her knees buckled. She met his gaze but didn't see light or life in there. All she saw was hatred, anger, and a void.

He ripped the locket from her and shoved her to the ground. "Don't you ever do this to me. You will not embarrass me." He brought his hand down again and the stars came back, but in more of a blinding streak. Her stomach lurched and she crumpled to the floor. The world around her went black. The last thing she saw as the darkness swallowed her was Claude standing over her with a smile tinged with malice and delight on his lips.

"This is how it ends, my enchantress. No one will find you. No one will care." Claude raised his arm a third time, but she had no fight left in her.

The swampy darkness surrounded her and she welcomed the rest. Was she dying? Probably, but the fight was gone.

He'd won.

* * *

Amanda opened her eyes, but instead of the comforting warmth of her bedroom or home, she couldn't breathe. Something swirled around her. She couldn't move. Had he paralyzed her?

Claude seemed to hover over her. He dropped something on her, but she didn't feel whatever he'd released.

Chill seeped into her bones. No, into her soul. No matter how hard she tried, her entire body was pinned.

Claude cackled and sat back. Was he in a boat? She managed to look around and noticed the gentle movement of the plants. Fish moved past her. Was she underwater? The moonlight pierced the space around her and she spied rocks.

He'd dumped her. He'd done the ungodly thing he'd threatened for months and killed her. But he hadn't succeeded if she could see him. Or was this her spirit rising and going to the next plane?

She recognized the form where he sat -- a boat. He held up her locket and turned the bauble in his hands. "I have her magic now. No one will stop me. I own it all. Mine."

He rowed away, leaving her in the water. Leaving her to suffocate? Or just rot with time?

She sat up, but her body remained submerged. She made her way to the surface and poked her head out of the water. She opened her mouth to scream, but no sound came out. She tried a second and third time to scream, but nothing. She couldn't even hear her voice in her head. Just silence.

She placed her hand over her heart, but instead of feeling the beating, nothing happened. Realization swept over her. She'd died. He'd managed to kill her shell, but not her magic or spirit. He'd silenced her.

For now.

Would anyone ever find her? Maybe, but maybe not. She rose out of the water and took stock, not only of what she'd accomplished, but where she was. The second she saw the tall oak trees and row of fence cordoning off the willow trees, she knew where he'd dumped her -- her favorite spot on the north end of the lake. The fingers of shallow water were always littered with leaves and other natural debris. Even if anyone came looking for her, if they knew where to look, they'd never see her. The tangles of branches, leaves and scattering of rocks would make it nearly impossible.

She perched on one of the boulders jutting from the water and wrapped her arms around her knees.

Claude had succeeded in the things he'd set out to do. He'd abused, intimidated and silenced her. He hadn't stolen her magic, but he'd killed her. Killed the dreams and wishes she'd had. He'd taken her life, but not her spirit.

A scream from deep within her ripped from her throat, but again, the sound was gone. She cried and mourned her losses. She'd never be the same.

Would Chloe look for her? Worry? Or would she move on?

Amanda continued to stare out over the water. She could drown herself in her own sorrows or she could move forward. For now, she'd allow herself to deal with her grief. If she ignored it, she'd go mad. That wouldn't do. Not because she didn't deserve a break with reality, but if she lost that control, she'd hand Claude the win he wanted.

He desired to kill and silence her? Fine, but he'd never, ever best her. She'd come back and make him pay. She allowed herself to cry while she planned. The truth would come out, and she'd make sure he never evaded punishment.

* * *

Time passed, and people used the lake. She watched from her perch, able sometimes to walk along the shoreline and to move around the people, but not visible. She eavesdropped on conversations and both connections and quarrels.

One hot July night, she spied a couple on the banks tangled up in each other, enjoying each other's bodies. She knew she shouldn't be watching, but the longing to have her life back was too strong. The longing and desire to be loved in the way the couple cared about each other swept over her. She'd never known that sort of connection.

As she watched them settle for the evening, sated and naked together, a vision filled her mind. She couldn't remember the last time her magic had worked and offered her such a picture. She saw the man plain as day. He wasn't translucent, and could hear her. He reached for her.

She tried reaching for him in return, but it was like he was right out of her grasp.

She memorized every detail about this man. His striking dark eyes and dark hair. He looked almost exotic, as if he knew of dark magic and could use it with ease. He had an odd tilt to his head, like he was listening intently to everything she said and had an air of mischief around him. Her grandmother would've called it good mischief. Maybe it was.

She longed to touch him and get to know him,

but she'd never seen him around the lake. As the years marched on, she knew everyone who'd visited her precious lake and he wasn't one of them.

Neither was Chloe. She missed her friend. Maybe Chloe had forgotten her. Even her family hadn't come looking for her.

She wasn't sure how many years had passed and she remained in the limbo of her existence. As time marched on, her skin tinged blue-green and she forgot how it felt to use her feet. She'd become a spirit.

At times, she'd heard whispers, then stories told by firelight about a woman in the lake who'd been killed there by her father. A woman who haunted the banks of the lake, ready to devour anyone who got too close or wandered too deep into the darkness.

Did they mean her?

She'd rather find the man from her visions.

No, she'd rather be human again. She'd rather be herself.

If only she could.

You will find love divine upon the right time.

Those words filled the forefront of her brain, but she gave them little attention. The love she sought was impossible. Who could love a woman who couldn't be seen?

Chapter Two

Present Day

Sawyer Gibson sat with his aunt at the nursing home and fiddled with his tablet. He didn't mind spending the hours with her, but when she slept, he got bored. He didn't like being bored, but his aunt's magic had been failing for a long time. This wasn't a new situation, her sleeping a lot and going in and out of lucidity. Most of the time, he let her ramble and spoke to her as if he were the person she thought she was talking to, not her nephew.

She'd drift into lucidity and believe he was an ex-boyfriend, or a co-worker from her days at the potions factory. Every so often she'd talk about a woman named Mandy. He'd never met anyone in her circles named Mandy, but she'd speak to him as if he were this Mandy and they shared big secrets. He didn't know what those might be, but he wouldn't stop her.

The nurse came into the room. "Just checking her vitals."

"She's been sleeping." He left his tablet on the side table. "How long do you think she's got?"

The nurse smiled. "I don't know. Could be a few hours or a few more days. Her magic is thin, but she's holding on."

"Thanks." He fortified himself. "I'm glad you're taking care of her. I appreciate your concern. You're good at your job."

She stared at him, then snorted. "Let me guess. You don't think you could do my job?"

"Maybe?" She'd confused him. "I wasn't trying to insult you. It's true admiration."

"Right." She ran through her battery of tests and checks, then tucked her pen away. "Look, it's not as much of a compliment as you think. It's not cool or kind, either. Maybe it is true admiration, but it's not needed and if you're trying to flirt with me, save it. I'm engaged." She turned on her heel and strode out of the room.

Bedside manner-wise, she lacked a lot. He'd been trying to flirt a bit, but obviously his skills were lacking, just like Virginia claimed. His ex-girlfriend hadn't been kind when she'd shamed him before walking away and the scars were still fresh.

"You don't need to worry about her."

He looked away from the door to his aunt. "No?" He smiled and slipped her hand into his. "I don't think she liked my trying to flirt."

"Then shame on her. You were being kind," his aunt said. "I could see that."

"Oh? I thought you were asleep." He scooted closer to her. "You amaze me."

"You're too kind." She tipped her head to meet his gaze. "You know, you'd be a good fit for my friend, Mandy."

"You keep talking about her. Who is Mandy?"

"Oh, she was my best friend." Her voice softened and she smiled. "Mandy was so sweet. She cared about everyone she encountered and wanted to help them. She wasn't good with magic, though. Hers was more the magic of reading spells. If you were fifty years younger, I'd set you up with her."

"You would."

"But I can't."

"Because she's the same age as you?" he asked. This Mandy did sound like a wonderful person. "Would she come to visit you? I could call her."

"I wish you could."

"Don't have her number?"

"No, she's dead."

"Oh." Well, now he felt silly. "I'm sorry."

"She died fifty years ago." She squeezed his fingers. "It was sad. We'd just talked and then she was gone. Her boyfriend said she'd run away, but I knew. You don't have a connection like that to someone and not know."

"When did you see her last?" If his aunt would keep talking, he'd extend the conversation as long as possible.

"In Eerie. She had a little bungalow on the north end with her boyfriend. We'd talked on the phone and I knew she was upset, but I couldn't help her. I bet you could." She closed her eyes. "I know you could save her."

He had a thousand questions, but she'd fallen asleep again. He'd lived on the fringes of Eerie for years and never heard of a Mandy. He picked up his tablet and tapped her name into the search bar. If nothing else, maybe he'd learn about her case. There had to be something.

He swiped through the results but saw little. No Mandy, no case, no mention of a runaway. It was odd. He had another possibility.

Sawyer created a bubble and sent a message to the Princess. If anyone would know something about a woman named Mandy who'd disappeared in Eerie fifty years ago, then it'd be her. And if she didn't know, the Princess would know who to contact.

A moment later, a portal opened to the hospital room. The Princess, along with her cyclops, stepped through. "How is she?" Piper asked. "My heart aches for her. She's been through a lot."

"She has." He lowered his voice and stood. "She mentioned a woman named Mandy. I don't know who this Mandy might be, but she gave me some details. I thought you might be able to help me."

"Sure." Piper rested her hands on her hips. "If I can't, then Diesel might."

"I might," Diesel echoed softly.

Good. Sawyer inched in closer. "So, this Mandy. She says this woman was her best friend and she'd talked to her just before she disappeared. She said it was fifty years ago and this woman, this Mandy, could read spells. Was she maybe a connection to the Fates? Have you heard of this person? Or this case? Her boyfriend claimed she simply ran away. I'm guessing he never heard from her again. Does this sound familiar? I asked my aunt when she mentioned Mandy if I could call her to be with her as she faded, but she said Mandy's dead. I don't know what to make of it."

"I don't either." Piper frowned. "But it's from before my time. I don't have the history of the town as memorized as I'd like."

"I know about it." Diesel hooked his fingers in his front pockets. "I've heard about the case."

"You have?" Good. He could get closure for his aunt. "What do you know? Is she really dead?"

Diesel shifted his gaze to Piper for a second, then back to Sawyer. "When my father was a younger man, there was a story going around town about a woman who'd disappeared. The story goes that she was afraid for her life and ran away from her boyfriend. The other story claims that the same woman was still afraid, but she never got away. The rumor is that she was killed and never found, but her spirit roams the lake."

"The Lady of the Lake?" Piper asked. She frowned. "I thought that was a tale to scare kids into going to bed."

"I thought it was an urban legend." But this was

Eerie, and anything was possible. Sawyer rubbed his chin. "I heard the story when I was little, but I also remember if anything was said about that, it wasn't around Aunt Chloe."

"I don't know if any of it is true," Diesel said. "I don't haunt the lake. Don't really like being on it even if it's not haunted. I don't like water."

Piper hugged him. "Which is why we don't vacation there."

"We don't vacation anywhere. You don't have time to take time off." Diesel sighed. "The best place to find out if any of this is true is to go to the Hall of Records or speak to the Chief of Police. If this really was a case of murder, then they'd have the file. If it's a runaway, they'd know. If it's never been solved, then they should know about that, too."

Piper nodded. "He's right. I didn't know there were any unsolved cases in this town, but I'm not shocked if there have been. Parts of Eerie aren't places I'd want to go in the daytime, let alone at night. Please, investigate this and let me know. I hate to think someone was harmed like this in my town, but I also hate to think it might be unsolved and there could possibly be someone's spirit out on the lake, roaming until she finds closure."

"I couldn't agree more." Sawyer placed the tablet back on the side table. "I'd like to get her some answers, but I don't think she's got time."

"No," Piper whispered. "I'd guess she's holding on long enough for you to agree to help her. Do that and let her rest. She's fought long enough."

"I will." He shook hands with Diesel, then Piper and waited for them to step back through the portal. Once the opening closed, he sank onto the chair.

"No!" Chloe sat up, but vacancy filled her eyes.

"You can't do that!"

"What?" He sat on the edge of her bed. "What's wrong?"

"No, you can't do that. You can't hurt her and get away with it. They'll find you. They'll destroy you," she said and pointed her finger at the wall. "Just you wait."

He had no idea who she was talking to, but whoever it was, they'd upset her. He debated slipping into the persona she thought was in the wrong. "I didn't do it. You didn't see me do it."

"Oh, I didn't have to. I saw the bruises. I knew she wanted to leave you. I knew she wanted to run, but you'd break her legs and spirit before she could. She had a vision and a plan, but you killed her," Chloe said. "You'll never get away with it."

"I already did." He played with fire, saying such things, but if it got her to talk more, then he'd do it. "I got away with it, and you can't do anything about it."

"Claude, you're a scoundrel." His aunt slumped back on the bed and drifted back to sleep.

He sank onto the chair. *Claude. Killed her. Hurt her. Abused.* It was all too much to digest yet made some sort of sense.

He needed to get her some answers. Piper claimed he should contact the Hall of Records. The last he knew, a faerie named Tasia was in charge. He picked up his phone. A bubble might be useful, but he'd rather have something a little more trustworthy. He checked the number for the Hall, then dialed.

Would someone answer? Did they even have a phone any longer? He wasn't sure. He hadn't been to the Hall since high school for a report.

The call connected and a male voice answered. "Hello? This is the Hall of Records. I'm Thaddeus. I wasn't expecting your call. How may I help you?"

Thaddeus? He paused a second. He didn't know anyone by that name but should get better acquainted with his town.

"Hello?" Thaddeus asked. "Is there someone there?"

"I'm sorry. I am. My name is Sawyer Gibson. My aunt Chloe Bitters is dying, and she's been talking about a woman named Mandy. I realize this is a long shot, but do you know of any cold cases or murder cases involving a woman named Mandy? Maybe Amanda? I have some details, but not many. I don't even know if this is a real story she's talking about or simply a figment of her mind."

"Let me ask Tasia. She's better with the scrolls than I am, but this sounds vaguely familiar."

"Sure." He waited as the call crackled. He might not have all the details, or any that were helpful.

"Hello. I'm Tasia. Thaddeus tells me you're looking for Chloe Bitters? What I can see is that her magic is fading. She's your aunt? Honey, I'm so sorry. It won't be long now," Tasia said. "She's the last of her line, and it appears you, Sawyer, are the last of yours."

"I know that." He didn't need to have his family history hashed out. "No, I'm asking about my aunt's friend. My aunt keeps talking about a woman named Mandy who may or may not have been abused by her boyfriend fifty years ago. My aunt claims this woman is dead, but I don't know for sure. I wondered if there was someone in Eerie fifty years ago named Mandy or Amanda and if she turned up missing or dead." He didn't want to keep recounting the facts he'd been told.

"Oh, the Lady of the Lake," Tasia said. "I've never seen her, but yes, I know who you're talking about. Okay, so fifty years ago -- I think it's more like fifty-three years, but who's counting? Anyway, there was a woman named Amanda Fortune here in Eerie. She and a woman named Chloe Bitters were best friends -- so, your aunt and this woman. Chloe was involved with a water nymph named Oliver, and Amanda, or Mandy, was dating a man named Claude. According to some accounts, Oliver had disappeared and it was supposed he went with Mandy, but they weren't together. Another account claims Claude was having an affair with Chloe and wanted Mandy out of the picture, so he killed her. Others say she ran off. The one thing everyone agrees on is that she haunts the lake."

"That makes no sense." He rubbed his forehead. "Why would she do that?"

"If it's believed that she ran off with Oliver, she joined him as a nymph, which makes sense. Some think that's her spirit haunting the north end of the lake," Tasia said. "But that's not the only story."

"Right, my aunt says Mandy was abused," he replied. "What if she didn't run off, but rather was killed?"

"That's possible, too," Tasia said. "She could be haunting the lake because she's buried there."

"That's awful." He didn't want to think about that.

"I mean, buried next to the lake isn't the worst thing," Tasia said. "She could've been drowned."

His blood chilled. "What if she was?"

"Drowned?" Tasia asked. "I mean, it's possible. I don't have any information on whether she was or not. What I do know is that she's not here."

"I get that." He bit back his frustration. "So is it true she was murdered, or that she ran away?"

"I don't know. The scroll for her family is

incomplete, but ends with her," Tasia said. "That doesn't mean she was murdered, but it also doesn't mean she wasn't. It simply means I don't have an end to her story."

He sighed. So much for getting closure. "So you say she's possibly the Lady of the Lake?"

"Yes, and she's supposed to haunt the north end. That's all I can tell you, but I do know that Claude is still alive -- he was her boyfriend -- and no one's seen Oliver since. Did she run off with him? Maybe. I don't know. Maybe you should come to Eerie and investigate."

"Maybe I should." If he wanted to get closure for his aunt, then he'd have to do it himself.

Chapter Three

Amanda wandered the woods along the north end of the lake. She didn't have much else to do. Campers were around, scattered about the grassy area, and even a few picnickers, but none of them could see her. She hated this existence. She had no one to talk to, no one to spend time with. She missed the simple interaction of being with other people.

But those were the things Claude had taken from her. He'd ruined her life, but he'd also robbed her of her future. She should hate him. Should be burning with the hottest, nuclear anger toward him.

She could be, but why? Would it bring her life back?

No.

She might as well focus on anything else but the past.

Something rustled in the woods and for a moment, she ignored the sound. Everything in the woods made noise. Animals, the wind, water… it all created disturbance. But this one was different. A shiver ran the length of her spine. She hadn't felt this way since that night.

She ducked behind a tree, knowing she'd never be seen, but wanting a private vantage point to locate the noise.

A hooded figure strode through the trees to the edge of the water.

The shiver increased when the figure leaned over and touched the rippled surface of the lake. She knew that hand and recognized the shark tattoo. Didn't have to see the rest of the person to know who stood there -- Claude.

She froze, not wanting him to know she could

see him. Could he see her? He hadn't for the last fifty years, but that didn't matter. He churned her stomach. She clutched the tree bark. The sooner he left, the better.

"She's dying," Claude said. "The last one to know what happened is dying. I can't steal her magic, too, but I can rejoice in her going. My secret went with you to the grave, but she figured some of it out. No one else did. I'd silence her, but I can't do that. Can't kill anyone."

He couldn't kill this person, but he'd murdered her! What a jerk. Amanda trembled, despite her best efforts to stay still.

"Won't be long now. She'll be gone and any last chance of anyone knowing will be gone. The cops didn't catch me. No one believed I could do it," Claude said. "They wouldn't have understood. I needed your magic. I needed to own you. You'd never have used that magic properly, but I could. We were expected to be together because you had to give yourself to me. It always had to end with your magic being mine."

She wanted to scream. He'd never loved her. Couldn't. Not when he wanted to destroy her.

"But now it'll be our secret. You gave me what I needed and you're where you were always meant to be." He patted the water. "Always."

He stood, then adjusted the sweatshirt, keeping his face hidden. He turned away from her vantage point and shuffled back through the woods.

Every cell in her existence screamed to keep away from him, but she followed. What else could he do to her? Kill her a second time? Was that even possible?

She navigated through the trees to the edge of the woods. She hadn't gone this far in so long. There hadn't been much reason. Now there was. She had to see where he was going and what in the name of Hera he was doing now that he'd come to haunt her.

Claude stopped at the larger picnic area in the park. A man sat alone at one of the tables and flipped through a book while holding a tablet. The guy seemed completely lost in thought.

Claude, now well over seventy years old but still the bully, shoved the book off the table and laughed. "Stop looking for the Lady of the Lake. She doesn't exist," he snapped and barely broke stride.

Amanda stopped short. The Lady of the Lake? There was someone else here? A kindred spirit? She had to find this lady and meet her. Maybe this other woman would know how to get away from the damn water.

"Thanks, ass," the man said and picked up his book. "Dick."

She wanted to find the Lady but was also intrigued by this man. She inched closer.

A child, running with a plastic disc turned just as she passed Amanda and her eyes widened. "Momma!"

Amanda paused. She wondered what had spooked the child. She ducked behind a tree and listened for the little girl and parent.

"Momma, I saw the Lady," the girl said. "Right there."

She peeked out from her hiding spot long enough to look for the Lady. She didn't see anyone.

"You're imagining things," the mother said. "The Lady of the Lake is a story made up to scare kids."

Amanda bit back a groan. That was a downer. A fib for kids…

The man looked up from his book. "It's not a story," he replied. He closed the book and picked up the tablet. "Actually, it's considered an urban legend, but there's fact behind the legend."

The mother rolled her eyes. "Don't butt in and scare my kid. She'll have nightmares because of you."

"But Mom, I saw her," the little girl said. "She had dark hair, blue skin and was pretty."

Amanda ducked back behind the tree. She really had to find this woman. Any company would be better than none.

The woman and her child left the picnic area and when Amanda emerged from her spot, she stepped right into the man's path. If she'd had breath, it would've stopped or clogged in her throat.

He was a beautiful man. Young -- compared to her -- and handsome. With dark hair, dark eyes and a studious look to him. The long-sleeved shirt accentuated his thin frame and the glasses gave him an air of sophistication. He didn't walk with a swagger, but instead a quiet confidence.

"Oh, my," she gasped. "Wow."

"Excuse me?" He met her gaze. "What did you say?"

She froze. He'd heard her? "I'm sorry?"

He cocked his head. "Where are you?"

So he couldn't see her? Good. She faded into the woods, rushing to the north end, to her safe haven. No one had seen her there in years -- if ever -- and no one would see her now.

"I know I heard you." The man drifted through the woods. "Please, don't hide from me."

She had no choice. No one else had believed she was there and this guy might be looking for the Lady of the Lake. She wasn't that Lady. She was nobody.

She glanced back and noticed the man. He'd bent over and rested his hands on his knees. He puffed as if he were trying to keep up with her. His bag slid forward and dangled along his side.

"I've done the research. I know the story. You're here. I can feel you." He stood upright but kept puffing. "She wouldn't lie to me. She led me here. Told me where I should find you. Told me to find you. I need to do this for her."

She balled her hands. "Who?" She snapped her mouth shut. She'd wanted to stay hidden, but her curiosity would get her into trouble again.

He sank onto one of the rocks at the edge of the water. "I hear you. Where are you?"

"I can't show you."

"Please?"

"No." If she could have this conversation with him, then something was different about him.

"Why?"

"I don't know you. Can't trust you." It was the truth. Others claimed to be looking for her, but they hadn't found her. Not the detectives, the amateur sleuths, or anyone else.

"You can," he said. He scrubbed the back of his hand across his forehead, then sighed. "When I was a little boy, my aunt told me about her friend, Amanda. She said her friend was a lovely person and so sweet, but she disappeared. For the rest of her life, my Aunt Chloe wanted to know what happened to her friend."

"Chloe?" She didn't venture closer, but the mere mention of the name pricked her curiosity again.

"My mother's sister. Do you know Chloe? Or Marie, my mother?" he asked. "My mother died five years ago, but Chloe held on. Her magic is fading."

"No," she whispered. Chloe had the strongest magic. She should be just fine.

"She told me you liked being here. She said this

was your favorite place and you'd spend hours among the trees and around the water, existing in nature. She said you might have even been part woodland nymph because you were here so much. She loved the nights you'd go dancing together, and the days spent talking and mixing spells," he said. "She said she was never the same after you disappeared."

"No?" She couldn't be excited. Not yet. She needed some detail only the true Chloe would know. Something only she could tell this man. "I can't trust you."

"I know you can't." He sighed again. "Why would you?"

The last man she'd thought she could trust had murdered her.

"She knew about the abuse and that you wanted to get away. She was trying to figure out a plan to get you out of that house without him knowing. To this day, she deals with the guilt of not working fast enough. You deserved better."

She emerged from behind the tree. "What did he steal from me?" If he knew this, then he'd spoken to Chloe. Only her best friend would remember she never let go of her locket.

"Besides your magic? He stole your necklace," the man said. "It was your favorite piece of jewelry."

"Why?" She held onto the tree for stability, even if her legs weren't holding her up.

"Because it came from your mother and was one of the few things you had to remember her by."

If she'd been standing on her feet, she would've collapsed. "Who are you?"

"Sawyer Gibson." He stood and held out his hand. "I don't know where you are, but I hear you and I want to see you. I want to help you."

"No one can help me." She stayed out of his line of sight. "You're wasting your time."

"Am I? I want my aunt to have closure. She asked me to find you so she could sleep. I don't know if that will really help her pass, but she misses you and I'm sure she'd like to see you one more time. I don't even know if that's possible." Sawyer turned, looking for her. "Please don't hide from me any longer. I doubt I can take you to her, but I can help you. I want to solve this. Please, let me help you."

She bowed her head. She had nothing left to lose. If he could hear her, then there was a chance he could see her. The little girl and various other children caught glimpses of her. Maybe he could, too. She stepped into his vantage point. "I'm here."

He looked about but didn't seem to see her. "Where are you?" His shoulders sagged. "I know this will work."

"Where did she say I was?" she asked. Chloe wouldn't have known she was buried in the lake.

"She doesn't know, but she's convinced you're The Lady of the Lake because your spirit must reside here. If you're Amanda and I've found you, then there's a chance you can have closure," Sawyer said. "Maybe I can get you some peace."

So *she* was the Lady of the Lake? *She* was the object of the urban legend and rumor? It didn't seem possible. And yet, it did. She existed at the lake. She'd never be able to leave. Unless Sawyer could help her move to the next realm or get her life back, she'd never have any peace. "I doubt that's possible."

"I'd like to try," Sawyer said. "May I see you again? Talk to you again?"

She saw no reason why not. "Do you know Claude?"

"No, I've never met him. According to what I've been told he's not a kind man, but I believe you're a kind soul who didn't deserve what my aunt claimed happened to you."

"You're flattering me." She didn't mind the kindness, though. She hadn't heard such words in so long that she'd almost forgotten them.

"You deserve it. You seem like a sweet, good-hearted soul." He tipped his head. "I still wish I could see you. I hear you, though, and I enjoy your company. I barely know you, but it's like we've known each other all my life. My aunt used to tell me about you, how you were willing to help anyone, rarely angry and quick with a smile."

"She makes me sound impossible," she replied. "I had my quirks and issues. I wasn't perfect."

"No one is." He smiled. "May I talk with you again? I'd like to help you. Would like to let everyone know you're not this terrible phantom, but a lost soul trying to find peace."

She had little to lose, and his words touched her. She could stay in the woods and slowly disappear into her feelings of abandonment and loneliness. Could let the darkness of the woods and water swallow her. Or she could allow a handsome, albeit younger, man to talk with her. He could help her get through the endless hours a little easier. Besides, he was cute. He seemed to even like her a little. Either that, or she intrigued him. She wasn't sure. Her ability to read the advances of men weren't sharp any longer. But if he was interested, so was she and that had to mean something.

"Well? Or did you leave me?" He laughed and sank onto a tree stump. "Why would you want to talk with me? You have magic and power. You can do things and all I've got are my notes, thoughts, and ability to be in Eerie. I'm nothing special. I can't do magic and can't create a spell."

"No?" She hadn't realized she'd been so quiet.

"Amanda?" He looked up and seemed to look her in the eye without realizing it. "You're still here."

"I am."

"You want me to leave or stay?"

"I'd like for you to come back. I forgot how lonely it is and how much I long for someone to talk to. If you'd like to visit again, I'd love it." She wished she could touch and reassure him.

"Then I will." He didn't jump up from his seat. "I look forward to it."

"I do, too."

He finally stood. "I should go, but I'll be back. I'll try to bring you some news."

"Wonderful," she replied. "Goodbye for now."

"Until then." He waved his arm around, as if to try to touch her. He grinned, then walked away, leaving her in the relative silence of the woods.

She watched him go and instantly wished she could leave along with him. The hours until he returned would be agonizing. But at the same time, she liked that she'd been able to break through. He'd seen her. If he could, then maybe he could help her.

He might get her closure.

Might set her free.

Could he even one day touch her? Make love to her?

At this rate, anything was possible.

Chapter Four

Sawyer left the woods and his phone buzzed in his pocket. *Shit.* He'd forgotten all about the device. But being among the trees and speaking to Amanda had been magical. Not only that, but he'd been able to see her for a split second. He'd been able to hear her. The Lady of the Lake was real, but she'd stolen a piece of his heart.

As much as that should sound odd, it felt right.

He pulled his phone from his pocket. He'd been forced to go old-school and use a phone.

He swiped to check the notifications. Missed calls. He knew the number and called it right back. He hurried to his car, then unlocked it and fell behind the wheel before someone answered the call.

"What's wrong?" He yanked the door shut. "Talk to me." He shouldn't be so blunt with the nursing home, but at this rate, his aunt had to be dying. They'd only call if something was truly wrong.

"Mr. Gibson, she's fading now. You need to get back here. She's only got a few hours," the nurse said. "I'm sorry."

"On my way." He abandoned the phone and drove as fast as possible while within the law to the nursing home. He had to make it in time. Had to share what he'd learned. Part of him wanted Chloe to move on. She'd grown too tired and needed that rest. He'd miss her, but he didn't want her to suffer any longer and the cancer was winning.

He screeched to a halt in the parking lot and scrambled out of the car, barely getting it locked before he reached the sidewalk. He ran into the building straight to her room.

The nurse stood in Chloe's doorway. "You're

lucky. Looks like you made it."

"Auntie." He slid to a stop outside of Chloe's room, then composed himself before entering.

She didn't open her eyes, but her fingers flexed. The machines beeped and the aura of pink around her faded.

He sat beside her bed and held onto her hand. "I saw her. Auntie, I found Amanda. You were right. She was killed and I'm going to find out who did it, but I did find her. She's on the other side, but she's where I can talk to her. She misses you and wants you to rest."

Chloe opened her eyes for a moment, then smiled. "I knew you'd do it. I knew you'd find her."

"I did. You were right -- she's a sweet person and didn't deserve whatever happened to her. I'm sorry I didn't look for her sooner, but I found her and she misses you, too." He caressed his aunt's hand. "She said you can rest now because I'll take it from here."

She smiled again and sighed. "I know. I love you, Sawyer."

"I love you, too." He brushed her hair from her face. "It's okay. You can go home now. Rest."

Her smile softened and she sighed a second time, then the machines buzzed and screamed. The pink aura disappeared and the sparkles in the room were gone. The slight tug she had on his hand went slack.

The nurses rushed in and nudged him aside.

He stood and moved to the perimeter. He didn't have to watch the scene to know what had happened. His aunt was gone. When he looked up toward the ceiling to blink back tears, he saw Chloe, but not in the form he remembered. She was now younger, vibrant, and smiling. Her blonde hair flowed around her shoulders and a pink dress accentuated her slender frame. A wicked glint filled her eye. She waved as she floated above him, then winked.

Although his heart ached, missing her, he found a simple peace at the same time. She wasn't hurting any longer, wasn't being eaten by the cancer. She'd found a new life on the other side and was moving on. She'd done her job, and it was his turn to do his.

He stepped into the hallway and wiped his face. It'd take some time to get over this loss, but he'd known it was coming. Part of him had mourned her ever since she'd gone into the nursing home. But for part of him, this was fresh. It was a deep wound.

One of the nurses came out of the room and sighed. "I'm sorry."

"We knew this day would come. You've done all you could and it was time." He nodded and tucked his hands into his pockets. "Thank you for letting me know to get here in time."

"She didn't need to be alone." The nurse stared at him. "Are you her only family?"

"The only one left. Her sister passed a few years ago and she was never married. She kept saying she was waiting for the right man. Said he was somewhere out there across time and space. Maybe she'll find him now."

The nurse narrowed her eyes. "You don't believe that romance garbage?"

"You don't?"

"It's crap. Guys come and go, they don't want what you want and don't like when you're blunt. They lie, they cheat and leave you with a broken heart. Yeah, romance is bullshit." She wiped her hands on her slacks. "And anyone who tells me there's someone out there across time and space is simply delusional."

"I don't know."

"If you tell me you're the one I've been looking

for, then keep walking. I'm not looking for love. I'm running the other way entirely. I don't date the family of patients and don't want to be picked up at the scene of their loved one's death." She shook her head and walked away.

He snorted. He hadn't been trying to come on to her. Before he realized what was going on, he was swept up by the other nurses, brought in to handle paperwork and his wishes for his aunt. He'd never seen so much paperwork, even if done through computers and spells. He'd been through this before with his parents, but he'd forgotten the sheer volume of busy work. Of things to write down and consider.

At least with his aunt, her body simply faded away. Nothing to bury, no stone to place unless he wanted to at the location of his choosing. She hadn't kept much and her estate had been liquidated to help fund her time in the nursing home.

He shook his head and left the building, needing the quiet of his car. She'd had a life and past, but it was all gone. Swept away with the dust of life and pushed from anyone's mind. Just another faded witch. It didn't seem fair.

Like it hadn't been fair with Amanda. She hadn't wanted to die or end up at the lake, but there she was. Would she have wanted to simply fade away? Could she?

At least with Chloe, he'd had closure. He knew she'd been given a fair chance and a life well-lived. Now it was his turn to do the same for Amanda. He had some information on her. She'd been with a man who'd abused her, was rumored to have ended up in the lake and hadn't moved on.

He left the nursing home and drove to his apartment. He'd dumped his money into caring for his aunt and put little away for himself. As he parked, he noticed a man outside the building.

"Excuse me?" He locked his car but kept his key in his fingers. "May I help you?"

"I'm Adam North with North, North, and Associates. We'd like to extend our sincerest condolences and would like to speak with you about estate planning." The man held out his hand. "Would you be willing to spare a few minutes to talk?"

"How do you know I need to speak to someone about estates?" he asked. He walked to the wrong apartment. "I haven't had a loss in my family."

"According to the rolls, your relative," he checked his tablet, "Chloe… I have the name here."

"If you have to look for it, then you don't. I've had a long day at work and would like to go inside to rest. I don't know what you're talking about concerning a loss in my family, so if you would excuse me I need to go inside." He sidestepped Adam North and rushed down the sidewalk to the stairwell leading to the second and third floors. He practically ran down the long outer corridor leading to his unit on the second level. If Adam North was going to talk to him, he'd have to do it later.

Sawyer ducked into his apartment and closed, then locked the door. What a pain in the ass. Here he was, grieving the loss of his family member and a damn attorney already knew as well as wanted to talk to him about his loss. It wasn't right.

He kicked out of his shoes and kept the lights off as he wandered through the unit to his bedroom. His heart needed time to heal.

He switched on the lamp, and the photo of his last girlfriend caught his eye. He picked up the framed photo. Heather hadn't been a bad mate. She'd kept him happy, smiled a lot and loved to socialize. She'd been loyal to him, too. Things should've worked out.

But he hadn't loved her and she hadn't loved him. They were passionate about different things and not about each other. He'd tried to love her. Tried to be the one she needed, but she wanted more out of life. Eerie was a dump town to her and she wanted so much more.

He didn't blame her. He'd never been able to explain his draw to his hometown. Like he had unfinished business here, but what? He wasn't sure.

When he'd broken up with Heather, she wished him well and promptly moved on to another man. He hoped she was happy.

He tucked the photo into a drawer. No point in looking at the past when he had to focus on the future. Besides, his aunt hadn't been a fan of Heather. Chloe hadn't disliked her, but she kept saying there was someone else out there for him.

He flopped onto the bed and stared at the swirls on the ceiling. He'd been the oddball in his family and friend group. He'd been the one who dreamed and wondered. Everyone else had grown up and married. Many had kids.

Where was he? Single. Alone.

It wasn't like he enjoyed being single. If given the chance, he'd love to find someone to share his life with while he figured out what he wanted to do with his next few years.

No one seemed to want him.

He didn't have magic and couldn't do much with his talents other than exist in Eerie. His skills were in math and accounting, not spells and conjuring. If one wanted to have their ledger totaled, then he was the man. Want magic created? Look somewhere else. He'd let his mother down with his lack of magical talent, and his father saw him as a confused young man.

His phone buzzed in his pocket. He'd probably forgotten something at the nursing home.

When he pulled the device from his pocket, he noticed the number. Not the nursing home, but a set of numbers he didn't know. He refused to answer. But as he swiped to ignore the call, he noticed the five other missed ones.

Hades, they were all from law offices. Did anyone not know Chloe had passed? And did none of them have the common sense to let him mourn in peace? He'd bet not.

He silenced the phone and left it on the side table, then turned off the light. If anyone wanted to bother him about his loss, they could wait until tomorrow.

He should be crying. Should be carrying on, but the tears wouldn't come. His heart ached, but maybe he was too numb to notice. He wasn't too numb to care. He'd simply known this was going to happen -- her magic would fade and she'd perish. Everyone did eventually.

No, not everyone. Amanda was still around, even if she was only there in spirit. And the vampires. They weren't dead -- not technically. And maybe the deities.

Hades, it was all such a mess.

He closed his eyes and tucked his hands behind his head. He crossed his ankles and allowed his thoughts to drift. Visions filled his mind of times with his aunt. Times he'd spent with her and the rest of his family. Good ones, not so good ones, plenty of laughs and magic, but also a few tears.

A vision of Chloe filled his mind.

"You've done as I asked and you've helped me. I'm on the other side," she said. "Now it's your turn. Don't cry for me. Have a light heart and move forward. Keep me in your heart, but don't let me weigh it down. There is someone waiting for you. You will find love divine upon the right time."

"Are you sure?" He wished he could hug her once more. "Auntie?"

"You will find love divine upon the right time," she repeated. "Believe your heart and trust the journey. Keep going and find the truth."

"About what?" He'd asked the question, but he knew the answer. She still wanted him to find out what'd happened to Amanda. "Yes, Auntie. I will."

"I know you will, and I know you'll find happiness." She smiled, then faded.

He opened his eyes and gasped. He didn't have magic, but he could have visions. Interesting. The conversation was just as if they'd been together in the room. A thought occurred to him. If he could conjure a vision of his aunt, then could he come up with one for Amanda?

He'd never know if he didn't try.

He reclined on the bed again and closed his eyes. He sucked in a ragged breath, then exhaled slowly, allowing the breath and his stress to leave his body. If Amanda was out there where he could find her, he would. Until then, he'd have to be patient.

"Amanda?"

He wasn't even sure she'd show or that he could summon her. All he had was a memory, really.

"You called me?" A figure came into his consciousness. Beautiful, slender, with long hair and shimmering eyes, she captivated him. Her skin was tinged bluish-green.

"Amanda." He'd know her anywhere.

She smiled. "Hi."

"Hello, my love." He wasn't sure why he'd said that, but he wasn't taking it back.

"A bit quick with such monikers, aren't you?" She laughed and the rich sound filled his ears. "We hardly know each other."

"It's me, Sawyer."

She laughed again. "I know you. I recognized your smile and voice. You know me?"

"I would've known you anywhere," he replied. He reached for her hand. "Walk with me?"

"I can hold my own hand." She flinched and kept a distance from him.

A wave of embarrassment washed over him. Of course she'd be hesitant to get close to him. The last man she'd trusted had abused her. He wasn't an aggressor like Claude, but she didn't know that. "I'm sorry."

"No need." She fell into step beside him. "Where are we?"

"My consciousness, I think." To be fair, he wasn't sure. "I've never done this before."

"What? Walk with someone?" She remained beside him but had inched a bit closer. "Or conjure something."

"Walked through my consciousness, but did I conjure this? I guess I kind of did." There were a lot of things he'd never thought he'd do. "I worry about you."

"Well, I should be the one worrying. I don't know anyone else who can conjure, but I used to be able to explain spells and read the Fates," she said. "But why do you worry about me?"

"You're stuck and I don't understand why."

"You mean at the lake?"

"Yes."

"Oh." She half-shrugged. "It's because I was murdered and dumped there. It wasn't my choice and I can't leave until I've been vindicated or given the chance to move on."

So she had been murdered… "He did this, didn't he?"

"No one else." She bumped shoulders with him, and he felt the action.

He'd actually felt her. Holy shit. It was nice to be touched, but even better to touch her. She was tender and soft and just as sweet as he'd expected.

"Oh." She paled. "Sorry."

"For what?"

"I shouldn't push it." She blushed, then inched back away from him. "Sorry."

"When was the last time you touched someone? Not looked at them or drifted through them, but a real touch?" he asked.

"Fifty years."

"Then touch me. I welcome it." He sounded desperate, but oh well. He craved this. He'd wanted to be desired by someone and knowing she might was even better. "I want to help you."

"By being… touched?" She laughed and her color returned. "You're peculiar."

"I am." He allowed her to slip her hand into his. "I like you."

"Ah, because you want to help me. You've developed feelings for the one you want to save." She shook her head. "I should've guessed."

"It's not that." He'd never get her to understand at this rate. "You intrigue me. Why would someone want to extinguish your spark? It makes no sense.

There is no reason for what he did."

"I suppose not."

"Amanda."

She stopped walking. A sad look crossed her face and her smile faded. "Some people are meant to do dastardly things. Some are meant to be the victim of those dastardly things. I'm not a martyr and never wanted to be a victim, but I became one. I accept my fate because others learned from it."

"You make sense, but it's not right."

"Some people are good at presenting themselves as kind souls, but they aren't. Some are rotten and it shows a mile away. I got unlucky enough to come in contact with one who could fake kindness and turn on others in a second."

He didn't like any of this. "That's not fair."

"No, it's not, but it's my fate. It was always going to be my fate. Remember? I can read the lifelines. I know when the cut comes because I'm of those Fates. I knew my cut was coming. I just didn't know it would end in the water and I'd be unable to cross over." She touched his arm. "I know you're upset as well. This boils your blood, doesn't it?"

"Yes." He couldn't explain his fury. He'd just met her, but he wanted to protect her.

"I can't explain why you're able to see me, even if only through your consciousness. I don't understand how you could conjure any of this, but it's your magic and it's strong. I admire your determination. I cherish the ability you have to be here with me, and I hope you'll be able to see me the next time you come to the lake. I take none of it for granted because it could be yanked out from under me at any time."

"That's not right."

"Maybe not, but you're taxing yourself tonight.

Get some honest rest. You'll be able to find me again. We're intertwined now. I need to go, but please rest." She leaned in and kissed his cheek, then disappeared.

"Wait." He reached into the darkness but felt nothing. His skin warmed from her kiss and the touch seared him to his core, but it wasn't enough. He needed more of her kisses. More moments with her. Wanted to hold her. Love and be near her.

But she was correct. He'd done magic, even if it was only in his own head. He'd conjured her. He'd made a connection with her. If he could do it through his mind, then he might even be able to do it in real life. The magic he'd tried to capture throughout his life was right there at his fingertips. He could spend more time with Amanda, right?

He'd never know until he tried.

Chapter Five

Amanda returned to the water and hid among the rocks. She'd never been able to leave the lake before, not since she'd died, but now she'd been spirited away to the darkness that was Sawyer's inner consciousness. She should've been fearful of the move but wasn't. He offered her a sense of safety.

How had he been able to get her out of her watery hell?

She sank beneath the surface and allowed her mind to wander. He wasn't afraid of her. The scary, ghoulish tinge of her skin hadn't turned him off. She couldn't believe he'd be so kind, or that she'd be able to ever find someone who'd like her. Being in the lake and dead sort of hindered her ability to meet anyone. It was too early to have strong feelings for him, but she was certainly intrigued. She'd like to be with him.

Was it even possible?

"Where are you?"

She knew that shout and remained hidden in the rocks. Claude had never been able to see her, but he seemed to know she heard him. Part of her wondered how he'd made it this far without being caught. He didn't know how to be quiet, and everyone within a five-hundred-yard radius had to be able to hear him having his fit. He might not be able to see her, but she refused to be where there was a chance he could. He'd done enough damage.

"Where are you?" he thundered. "What did you do?"

What *had* she done? She'd left him alone.

"You got him looking for me, you bitch."

She didn't understand what he meant, but someone was on his case and good for them. He needed to be afraid. He'd done enough violence that it was time he paid for it.

She winced at the memory of his hands on her. The violence, the pain and the screams. He'd been so cruel to her. Yet, he seemed to believe she owed him.

"You sent that fool to find me. He won't get any information and they'll never find you. You're dead," he growled. "Stay dead."

She wanted to ask him why this all bothered him so much. He'd had a life. He'd moved forward. What did he have to lose? She'd paid with her life and had no power over him.

"You want to best me. I told you. I will not be bested. I'm still alive and I have a family. Don't take that from me."

The gall! He had a family? What about hers? *Don't take it from him?* Like he'd taken her life? What made him so much better than her? What about the life she'd wanted to have and would never?

He had the right to treat her this way because he was a man? Bullshit. Or because he didn't want to be caught for his crime? Probably a combination of all of the above.

He believed he mattered, but she didn't.

Bullshit. She did matter. And if Sawyer wanted to figure this out, wanted to somehow turn Claude in for what he'd done, then good. Claude deserved it.

"You sent him and got him stirred up, but if you keep that going, I'll make you pay. I'll end his life and leave his body somewhere away from yours. Do you want that on your soul? That you got him killed?" Claude asked.

What a jackass. Everything ended in death because he had to win.

Not this time.

"Want to save him? Then tell him to leave me alone."

No. She'd had enough of his threats.

"Don't challenge me."

How could she if she was dead?

"If he gets too close, I'll kill him or tell him you wanted him dead. It was mercy -- he doesn't need to know the truth. I'll tell him you wanted me to do it for you. Wanted me to get out the truth that you killed yourself. It was a suicide and you caused this. You begged me to kill you and now you're begging me to kill him."

He'd never stop. He'd destroy and twist everything until he could get rid of his guilt. Until there wasn't anything left.

Let him.

He growled. "I'm an old man. No one will believe I killed you. Not after so many years. They'll think he made the story up. You keep your fucking mouth shut or I'll make sure you pay again, with his life."

She'd love to see it. He was correct -- he was an old man and he might have magic, but not much. What could Claude do? Kill someone else? Sawyer? For all she knew, she wasn't the only one he'd murdered back then.

"You keep quiet," he snarled. "If you know what's good for you, you'll keep your trap shut and put him off. You were always a good girl. You followed directions and took orders well. Keep doing that and don't you dare cross me."

With that threat, he left. She remained beneath the water until she knew he was gone. He couldn't kill her again, but he could harm Sawyer.

She should tell Sawyer to back off, but if he could

uncover proof of her murder, then let him find it. She wanted closure.

She mulled over what Claude had said. He was an old man. Cruel, too. He'd hurt her. Had he done the same to his wife? His children? Tormented and abused them? She hoped not.

Or was he kind to them?

He'd told her to stay a good girl who took orders. Translation: he wanted her obedience. Fat chance. Being a good girl had gotten her killed. It'd gotten her abused.

She deserved better.

Could Sawyer give her better? Maybe. She wanted to believe she could save herself, but she wasn't naive enough to think she didn't need help.

Sawyer could see her. He'd heard her. If he could use her information and find more help to nail Claude, then she'd take it.

She had no idea how long she'd have to wait to see Claude pay.

The night meeting with Sawyer, though, buoyed her. He'd found a way to lift her spirits and warm her heart. If she hadn't been so scared of him, she'd have tried to get closer.

Her heart wanted to learn Sawyer all over, but her head screamed for her to slow down. Men hit. They hurt. They screamed. They lied.

And she'd been left to pick up the pieces. Her father claimed to love her, but he'd accepted Claude's bride price, and Claude settled everything with his fits. She didn't want to be with another man like that. Would Sawyer be that way? She doubted it. He would've shown his true colors by now. He'd have demanded more. Then again, she'd been fooled in the past.

As she remained there in the water, she heard a voice.

Mandy?

She knew that voice, remembered, even though she hadn't heard that crystal clear sound in so long. "*Chloe*?" She surfaced from the water to see Chloe, albeit misty, on the rocks at the edge of the lake. "Chloe."

"The very same." Chloe sat on the largest rock. "I'd love to get closer, but I can't. I'm here in spirit form, I guess. So this is where you've been? All this time?"

"I have." She couldn't believe her eyes. "You're here. You're a spirit?"

"For a short time. I was able to cross over for a bit because I used a spell -- one of the last I've got -- to find you. I've only got a few minutes, I suspect." Chloe sighed. "I can't hug you, so imagine a big hug. I'm sad you're truly dead, but I'm happy I can talk to you for a little while."

"I'm glad to see you, too. Why didn't you cross over and stay there? Be happy. Isn't Walter over already?" She'd heard whispers that Walter had died over five years before.

"He is and I can't wait to see him, but I had to say a few things to you first. I needed to see you with my own eyes." She swept her gaze over Amanda. "You're still beautiful."

"I'm not exciting." She wasn't anything special.

"You'd be surprised how exciting you are," Chloe said. "As the years went on, my memory faltered, but I never forgot you. I never forgot what happened. I wasn't able to tell everything, but I got my nephew on the case, so you will get vindication."

"Sawyer?" She remembered him saying he was

Chloe's nephew, but it still shocked her. The whole thing was real.

"I knew he'd found you. He said he had."

"He did." Now her attraction to Sawyer embarrassed her. He was so much younger, and practically family. She'd considered Chloe the sister she'd never had. She shouldn't be attracted to Chloe's nephew.

"He's quite the looker, isn't he? And he's single," Chloe said. "I know you've noticed."

"He's single?" He shouldn't be. He was too kind to be single. "You're sure he's not got a wife hidden away somewhere?" He was so out of her league, and should be out of her reach.

"Never married. That poor boy wanted to, but the girl wasn't ready and wanted to run off with a guy she'd known before. I knew the moment I saw her she wasn't going to make the relationship work, but he got his heart broken. Doesn't matter now. I knew he'd find you," Chloe said. "He'll help you, and you'll get out of this hell."

"Chloe." Her friend always had fantastic ideas that weren't possible. "That's a lot to put on someone who is fifty years younger than me and may not even be able to do whatever you think he can."

Chloe narrowed her eyes and the corner of her mouth quirked. "Claude's been going around town for fifty years claiming you ran away. Like hell. You were killed and he knew it because he's the one who did it. Sawyer will sort it out."

"Chloe." It wasn't a surprise Claude was that big of a jerk. He wasn't about to take credit for what he'd done. Not when he could blame anyone else. "Everyone thought he was a good guy and a catch. Did they feel bad for what happened? Because he lied about it all."

"They did. They bought his story and he married Maria Dellacorte with what seemed like everyone's blessing -- the poor guy had found love after being jilted. Then they had three kids and he had a life he took from you."

"I expected he did."

"I can't get you closure on my own, but Sawyer can help you and he wants to. He likes a good mystery and there's no better one that this."

"He seems nice."

"Nice?" Chloe asked. "Just nice? He's sweet on you."

She gasped. "I'm stuck in water, in limbo, I'm old enough to be his grandmother and can't exactly leave this muck. He can't be sweet on me. It's illogical."

"We're in Eerie. Everything is a little sideways. I shouldn't be back to see you. The magic and spell shouldn't exist, but it does." Chloe grinned. "It's working out the way it should be."

"I know."

"But?"

"I'm old."

"He's an old soul."

"Chloe." She didn't understand.

"He's the man you should've been with all along. He'll take care of you. So what if it took a few years to connect? So what if there's an age gap? Good Hera. You're the same age as he is -- you were simply left in a sort of stasis. You haven't aged, even if time has passed. Let him help you, get some closure, and if he wants to get some with you, then let him. You do deserve it."

The words all cut like a knife through her soul. She did deserve closure but never felt worthy.

"You don't buy it, I can tell." Chloe nodded.

"You know me well." She'd been fine before the push to connect with Claude. Being forced into that relationship changed her. Made her shut down.

"Do you remember when we were in school and Gus Townes hit on you?"

"Yes." She'd been so flattered until she found out his attraction had been a joke.

"He did that because he was a jerk," Chloe said. "Claude was a jerk and because of your father, you were primed to meet nothing but jerks. They're all gone except Claude, and he's not going to win because Sawyer isn't a jerk. He's the exception that proves the rule."

"You're pushing me rather hard."

"I know."

"Why?"

Chloe sighed again and rubbed her hands together. "I feel the magic running out, so I can't stay much longer."

"And I'm wasting your time. I'm sorry."

"No," Chloe said, her voice soft. "Sawyer has magic like yours. He can read the Fates, but he doesn't understand it. He's always been able to interpret the lines of the Fates and is intuitive with situations. He needs you to show him how to use his magic and talents. Save him from himself. He's trying to turn inward and he shouldn't. You both need someone who is kind to prove this world isn't completely cruel. Be that for each other."

"Chloe." It seemed impossible. "I had my chance and chose wrong."

"You were given the wrong circumstances and this is your chance for a redo."

She should argue, but Chloe had begun to fade.

"Oh no."

"I knew this would happen, but I got everything I needed to say out. Cherish him and help that boy learn his magic. If you fall in love, then even better," Chloe said. "And remember, this isn't goodbye but 'so long for now'. I'll be watching you and you'll know I'm near. Don't screw this up. Take what you need with Sawyer and make no excuses. Get what you deserve and enjoy him."

"Chloe."

"You will find love divine upon the right time," With that, Chloe fully disappeared.

Amanda sank back beneath the water and contemplated what she'd been told. She had so much to think about. Sawyer wanted her? Claude wanted her dead. He wanted everyone dead. It was time she took control of this narrative. She'd been allowing Claude to run her life and now her death, but why? He'd done the damage. He'd killed her and maybe others.

She needed to see Sawyer and straighten this all out. If she could get closer to him and enjoy his body and mind, then even better. Was she in love with Sawyer? Hades, it was way too soon to know that, but she'd like to get to know him better. Would love to touch him. Kiss him and find out if the crackling in her veins was real or a figment of her imagination. Did he feel the same way about her?

He might.

Might not, but he might.

And she wanted to explore those feelings.

If she could save him from himself, then he'd save her right back. She didn't want to live in the lake any longer. She wanted to be loved. If there was a chance he could fall in love with her, then she wanted to give it a try.

Chapter Six

Sawyer returned to the Hall of Records. If he didn't get answers now, he'd raise hell until he did. He wandered through the Hall to the tables and located the scrolls pertaining to his family. He knew his own life story, but he'd always wanted to learn the generations before his grandparents.

"So you're looking for your family." Tasia appeared out of what seemed like nowhere. She opened a scroll for him. "Your parents, Maria and George Gibson, had magic and created confections."

"I knew that." He'd grown up eating those sweets and wishing he didn't like candy so much. "My aunt is Chloe Bitters, and she was one of the beings who communed with nature."

"She did. She never married and was content to work on her land. We have her to thank for her three variations on the Peace Lily." Tasia leaned on the table and folded her arms. The move bunched her breasts, practically forcing him to look at the display. "You also had an aunt named Alessi, but she died when your mother and Chloe were fifteen and fourteen respectively."

"Right." He sighed. "But I'm still looking for information on Amanda Fortune. You said she was connected to Claude Revere. What do you know about Claude Revere?"

Tasia stood, then retrieved another scroll. "Well…" She frowned as she read the yellowed paper. "That's odd."

"What?" He didn't want to get his hopes up.

"Well, it says here that Claude Revere died seventy years ago in an accident. He was a sorcerer who miscalculated one of his spells and incinerated himself." She crinkled her nose and brow. "Sounds like a terrible way to go."

"But the guy who was with my aunt's friend wasn't dead. Either he's immortal, or there's something wrong." He tried to look at the scroll, but Tasia held it just out of his reach. "Are you sure?"

"I'm positive." She flicked her gaze to him, then back to the scroll. "I'm going to check something." She left him alone to his thoughts.

Something didn't add up. Claude wasn't a dead man. He wouldn't need Amanda's magic if he were immortal. Then what did he need?

"Holy shit." Tasia rushed back to him. "You're never going to believe this."

"Oh?" He closed the notebook he'd brought along for jotting down information. "What?"

"So Claude most certainly died seventy years ago. There's proof he died, but his line died with him. No one thought about it because he was the last of his family, but about fifteen years after he passed, another Claude Revere shows up and he's not the same man," Tasia said. "According to the scrolls, this Claude is really Angus Breen and he's one of the trolls. The Breen clan is long known in the troll colony, but after his parents died when he was fifteen, Angus disappears, but a new Claude shows up."

"So he stole the identity of a dead man?" That pissed him off. But more than that, it made him want to have Amanda there to hear the information. She should be there. Should be learning this along with him. *I want her here.*

No, he didn't just want her there. He needed her to be beside him. Wanted it with every last cell in his body. *I need her here.*

Tasia blinked, then jerked in her seat. "How did

you do that?"

"Do what?" He shifted his gaze to where Tasia stared.

Amanda sat beside him. She rubbed her bare arms and seemed to shiver. "I don't know how I got here. Sawyer? Is this a dream?"

"Not for me." He wasn't sure how he'd managed to bring her to the Hall, but hot damn. She was there. He yanked his jacket from the back of his chair and draped the garment around Amanda's shoulders. "Hi."

"Hi." Amanda tugged the jacket around her body. "Hello."

"Oh." He'd forgotten his manners. "Tasia, this is Amanda Fortune."

"The Lady of the Lake?" Tasia blurted. "She's real?"

"I am." Amanda seemed to sigh. "I'm guessing you never thought you'd see me."

"No, I didn't.'" Tasia's jaw slackened and she gawked at Amanda. "I just never thought… I'm sorry. I'm Tasia and I'm in charge of the Hall of Records. I keep the scrolls and the stories of Eerie. I'm quite honored to meet you."

"As I am you." Amanda remained in the jacket and tucked into herself.

"So, we found out old Claude isn't really Claude," Sawyer said, barely able to contain himself. "He's really a troll named Angus."

Amanda's eyes widened. "What? I know I heard you wrong. He's what?"

Tasia nodded. "A troll and from the Breen clan. About five years before he connected with you, he changed his name from Angus Breen to Claude Revere. He assumed the identity of the dead sorcerer."

"So now we know he's a liar," Sawyer said. "Which proves he's got a track record for lying."

Amanda paled and sagged in her seat. "Hera…"

"What?" Tasia cocked her head. "It's a shock?"

"Yes, but…" Amanda averted her gaze. "He told my father he was a sorcerer and he could provide me with a good life. My father accepted the bride price Claude offered to marry me. I didn't like him but I was told he could take care of me. He'd provide because he was a sorcerer. I was duped."

"Everyone was," Sawyer said and rubbed her back. He liked that he could touch her, but hated that it had to be in this moment. "He wanted everyone to think he was something he wasn't."

"He stole from me and my family." Amanda shook her head. "I don't know what to say."

"Say he's an asshole," Tasia said. "He lied."

"He did," Amanda whispered.

"He did something wrong, not you." Sawyer continued to rub her back. If he'd been able to bring her here, then maybe he could take her back to his apartment. Maybe even save her from being in that stupid lake for a while. It couldn't hurt to try.

"Amanda?" Tasia asked. "What's wrong? Sawyer's right. Claude lied, but it's not your fault."

Sawyer blinked to get his mind back on the situation. He had to focus. "I get why you're upset. Not only did he lie to your family, but he stole from them, then he stole not only your innocence, but he abused you. For what end? He didn't get your magic."

"He stole my life and never paid for it," Amanda said. She cleared her throat. "That's what pisses me off. He got everything for free and lived his life."

"That jackass." Tasia snorted. "I knew I didn't like him."

"He got away with it for this long, but not forever," Sawyer said. "You can prove he stole that ID?" he asked Tasia.

"I can look through the scrolls, but I don't know if the police will permit it." Tasia drummed her fingers on the table. "Why don't we ask them?"

"Yes." Amanda clutched the jacket.

"I'll be right back." Tasia left him with Amanda.

"I won't let him get away with this. I don't give a rat's ass if he's an old man. He committed murder and lied about it to everyone," Sawyer said. "I don't back down easily, and he's picked the wrong man to piss off."

"He's threatening to kill you, too." She sagged into herself again. "I didn't want to tell you because I wasn't sure he'd be serious, but he's come to the lake ranting. He can't see me, but he knows I'm there. He's probably talking to my body or whatever, but it doesn't matter. He goes there to shout."

"Oh?" He snorted. "Then we use that to nail him."

"What?" She stared at him. "If you confront him, he'll harm you."

"Let him." A plan formulated in his mind.

Tasia returned a moment later with a man in a suit. "This is Detective Schmidt. He's part of the cold case squad."

The detective offered his hand to Sawyer. "Good to meet you. Sawyer Gibson?"

"Yes, and this is Amanda Fortune." He gestured to Amanda. "You might know her."

"The Lady of the Lake." Schmidt sank onto the chair. "Holy fuck. I thought that file was mislabeled. You do exist."

"Like Santa." Amanda tucked into herself. "I

have a police file?"

"You do." Schmidt shifted his gaze between Amanda and Sawyer. "I honestly never thought I'd meet you. You're supposed to be a legend and that file has been overlooked for years because none of us had any connection to the case. I'm sorry to say we thought it'd be cold for good."

"I guess we'll prove you wrong." Sawyer resumed rubbing her back. "We have new information for you."

"I'd like to see it." Schmidt created a bubble. "I'll record what we discuss, if that's permissible."

"Sure." Amanda half-shrugged. "I have nothing to hide."

Tasia pointed to the scroll and explained what she'd learned about Claude's true identity. "As you can see, he lied."

"I do see that." Schmidt nodded.

"And if you want to catch him, or at least get him to talk, then set up surveillance at the lake. I can show you where he visits and where he left me," Amanda said. Her voice grew stronger as she spoke. "He demands I comply, even if he can't see me."

Schmidt's brows rose. "What a dick." He nodded. "Okay. I need the location and we'll set up trail cams. I'll probably get a couple officers posted out there as well."

"Can you do anything if you get him to confess?" Sawyer asked. "Can we nail him?"

"I can't guarantee anything, but I'm going to reopen the investigation and sort through this. This is the biggest cold case we've got, outside of the disappearance of Oliver Waymont."

"Oh, he didn't disappear," Amanda said. "He thought he got Chloe pregnant and left to get a better job. He said he'd come back for her, but he was killed in a logging accident. His spirit came to me after he died because he couldn't break through to Chloe. I never got the chance to tell her the truth."

"She wasn't pregnant, not that I know of." Sawyer folded his arms. He'd believed he'd learn things when he came to the Hall. Of course, he would. But now he had renewed energy to not only solve Amanda's murder, but to bring the bastard to judgment.

"I can look most of that up, but I may need a release of medical records for Miss Bitters." Schmidt closed the bubble, then flicked his fingers. "I've got my partner on this case as well now, but we need a little time. As soon as I can scramble officers to the lake, I'll have them there. I realize it's been years since the murder, but I want to find you and make this right."

Amanda nodded. "Thank you."

"I'll be in touch." Schmidt pushed his chair in, then left.

Tasia allowed the scroll to roll back closed. "Well, we've got some action. Hot damn. You might get to leave that lake after all."

Amanda paled again but said nothing.

"Maybe," Sawyer replied. He understood Amanda's fear. If she was freed from the lake, where would she go? Could she cross over? Or would she be in limbo somewhere else? Neither she or he had considered the next step.

"I have to put this away. If you need any other help, please let me know." Tasia strolled away, leaving him in silence with Amanda.

"Hey." He held out his hand. "Can we talk?"

"Sure." She didn't look at him. "My mind is a mess right now. You could tell me anything and I might believe you."

"I'd like to take you to my apartment. We don't need to stay here, and I don't want you to go back to the lake." He wanted the chance to check the fate lines to see where this would go.

"Is it possible?" she asked. "I don't know how I got here."

"Sheer will of my mind, I believe. I wanted you here, and you showed up. I can't explain it, but I love it. I didn't want you in that cold lake." He slipped her hand into his. "We need to make a plan and piece through this mess. It'd be nicer at my place and private, too."

"It would be." She finally looked at him. "I'm scared I can't leave here."

"I think you can go wherever I am." He laced his fingers with hers and helped her from her seat. "Come on. You've been in too many dank, dark places lately. It's time for some light."

"What if he sees me?" She tugged him to a stop. "If the detective could and Tasia could, then he might be able to, too."

"Good point." He had to come up with a story to cover them. "He knows who I am?"

"He says he does."

That changed things. "You know what? Let him try. He won't do anything in broad daylight because he'd have to admit what he did years ago. It'd draw too much attention."

"Are you sure?"

"I am. You said he didn't want to risk his family. A public display would do just that." But he'd parked right outside, and they could get to his car without much notice. "Let's go."

She didn't argue, but allowed him to tug her

through the Hall to the entrance. He hurried to his car and unlocked it before he reached the door, then helped her onto the passenger seat before rushing to the driver's side.

"I can't believe this is what it's like to be real again." She bounced on the seat. "I haven't been in a car in so long."

"Fifty years?" He engaged the engine, then shifted into gear and drove away from the Hall. "It's time we do some new things."

"What are you doing that's new?"

"Driving with you not wearing a seat belt, but I don't think it matters since you're…" Shit. He couldn't say that.

"Dead? A zombie?" She turned in her seat to face him. "A spirit?"

"I wasn't trying to insult you. I misspoke." He drove through the town to the outskirts and his parents' cottage. He hadn't been willing to sell the place but wasn't sure he could live there. Now, he thanked his hesitation because it allowed him to have a place to hide with her. To give them some time to exist and talk.

"I know." She shook her head. "I haven't been here before. Eerie was so much smaller when I was alive. I feel like a stranger in a strange land. When were these cottages built?"

"Thirty years ago?" Before he was born. "My parents bought it from my father's parents. All I know is that I inherited it when they died and I haven't wanted to stay here until now."

"Why?"

"Being with you makes it feel like home." He should've kept that to himself, but he couldn't help it. She gave him the warm fuzzies. She made him want things that could be impossible. She made him better. He refused to let her down. Now that he'd connected with her in the flesh, he didn't want to let go.

If they caught Claude, then he wouldn't have to.

Chapter Seven

Amanda marveled at the world around her. She'd been in the lake for so long that she barely remembered what anything looked like besides it. The sheer volume of colors and light amazed her. She'd grown up in this town and remembered the brightly painted buildings, but it was like she was seeing it all for the first time.

Eerie was a kaleidoscope of color and the sounds were nearly deafening, but wonderful. The smells from the candy factories and bakeries were mouth-watering. She'd forgotten people converged on the circle in town to play instruments.

But right now, she couldn't enjoy her time. She had to be careful. Had to hide. For all she knew, Claude was lurking around every corner.

It was just like Claude to instill fear, even when he wasn't physically around. He'd done that through the entirety of their relationship. She'd had to defer to him to make decisions, had to get his permission to leave the apartment or speak to her friends. He'd run her life, and she'd thought it was how relationships should be. One had all the power and the other followed along blindly.

So foolish. If she could cry, she would have. She'd missed out on so much because she'd been taught to believe what her parents and her partner told her.

"You okay?" Sawyer asked. He held her hand but didn't leave the car. "You look odd, like you're sad, but angry and scared at the same time."

"You'd be surprised at how close to the truth you are." She steeled herself. "This is your place? Can we go in before we talk? I don't like being outside right now."

"Sure." He hurried from the car and rounded the hood to the passenger side. She opened the door and exited just as he reached her. He tapped a button on his keys, then rushed her to the cabin. "My parents had this place and after they died, I didn't want to come back much, but it feels like the right place to be now." He ushered her inside and shut the door behind them.

Before she could speak, he darted in and out of the rooms before rejoining her in the living room space.

"Is it safe?" She rubbed her arms, feeling a chill she guessed wasn't really in the space. It was the coldness of the water permanently in her bones.

"Very safe." He hesitated in front of her. "You're trembling. May I hold you?"

He'd *asked*. He hadn't demanded. She liked his tenderness and missed being held, but also being kissed, loved and appreciated.

"You're crying." He slipped her hand into his. "I wish I could make things better for you. I don't know how to make it right any faster."

She *was* crying? She wiped her face with her free hand and noticed the dark blue on her fingers. Were her tears the same as the deepest lake water? "I didn't know I could cry, but I can't handle this burden any longer. I'm tired."

"I know you are." He guided her to the sofa and sat, then tugged her onto his lap. "I don't like being forward, but my heart is breaking for you. Let me hold the burden a while. Let me help you."

She sank onto him and the weight of her situation as well as the weight of her sadness hit hard. She sobbed against him.

"I don't know how you feel, but I'm here. I'm not going anywhere," he murmured.

She appreciated his strength and resolve. After allowing herself to grieve her lost life, her sad existence and another moment to pity herself, she quieted and clutched at his shirt. "I'm old enough to be your mother."

"Nah." He rubbed her back and continued to hold her. "You're just right."

"I'm dead."

"And I'm not good at magic, but I was directed to you and I can't imagine being anywhere else."

"What are you going to do if I can't leave the lake? What are you going to do if we get him caught and I move on?" she asked. "What will you do if you get tired of me?"

"You ask so many questions because you're trying to protect yourself. I understand why you're so guarded and I would be, too. You've seen the worst side of life and expect it to come back to you. I'm not like that and I'll do whatever it takes to prove to you I'm not going to hurt you. I'm not him."

She sat up and met his gaze. "Sawyer."

"I love when you say my name." He trailed his index finger along her jawline, then her cheek before tracing the line of her chin. "If you can't leave the lake, then I'll build a cabin right there next to you, maybe even over the spot where you rest. If you move on, then I'll stay here in this cabin and help others who are in your position until I close my eyes the last time and can join you. I won't tire of you."

She wanted to argue, but the words weren't there. He'd make her cry all over again.

"I won't make you do anything you don't want to do, but I would love to kiss you. I want to hold you and show you that all men aren't assholes." Sawyer cupped her jaw. "Some of us are kind."

"I know you are." She rubbed against his palm. "We've barely known each other, but I want to do some very naughty things with you."

"I won't stop you." He rested his forehead on hers. "You're the woman I've been looking for and the one who haunts my dreams."

"I did enjoy seeing you that way." She laced her fingers with his. Heat she hadn't known in so long flooded her body. She shifted on his lap, wriggling on the bulge growing in his jeans. "I'm scared."

"Of me?"

"No, that this is simply an itch to scratch. I'm scared to make a move and that you'll regret it."

"You could regret it."

He made a good point. He also hadn't pulled away when she showed fear.

"My mother once told me I had this ability to read futures and I always thought she was full of shit. I don't know anyone's future. All I can do is sort of understand where the road will take them and make suggestions. Whether they follow is up to them," he said. "I don't know how to use this magic to make any kind of way for myself. Don't think it'd be a means to support myself. But I can see that the fate lines meant for us to come together. We're entwined."

She stared at him. She'd felt that, too, but hadn't wanted to say anything and jinx it. She remembered what Chloe had told her before she'd moved on. She was supposed to help Sawyer use his gift.

"You look peculiar, like you're deep in thought again." He half-smiled and didn't stop caressing her jaw. "What's on your mind?"

Her ability swore she'd not only sleep with Sawyer, but she'd lose her heart to him. They'd begin a love affair that had no foreseeable end. Did he sense it, too?

"Amanda?" He caressed her bottom lip with the pad of his thumb. "You see it, don't you? Our fate lines connecting and twisting together in a tangle that can't be undone."

Like he could read her mind. "Maybe."

"I've made mistakes in my life, but this doesn't feel like one at all. Feels like the most correct thing I've ever done." He nuzzled her cheek. "I don't want this to end and can't see that it will."

"Then let's not end it." She tilted her head and feathered her mouth over his. She closed her eyes as she drank in the warmth of his body. She slid her hands over his shoulders and shifted enough to straddle him. The heat from his crotch seeped into her being. The headiness of being with him, combined with the tenderness of his kiss, spurred her on. She threaded her arms around his neck.

He held onto her waist and kissed her with matching ferocity.

She kissed and tasted him, loving the connection they'd created. Her skin tingled and she could swear the warmth engulfed her. She felt alive. How could she not? He tasted like mint. When he kissed her, she wanted more. She opened to him, thrilled to suck on his tongue. He knew how to kiss and turn her feelings inside out. A whimper bubbled in her throat.

She clutched at his shoulders and held on tight. She never wanted this ride to end.

Sawyer slid his hands along her back, then down to her thighs before he eased one hand to her breast.

She arched into him and placed her hand on his. She loved being touched. Loved being teased this way. Another whimper bubbled in her.

He broke the connection. "Need me to stop?"

"Never." She allowed one strap of her sundress to slide off her shoulder. Within seconds, the other strap fell, too.

"My God." He traced the line of her cleavage. "I…"

The front of the sundress slipped, exposing her breasts. She paused, wondering what he thought. Was she good enough?

His lips parted and he stared at her boobs but said nothing.

She placed his hand on her bare skin over her nipple. "I'm sorry I'm cold."

"No." He snapped his gaze to hers. "You're not cold."

Embarrassment washed over her. She wanted to hide herself but refused to back down. "I know I'm not the best."

"Who says?" He toyed with her breasts, teasing and caressing her nipples. "You're magnificent."

"I'm blue-green." The words from her past flicked into her mind and she couldn't shoo them away.

Sawyer tugged her closer and simply held her. He rested his hands on her ass. His breath tickled her cheeks. "I have no idea what you've been through, but I'm not him and I'll work for the rest of my life to make you know how much you mean to me. Any man who sees the woman sitting on my lap and doesn't see her worth is not paying attention. I see you and I know what you can do. You're more than you realize."

She'd always wanted credit for being alive. For being funny or sweet or silly, not a bother. Sawyer saw the real woman. She wasn't a monster or a myth, but a being desperate for love.

"Come here." He kissed her, sliding his tongue

along hers. At the same time, he rocked her on his lap.

She could get used to this. Hades, she hadn't thought she was capable of having sex -- being a ghost or whatever the hell she was -- it didn't seem possible. With Sawyer, anything was.

She broke the kiss and wriggled her dress down to her waist. "Make love to me."

"I want nothing else." He scooped her into his arms and carried her to the bedroom. Once he placed her on the bed, not thrown, but placed, he tugged his shirt over his head. As he moved, his muscles flexed and his nipples peaked.

She followed the trail of hair from his pecs down to his navel, then below his belt. She scooted to the edge of the bed and shrugged the rest of the way out of her dress. The garment landed on the floor without a sound and she noticed the odd pattern of the fabric. For the first time since her demise, she wasn't wearing the terrible pattern of her death, but the loud, exciting one from before. Her skin was still blue-green, but when she caught sight of herself in the mirror -- so much better than in the moving water -- she gasped at her own smile.

"Yes, sweetheart, you're gorgeous." He unbuttoned his jeans, then shoved the denim and his underwear down his legs.

Her mouth watered as he silently demanded her attention. He had enough to please and it'd been so long since she'd been delighted like that. She opened her legs and balled her hands at her sides.

"Don't you dare tense up on me." He grinned and kicked out of his shoes, then the wadded-up clothing. He stood before her in nothing but his socks. "Do I measure up?"

"You do." She forced herself to relax her hand

and reach for him. The second she wrapped her fingers around his cock, electricity shot through her. She stroked him and met his gaze. "Sawyer."

"Right here." He inched up to her, then cupped her jaw in both hands. "I can't wait to kiss you." He nudged her onto her back and leaned over her.

"Do more than that." She scooted back up onto the bed and stretched out beneath him. The heat and tingles in her body ratcheted up. She trailed her hands along her inner thighs. "Please make love to me."

He said nothing and instead kissed a line of fire along her belly to her breasts. When he sucked on her nipple, she tensed and threaded her fingers into his hair. "Sawyer."

He still didn't speak. Each nibble and lick along her breast scattered her brains. She slid her hands down his ribs to his hips. She wasn't sure she could wait much longer. Hera, this was going too fast and her head swam, but she didn't want to stop. She had no idea how much longer she'd be above the water and away from the lake and she intended to enjoy every second.

He let go of her breast with a pop, then crawled off the bed. He padded around the room, then opened a drawer.

"What are you doing?" she asked, glad to have a second to catch her breath. For the first time since she'd died, she had a kind of breath in her lungs. Nothing made sense and this could be the biggest, most detailed dream of her life, but who cared?

"I was going to retrieve a condom, but I don't need to. I don't want a barrier between us."

They might not have this chance again, she wanted to say, but didn't.

Sawyer crawled onto the bed and settled

between her legs. He rubbed his cock across her pussy lips.

She grasped his shoulders. Nothing else mattered. Not that she could be whisked back to the lake at any second, not that anyone was chasing her and not that she was quickly losing her heart to Sawyer.

Words came to mind and she paused. *You will find love divine upon the right time.* Was this the right time?

Sure felt like it.

Sawyer nudged against her cunt, then eased into her. He moved slowly, sinking into her body. She gasped at the snug fit. But it was like he'd been made for her. She bucked into him, encouraging him silently to move.

"My God." He braced himself on one hand and knees, then held onto her hip with his other hand. He began to thrust. He moved in and nearly out of her pussy, building into a steady rhythm. "Amanda."

She focused on him, but sparkles filled the air. Swirls of blue, green and silver fluttered around her. The flecks of color landed on his shoulders. He moved faster, the sound of skin on skin echoing in the room. She held on for dear life and admired the colors they'd created. This was the manifestation of their magic.

"Sawyer." She arched her back and embraced the good feelings. The swirling in the room matched the swirling in her belly. She cried out and swore she saw fireworks behind her lids. She'd never felt this way before. Never wanted to combust like this before.

"Yes." He leaned over her, his forehead on hers as he pumped his hips. He trembled, then tensed. "Come with me. Come for me."

She didn't need to be coaxed. The orgasm was

right there. It was happening too fast, but that didn't matter. There was no way to hold this back ever. She cried out and embraced the climax. The warmth increased along with the sparkles.

"Fuck, yes." He pistoned into her until his movements turned feral and he tipped his head back. He surged into her, filling her with his seed. A final burst of sparkles exploded over them, then the glitter seemed to dissipate. He added a couple more thrusts, then stilled. His breath tickled her face again and he bowed his head.

She wanted to speak, but the words were gone.

He rested his face against her neck. "My legs are jelly."

"That sounds like you liked it." Her words came out sloshy and didn't sound intelligent in her own ears.

"I did. Very much." He pulled out, then collapsed next to her on the bed. "You wore me out."

"I did?"

"The sheer frantic pace."

Made sense. "I don't know when this dream will end."

"Who says it has to?" He tucked her to his chest. "I'm not ready to give up. I want to have forever with you."

"You do?" She rubbed on him, loving the feel of his naked skin against hers. "Sawyer."

"We're going to make this work. I have no doubts." He kissed her. "None."

She wished she had his belief. Just like a certain fairy tale, she knew she had a shelf life and once it was up, she'd have to go back to her watery hell.

Couldn't she have just a few more hours? *Please*?

Chapter Eight

Sawyer wanted to hold her forever, but even he, in his post-orgasmic haze, knew she could be pulled away from him at any time. The thought of having to lose her to the lake pissed him off, not that he'd show her. It wasn't her fault.

"Sawyer?"

He opened his eyes and smoothed his hand over her hip. The second he looked at her, he knew. She'd begun to fade. "I want you here. I need you to be here." It had worked before. Why wasn't it keeping her there now?

"I don't have control." She held tight to his wrist. "I don't think I have a choice. I have to go."

"I know." He couldn't lose her. "I'll fix this. Our lines are tangled and this isn't them coming apart." Couldn't be.

"I'm sorry." When she reached out to him, her hands swiped through his body. Her eyes shimmered with unshed tears. "Sawyer…" Her voice faded into the darkness as she disappeared.

"You will find love divine upon the right time," he replied, not even sure where the words had come from. "I will find you." He sank down on the sheets and bit back a growl. As much as he wanted to complain that this wasn't fair, he didn't have time.

He needed to get her killer caught. He was taken by her. The thought brought a smile to his mind. He'd been entranced by the Lady of the Lake. It didn't seem possible, but at the same time, it was just right.

"I know you're in there."

He sat up and yanked the sheet over his lap. He knew the voice. *The Princess.* What was she doing there? "Just a moment."

"Take your time," Piper said. "I'm sort of jealous of everyone having cabins. Everyone has a hideaway surrounded by trees and the music of nature. I really need to get one of these."

He'd planned to languish in the glow of making love to Amanda. Take his time with her. That would have to wait. Now, he scrambled to get dressed and rushed, barefoot, out to the living room. He bowed his head. "Princess."

"Please don't get formal." She'd perched on the couch. "I'm serious about this being a great place. I don't want to have a whole extra business, but I want a cabin."

"You could create yourself one." Sawyer turned his attention to her. "How may I help you?"

"You're not customer service." She scooted back on the cushions and crossed her legs. "So, you've got a few questions and it seems like it was handled at the Hall."

"About Amanda? Yes. Claude... er, Angus, did it. Has to be him," he said. "The walking turd abused her. I don't know how he killed her, but according to Amanda he dumped her in the lake, which is why she's still there. I just can't figure out how he did it."

"I don't know that you need to know." She sighed. "You're already mad and knowing won't change that. It'll probably inflame you more. Truth is, you don't need those details."

"Do you know?" he challenged. His ire rose. "Can you catch him? Do you know how that animal attacked her and left her alone in the water? Was she alive when he dumped her? Does it even bother him that he did it?"

"I can't answer those questions, but we're going to work together with the police so we can. I know your plan and it's a good one. He's reportedly lingering in the woods, hollering to scare people off. He's been written off as a weirdo by witnesses to his strange behavior. I mean, there are all sorts in this town, so people talking to themselves isn't really that strange. Hell, if you come to the castle at the wrong time, I'm probably just as guilty of talking to myself because I'm trying to remember everything I have to do that day."

"You're being too hard on yourself." And getting a bit off topic. "So we're working with the police?"

"Yes. I've got guards stationed in the woods where she's reportedly been seen. The police are around there as well because I want to hear what he'll say without the assumption anyone's listening," Piper said. "But to do that, he has to assume she's there. If he's going back to the scene of the crime, then either he's guilty and can't live with what he's done, or he's one of those who has to visit the scene of the crime because it's a thrill. My guess is it's the first rather than the latter."

"I don't understand." Why wouldn't Amanda be there? She was locked in the lake like a tomb… because it was. "Princess."

"I can't answer everything because I can't get into his head and don't think I want to if I could," Piper said. "Right now, you have a bigger issue to worry about."

"Than Amanda? And getting her out of that water?" He doubted anything was more important.

"You've got a talent, and magic. You do understand your power? Right?" She tipped her head. "You truly did conjure her, but you also helped to free her -- even if it was only for a small period of time."

"I did?" It wasn't just a figment of his

imagination or a dream? "We really..." He'd better not mention that in front of the Princess.

"You did." An odd smile curled on Piper's lips. "I love it when a para doesn't understand their power and finally has it explained. It's like a light comes on and the world opens up."

He should question her, but how? "What do you mean? I can conjure and read the Fates. That's not news to me."

"No, it's not," she said. "But you don't realize you have the power to raise the dead."

"Because I conjured Amanda?" That wasn't exactly raising the dead -- it was freeing the woman he'd begun to fall in love with.

"Yes, but she's not the only one."

He frowned and his stomach churned. "Are you going to have me go along raising the dead, when I don't know how?"

"You do know, but only if you want to." She eyed him and the smile increased a little. "It takes a certain para to understand what's involved with raising the dead. You wanted to find her killer, yes? So you searched. The attraction happened because, let's be honest, your aunt already knew you had a type that Amanda fit and Amanda needed someone who could be who she deserved, which is who you are. The Fates already had you both entwined."

"I told her that." But it was nice to hear it from the Princess, too.

"I know you did." She folded her arms. "See? You're more attentive than you realize."

"Maybe, but are you saying I'm not supposed to end up with her?" He'd have to argue that one. "I'm confused."

"You're letting your fears and worries get the

better of you and not listening to me."

He kept quiet, but who could blame him? He couldn't make sense of what she was trying to tell him.

"I can't give you a definitive answer about your future. That's not my magic. You should end up together because you're darn adorable that way, but I can't control that line of the Fates. You both have free will and can change your mind. But you have my vote to be a couple. If there's a way for it to work for the long-term, I'm behind you."

He appreciated what she had to say. At least on his end, he wanted the pairing with Amanda to continue forever.

"The thing is, she's saved you, too. You brought her out of that watery hell, but she's got you out of your quagmire, as well."

"She has?" He didn't doubt it. He had a purpose and found the zeal he'd thought he'd lost.

"If you're successful in this mission, would you be willing -- with her help, as a team -- to be special envoys to the crown to assist in solving other crimes like this?" Piper asked. "Your own Cold Case Unit of sorts."

"Us?" He wasn't a police officer. He didn't know the first thing about investigations. "Would they even allow it?"

"Good question," Piper said. "You wouldn't be with the police, but you'd be working beside them. You'd actually be part of the court."

Him? Part of the court? "As in the royal one?" His aunt would've killed to be involved with the court. She'd been such a fan of Piper and everything she and Diesel were doing to revive the town.

"The very one."

"I'd have to talk to Amanda. I'd also have to

have insurance that Amanda can stay on this side of the lake -- the topside -- and have the chance to continue our relationship," he replied. "I know you can't ensure it, but I don't want to do the job alone."

"Understood." Piper left her seat. "It's funny. When you're floating around out there on your own, you don't realize how much better life can be with that one soul who makes you better. When you find them and get the chance to see the brighter side, it's a whole new thing."

"That world opens up," he said. "She opened my eyes and made me want more than I really deserve."

Piper grinned. "That's when you know the magic is true."

He sure hoped so. "What do I need to do now? Should I go to the woods? I'm worried that if we waste too much time, he either won't show or he'll make a move before we can see him."

"That's already handled. We were able to use the royal court to track him." Piper laced her fingers together. "Why don't you head to her side of the lake? I have the feeling your presence will draw him out."

"I'm sure."

He exhaled and before he finished his breath, Piper was gone. In like a flash and right out like one, too. He finished dressing, then put on his shoes and grabbed a light jacket. He hadn't asked Piper if he should bring something to defend himself. If there were already people there to watch for Claude-slash-Angus, then would they also be there to protect Sawyer?

As he walked through the living room, he noticed the anniversary photo of his parents over the fireplace. "I'm going to make something of myself," he said to their picture and memory. "I'm not going to float through life trying to find my place. I know it. I'm home." He'd spent so much time existing, not really settling anywhere or with anyone. Yes, he'd had a bad breakup, but he'd be more devastated to lose Amanda than he'd been with any other lover.

He tucked his phone into his left pocket and ensured he had a butterfly knife slipped into his other pocket. Better to have something than nothing. He locked the cabin, then followed the trails through the woods.

For the first time since he'd been a little boy, he drank in the view around him. The trees towered, but the leaves were streaked with brilliant color. So much green and brown but also yellows and gold as the light caught the bark differently or the leaves moved. The sounds of the woods were more definite. He swore he heard not just the squirrels and birds, but the chipmunks and foxes in among the trees. There was a magic to the woods he hadn't noticed in a long time -- maybe never. He'd been too wrapped up in everything else.

He also heard something else. Voices. Not Amanda's or someone arguing with her, but voices crying out. Low sounds, soft ones, people trying to get anyone's attention.

I'm here. Someone please find me. I'm here.

He stopped and glanced about. He didn't see anyone, but he'd definitely heard the voice. A realization swept over him and his breath clogged in his throat. Was this the kind of thing Piper meant? Could he really hear the dead?

"I haven't forgotten you. I need to solve this problem first, then I'll be back." He withdrew his knife and carved a crude X into the maple tree before him. "Promise."

He couldn't be sure, but he swore he heard a soft *thank you* in return.

Part of him couldn't wait to tell Amanda. They had a job and were being invited to the royal court. But part of him just needed to be sure she was safe and would be in his arms tonight.

He kept on through the woods and might have heard a couple more voices. Hera's ass, how many people were left for dead in the damn woods? If anyone knew, they'd probably stop visiting the lake for sport and recreation.

Sawyer rounded the lake and followed the trails to where he'd first encountered Amanda. His heart beat faster at the memory of their meeting. He hadn't been able to see her, but he'd been entranced. He knew she'd be a tender soul and once he finally did lay eyes on her, he'd fallen a little in love.

Although he couldn't see the others, he felt their presence in the woods. He hid behind a large growth of underbrush. Twigs snapped and something clicked behind him.

"So you came out here."

He glanced over his shoulder and tensed but resolved not to show his fear. "So did you." He gathered a strength he wasn't sure he had. It was time to face Claude-slash-Angus.

"I told her to be a good girl and not talk to you." The man had a gun. He waved the weapon at Sawyer. "That aunt of yours. She's trouble, too."

"Can't be much trouble. She's dead." Sawyer kept his hands visible for now. Maybe if Claude-slash-Angus didn't think he was a threat, he wouldn't get hurt.

"The old bat finally died? I'll be."

"How didn't you know, Angus? It was in the

chatter around town. Everyone knew." He'd intentionally called the bastard out. Would he take the bait?

"I don't know an Angus, but you know that. She's probably told you."

"Oh, so you're Claude." He nodded once. "The rat that killed her."

"Aren't you cute?" Claude asked. "You're trying to get me to admit to something I didn't do. Don't you know I was the grieving partner? She ran off with Oliver and left me here."

"Really?" Such bullshit. "That's not what I read. But you already knew I did my own research."

"What'd you hear, then?" Claude crooked his brow. "It was all over the news."

"It was," he said. "According to the stories, you and Amanda were going to be married, but hadn't set a date. You had cold feet or something like that. Then she got tired of waiting and ran off with Oliver, the man she'd been having a passionate affair with. Chloe stuck up for them because she'd rather see her best friend with her boyfriend, than see her with a piece of shit. You were the poor man left behind and everyone felt bad."

Claude's eyes narrowed. He growled low in his throat. "What do you mean piece of shit?"

"I'm sorry?"

"You called me a piece of shit."

"Oh, that." Sawyer chuckled. "The news stories claimed you beat the hell out of Amanda. Claimed she wasn't doing what you wanted and you abused her. Or is that all wrong?"

"The whole damn thing is wrong. I never touched her."

"Why was she seen that day with bruises?" He

was making this part up as he went along, but if it snagged Claude, then good enough.

"Couldn't be. She never left the house without my permission."

Sawyer snorted. "Oh really? But you said you weren't cruel to her. Not allowing her to leave the house without your knowing seems wrong."

"You won't corner me."

He sighed and shifted his weight from his left to his right foot. "Oliver was found dead not even a year later. He was stabbed to death." He intentionally lied to see what Claude would say.

"Serves him right. He left with my woman." Claude raised his chin, an air of indignation around him.

He should've guessed Claude would fall for it. "*Woman* or *property*?" Sawyer asked. "If you cared about her, then why do you come out here to talk to her? Why are you telling her what to tell me to do? Is she still alive and you've got her stashed out here?"

"I'm talking to her spirit. She loved being here and this is the logical place she'd go. She's probably living out here with the trolls."

"Then you'd know where she is because you're from the trolls," Sawyer said. "You see, in my research I found reliable information that states you were never named Claude. You aren't a sorcerer, or whatever the hell you claim to be. You're from the trolls, and your name is Angus Breen. You weren't getting anywhere in life and didn't want to be of the trolls any longer, so you turned fifteen, changed your name and took on the identity of a dead sorcerer. No one questioned because they didn't realize the man whose ID you took had been gone for more than twenty years. Why would a kid take someone's ID?"

"Exactly. Why would I do that? Because I didn't," Claude snapped. "I've never heard of Angus Breen."

"No? Then if you were truly a sorcerer, why would you need to take a locket from another magical being? You wouldn't need someone else's magic. Yours would be enough."

"I never took her locket." Claude's face drained of color for a split-second, then he resumed his poise. "They never found it anyway."

"Because you have it." Sawyer shook his head. "I'm tired of arguing with you. None of what you say adds up. You tried to take her magic, but you were wrong because the magic wasn't ever in that locket."

Claude narrowed his eyes again. "I knew it. She duped me."

"*Duped* you?" Sawyer wanted to click his tongue but instead held onto his restraint. "You're the one who comes out here to the lake to shout at her. Not just talk to her or cry because you miss her. You *shout*. You carry on. There are so many witnesses to your behavior. A man who isn't guilty wouldn't be screaming like that. Wouldn't be threatening her. What do you say to that?"

"You're full of shit."

"Why would someone make up seeing that behavior out of you?" Sawyer asked. He noticed the flick of movement from the corner of his eye. The others from the court? The police?

"Because they hate me and they're jealous of my abilities. I'm the most powerful sorcerer you've ever seen." Claude stepped closer to Sawyer. "Anyone who claims I've been shouting at her is lying. They're trying to get me into trouble. I never killed her. Never touched her. I barely loved her."

"*Barely* loved her?" he repeated. The fucking asshole.

"Her old man was hell-bent on getting her out of his house. I paid dearly to take her off his hands." Claude laughed and waved the gun. "No one else wanted her so I took pity."

"Interesting." Sawyer considered his words very carefully. He cleared his throat and noticed the movement again, but this time on his left and right. "So, the story that you were Angus Breen of the trolls and wanted money, so you lied about who you were, assumed someone else's identity, lied to Amanda's family, offered her father a bride price you never paid, kept her a virtual hostage in your home and swore she was worthless is all…"

"Lies." Claude shrugged. "It's all lies."

"Funny." Sawyer massaged his temple. "The Hall of Records bears out the story about you lying."

"The Hall of Records should be blown up. It's an ancient building that no one visits." Claude glared at him. "No one believes the shit coming out of there."

"You're fighting this rather hard. Makes me think there's a little more truth to the story than you're letting on." Sawyer stood tall. "The truth is that you're the one who's lying. You thought you'd found a para who would give you the magic you so desperately needed and when you realized she wouldn't, you took it out on her. You abused her because you were angry with yourself, but you were too proud to simply let her go."

"She'd have told someone."

Sawyer didn't let on that Claude had finally tripped up, but the fucker had made a huge mistake. "What if she had?" Sawyer asked. "Who would believe her over you? If you're supposed to be this big strong sorcerer, then they should be in fear of you."

"Damn right."

"Then who should they believe?" Sawyer asked. "If you're not lying and she's not telling the truth, then why would it bother you what she said?"

"You have no idea what you're talking about," Claude said. "Who's going to challenge me?"

The wind whipped and a roar echoed in the woods. Leaves blew sideways and birds scattered. Amanda strode right out of the water and flicked her hands.

"What in the hell is that?" Claude screamed. "I told you to stay dead. I told you to cooperate."

"What are you going to do about it?" Amanda snarled. "Kill me? Again?"

Sawyer bit back a grin. He loved seeing her so powerful. He admired her strength and resolve in standing up to her bully. Claude had chosen the wrong woman to torment, and it was time for him to pay for his sins.

About fucking time.

Chapter Nine

Amanda wasn't sure how she'd managed to appear to not only Sawyer, but also Claude in this moment, yet she had. Was it the sheer fury in her veins? Had to be. The anger from being silenced all these years? Definitely. Knowing she'd been prevented from having a life while Claude had his? Absolutely.

"You've already killed me. You can't kill me again," she thundered. "You stole my life and now you're lying through your teeth about what happened."

Claude paled. "You can't be here."

"Want to bet?" Sawyer asked. "You fucked with the wrong woman."

"You're dead. You can't rise again." Claude shuddered.

If she wasn't mistaken, he'd also stained his trousers. Good. She wanted him panicked. She stepped toward him and flexed her hands. "You've been coming to my lake, where you drowned me, for years. You shout at me, you give me directives and expect me to comply. You knew damn well what you'd done. You've always known. But like the coward you are, you couldn't own up to what you did."

Claude's mouth opened, but no sound came out.

"You wrapped your hands around my neck, stealing my breath until you thought I was dead, then you tossed me here in the lake. The rocks were insult to injury. I wasn't dead yet, but the rocks, smashed onto my body, finished me off. You knew what you were doing, then you had the audacity to lie about it," she said. "Say it."

He shook his head and trembled more. "I didn't."

"Then say it." She curled her fingers, summoning a magic she didn't know she possessed and unsure of what that magic would do, but damn sure happy to have it. "Say what you did."

"You've been lying to everyone. Stealing pity and wearing your victimhood like a crown, but it's not yours to have," Sawyer said. "You're the monster, not the victim."

"You used your words and fists to keep me silent. Does anyone know how you'd slap and hit me, then blame me for the violence?" she asked. "Or do they know how you'd lock me in my room until I complied? You called me names and threatened to give me back to my family because I was worthless. Did you ever tell my father the truth?"

Claude turned to run but was stopped by the Princess. She held a gleaming crystal spear right at his throat.

"You think you're going to run?" Piper asked. "Oh, no. You're going to take every last bit of your medicine. I believe she told you to admit to your sins. I've got the whole of the Princess's Army out here. The police are listening. Have been for years. It's all up to you. Give her what she deserves -- the truth, right from your lips."

Amanda embraced the electricity in her body. She'd been waiting for this answer for years. She needed to see him squirm. She tipped her head. The longer he kept his mouth shut, the longer he pissed her off. "Say it."

Claude full-on soiled himself. "You can't take my life from me. Can't take my kids or my grandkids. Can't make me say this."

"Oh, but we can." The Princess snapped her fingers with her free hand and held the spear to his throat. “Take this poor fool in. He’s making a mess of my woods.”

Amanda shook her head. Her chance was slipping through her fingers. If he was taken into the police office, he’d never talk. There wasn’t enough fear to get him to speak. He’d cling to his lie of being the victim. “No…”

Piper opened a portal to the police department. “Everyone through. I’m tired of this shit. It ends today.” She gestured to Claude, who, with several officers surrounding him, made his way through the portal. As he stepped into the sterile room, he tried to run, but the officers tackled him.

“Your turn.” Piper pointed to Sawyer. “And you.”

Sawyer turned to Amanda and offered his hand. “Come with me, my love.”

Could she leave the lake? She’d created a terrible disturbance. She hesitated before accepting his hand. Instead of being a vapor or simply disappearing around his fingers, she could grasp him.

He smiled. “You’re still blue-green and beautiful, but now you’re corporeal. I’ve got you.”

She stepped with him through the portal and wobbled at the bright light, plus the pungent scent of cleaner.

Piper closed the portal and tapped her spear on the floor. “Now, we’re missing at least a couple people. Do you want a full audience for your confession, or will you give one, then explain to your family what you did?”

Claude glared at her. “Never.” He thrashed as the officers placed him in handcuffs, then cuffed him to the wall. “Let me go. I don’t belong here.”

“Ah, so the family option.” Piper snapped her

fingers. Claude's wife, plus two sons, appeared in the room.

"What's the meaning of this?" the wife asked. She glanced about the space. "Claude? Why are we at the police department and what in the name of Hades is that?" She recoiled from Amanda.

"Is it All Hallows Eve and no one told us?" the older of the two sons said. He looked like a twenty-year-younger version of Claude and had his same cruel streak. "She loses the costume contest."

Piper rolled her eyes. "Enough." In an instant, the boys, along with Claude's wife, were silenced. In fact, where their mouths should be was simply flesh. No opening. "You will listen and you will deal. I hate being interrupted and I really hate insulting men."

Claude snarled and spit at her. He turned his anger to Amanda. "You were supposed to stay dead."

"I didn't." Amanda let go of Sawyer's hand and folded her arms. "Care to tell them what you did? I'm still waiting for you to say it."

The irritation on his wife's face melted away to fear, then shock and embarrassment.

Had she thought maybe he'd done it? Maybe had an inkling all along? Amanda crooked her brow. "I'm waiting."

"You'll wait forever," Claude spat. "I don't talk to bullies."

"That's rich." Piper stepped up to Claude.

"I'm cuffed and bound to the wall. Who's the bully?" Claude snapped. "You're hurting me."

"You're a liar." Piper turned to Amanda. "Would you like a chance at him?"

"Very much so." Amanda swept her gaze over Claude's family. She remembered seeing Maria during their relationship and wondering why the woman hung out with Claude so much. Now she knew why. They might not have been in a relationship at the time, but it was brewing. She turned her attention back to Claude. "Who are you?"

"Claude Revere. I once loved you, but now that I see you're truly a vengeful monster, I'm glad I was ghosted by you," Claude said. He couldn't look at her. The smirk on his face belied his true uneasiness. He'd probably start laughing, too. He never could keep a straight, bland expression.

"The scrolls attest to you being Angus Breen of the troll clan. You've been lying to everyone for all these years. Does Maria know you killed me?" Amanda asked. "Or was she in on it?"

"I bet she knew," Sawyer said. "Bet she knew and encouraged it so she could have your place."

"Don't you ever say that. Keep my wife's name out of your mouth," Claude snapped. He lunged toward Sawyer, only to have the chain hold him back. "Fuck."

"It's not so comfy when you're the one in the hot seat." Piper matched Amanda's stance and folded her arms. "I'm tired of this nonsense. Daniel? Hit him with the truth serum."

One of the officers stepped forward and blew sparkles into Claude's face. Claude, for his part, shook his head, but the sparkles settled around him anyway.

"Now, answer her questions," Piper said. She gestured to Amanda. "Take it away."

"Why did you change your identity?" Amanda asked.

"I wanted to be someone. I hated being a troll, and saw the witches as a way to get out." Claude paled. He shook his head. "I figured out that your family was of an old class and had ancient magic. If I lied and took yours, then it might give me more credibility and make me into the sorcerer I was dying to be."

Maria sank onto a chair and both sons stood in stunned silence.

Sawyer remained beside Amanda and softly rubbed her back. She appreciated the gesture. She'd known they'd get answers, but hearing Claude admit the truth still hurt. "So you thought you'd steal my magic and make yourself someone?"

"Yes." Claude trembled. He shook his head again. "Your father was so upset that you were a girl, he had no problems in offering you up to me. He didn't know until right before he died that the money I'd promised him was a farce. I never had that money. I was going to use your magic to make it, then make him think he'd been given the cash, all while keeping it for myself."

She should've known. "And what of me?"

"You were too spirited. You didn't listen to me and when you did, it wasn't right. I had to put you in your place. Had to take away your locket so I could have your magic. I didn't care about you or what happened to you." Claude paled. He sank to the floor and his arms hung from the cuffs on the wall. "I always wanted to kill you. You were in the way. I hated you. You had magic and credibility. You were sweet and kind. People liked you, but they hated me."

She leaned into Sawyer, not sure she wanted to hear the rest of the words. Claude had broken her heart before and was doing it all over again.

"I met Maria and knew I wanted to be with her, so I tried poisoning you, but it didn't work. Tried locking you up and that didn't work. Chloe would ask about you or she'd switch your drinks. She knew,"

Claude said. He tried to snap his lips shut, but the words continued to tumble from him. "I got so angry I put my hands on you for the last time. I hated that I could hurt you and you'd simply take it. You didn't lash out. You just cried and that pissed me off. How could anyone be so… perfect?"

She hadn't been perfect. She'd been scared.

"I fed off the fear in your eyes. Lived for your screams. I came to hate you so much that I finally gave in and put my hands on you. I thought the life had drained from you, but Maria was coming to the house and I couldn't let her see what I'd done. I put you in the wheelbarrow and carted you to the lake. I knew where no one would look for you and worked on my story along the way. I dumped you there, then put the rocks on to keep you from floating, then left. I hated you, but I felt free. Even proposed to Maria that day."

Maria, for her part, wept. She buried her face in her hands.

"You weren't supposed to come back. You were supposed to be dead. Supposed to rot there and let me have my lie. The magic was supposed to be in that damn locket and give me the chance to have the life I deserved," Claude said. "I had to go back and speak to you because you were the only one who listened without talking back, just like in life. I did it. It was my fault. I wanted more than I deserved."

Amanda gritted her teeth to keep from screaming. The truth did help, but it wasn't going to heal her today. Wasn't going to take away her anger. It simply explained the parts she didn't know. She didn't have peace. All she had was a heavy heart, saddened by what he'd done and his callousness in doing it.

"Got that on camera?" Piper asked. "Guys?"

"Camera, bubble and audio," Daniel said. "And

copies already made."

"Beautiful." Piper tossed the spear into the air a few inches and caught it. "The truth serum always works. It's so simple, too. It's a threat. No magic, no change. Simply the threat that the truth will come out and it does."

"Fuck you," Claude shouted.

"Oh, no. I'm married. Get him out of here." Piper shook her head. She turned to Amanda and Sawyer as four officers hauled Claude from the cramped space. She snapped her fingers, giving Maria and the boys the ability to speak again. "I suppose I ought to let them give rebuttal, but I'd like to have a word with you two, as well."

Amanda didn't want to talk to anyone. She needed time to process what she'd learned. It was all too horrible and she'd been in the middle of the situation. At least she had Sawyer there to hold her.

Maria stood. Tears streamed down her cheeks. "I knew what he'd done. I knew he'd been so underhanded, but I thought it was sexy that he was bad. Thought he'd never do that to me, but I knew. I remember."

"Ma, you can't cop to that. You'll be in trouble, too," the taller son replied. "Dad was lying."

"No, he's not, Elijah." Maria flicked her gaze to Amanda. "I'm sorry. It's not enough and it's far too late but I'm sorry."

Amanda wanted to reply, but the words weren't there.

"Ma." The shorter son shook his head. "You told us it was her fault and we should be afraid of her. Maybe it was Dad we should've feared and you, too."

"I oughtta smack you," the taller son said. "Dad didn't do it. It's all a lie."

"Elijah. Leonidas. Enough. He did what he said and I knew about it. We all have to live with the truth, and that's all there is to it." Maria stood and offered her wrists. "I'm surrendering myself."

Daniel and another officer ushered her from the room.

"You haven't heard the last of this," Elijah shouted. "I'm getting a lawyer."

Leonidas sighed and rolled his eyes. "He's all bark and no bite. I'm sorry." He followed his brother from the room.

"That was explosive." Piper flicked her fingers, making the spear dissolve. She massaged her temples. "Now, where was I?"

"You said something about speaking to us," Sawyer said. "I don't know what to do."

"I'm going to send you back to the cabin where you can have some silence and digest what you've been told. I know it's a lot." Piper opened a portal to Sawyer's cabin. "Before you go, Amanda? You're no longer a prisoner of the lake. You've been freed. Your body no longer resides in the water. You are truly free."

"Free?" She murmured, "What do I do?"

"You've got a whole new chapter to your life. I guess it's up to you what you'll make of it." Piper nudged her and Sawyer into the cabin. "The police and my guards will take care of your case. You rest and we'll keep you updated, but before I forget, I'd like to offer you and Sawyer a spot in the royal court. We could use a couple who can communicate with the dead and help solve these kinds of cases. The offer doesn't expire, so take your time and discuss. I need to get back to the situation here. Try to rest."

Amanda shook her head to make sense of what

had happened. It was all so fast and confusing. The sheer volume was too much. Before she could say a word, Piper stepped back through the portal and closed it.

Sawyer rubbed her palm with the pad of his thumb. "Want to sit?"

"Not sure I can do much else." She sank onto the sofa. For the first time since she'd been killed, she could feel the couch. Could feel the lumps in the cushions and smell his cologne. This wasn't a dream. Wasn't even a part of her imagination.

This moment, even Sawyer, was real.

She scrubbed her face with both hands. A whimper vibrated in her throat. She cried out. "I hate this."

"What?" Sawyer caressed her back again. "Me?"

"No." She drew a breath into her lungs and paused. She could breathe. She had air in her lungs again. She opened her eyes and stared at her hands. Still blue-green. "I'm alive, but I'm not."

"Who says you're not?" He met her gaze. "Sweetheart, you're beautiful."

"I'm not… I'm not like I used to be." Wasn't she supposed to be flesh-colored again? At least look alive?

"Who says you need to be? This version of you is beautiful. It's the version I fell for." He smiled and nodded softly. "I can't imagine you being any other way -- blue-green, sweet, strong, and determined."

"Sawyer." She was supposed to be beautiful, not a monster.

"I see not only the beauty you have on the outside and trust me, you've got my attention." He placed her hand on his crotch. "You're the one who turns me on."

She didn't recoil, but caressed him. She'd made

him hard? Even looking this way?

"I also see the woman inside. I see your soul and it's just as beautiful as the outside," he said. "No lies."

"Your aunt said you had a type." She rested her forehead on his and continued to stroke him through his jeans. "She also told me I'd find love divine."

"Upon the right time?" he asked. "Told me the same thing."

"She did?" She sat up and stared at him. "It was in a line of the Fates that I read. She wasn't there."

"I don't know how she knew, but she did. She's the one who told me." He half-shrugged. "I don't care how she knew. What I care is that she was right. I found the love I wanted and the love I deserved when the time was right. When I found you."

"And you want to go on this journey with me?" It didn't seem right but felt perfect.

"I do." He winked. "I might even have a job for us. You heard the Princess. She wants us to join the court and she's the one who told me you and I can communicate with the dead. It's already happened. When I was crossing the woods to find you, I heard from someone."

She tensed for a split-second. "I might not be enough to keep you satisfied. I wasn't for him."

"Because he was a dumbass. I know who has been put into my path and I don't want anyone else." He curled his fingers under her chin. "But I'd like you to be my partner in finding this poor soul and giving them the same closure you were given."

The offer was tempting.

"But, before we proceed, I want to make love to you. I want to sink into that sweet pussy of yours, taste you, make you cry out, feel your nails on my skin and your breath on my cheek. I want to hear you call my name when you come and play with your tits. You're my vision of perfection, beauty, and sexiness all in one."

She'd been given a second chance and the ability to have a life once again. She could have the love of a lifetime with him. Could have her heart's desire. All she had to do was accept her abilities and her distinct coloring, but also Sawyer. She wished Chloe was still alive to see how far she'd come. Wished she hadn't lost so much time.

But she had the chance now and a partner to share this part of her life with. Why not embrace it?

"May I make love to you?" Sawyer asked.

"Like I could tell you no."

Chapter Ten

Sawyer scooped her into his arms and carried her to the bedroom. He'd never done anything this exciting or right in his life. The more he looked at her, the more things made sense. He'd been looking for her all along. He placed her on the bed and admired the view.

She might not think she was beautiful, but he loved the pale blue-green of her skin. The way her lips parted when she wanted to say something but hesitated. The swell of her breasts. How she'd given him a chance when few others might have.

She made his heart beat faster. His blood rushed through his body. She made him hard as a rock and determined to be with her.

"You're staring at me." She propped herself up on her elbows. "I do have to admit it's strange to be… full-bodied."

"Not a mist? Or a dream?"

"Or a zombie."

"You weren't a zombie." He tugged his shirt over his head. He'd just been with her that night, but it felt like ages ago. He needed her now.

The chilly air swept around him and his nipples peaked. He wanted to present the best image for her. Wanted her to crave him, too.

"How do you know I wasn't a zombie? I was one of the undead." She sat up and tucked her legs under her. "It is nice to be able to use my legs, though. Not be a spirit."

"You're great as a spirit and in this form. I'm entranced by you no matter how you look." He unbuttoned his pants but left the garment around his hips. "But you were never a zombie. Did you eat brains?"

"No." She crinkled her nose. "I didn't eat."

"Then you couldn't be a zombie."

"A specter?"

"Does it matter?" He crawled onto the bed, nudging her onto her back and straddled her. "Doesn't to me. As long as you're here, you're with me, I don't care what form you take. I just need you."

She draped her arms around his shoulders and a slight smile curled on her lips. "I don't understand why you like me so much, but I can't look away from you."

"Maybe it's because I'm falling in love with you." He nuzzled her throat, then kissed along her neck to her collarbone. She tasted like sin and sex. Like raw passion in the flesh. "I've never met anyone like you, and I can't imagine my life without you."

"Even now?" She arched into him and threaded her legs around his hips. "We just met."

"Feels like a lifetime to me." One he'd happily revisit over and over. "I can't explain it." He moved the straps of her dress, exposing the upper swell of her breasts. The more he kissed her, the more the heat in his body ratcheted up.

She clutched his shoulders and stopped him. "Like the fate lines brought us together and we were supposed to be in this moment?"

"Yes." He tipped his head and met her gaze. "Exactly that. I've had the Fates pushing me in a certain direction. Felt like I'd been floating and existing until my aunt sent me looking for you. Like it had to be the right time to find each other."

She stared at him and a slight blush crept across her cheeks. "You felt like you were a shadow of yourself?"

"Yeah, I kind of did." He'd never thought about

it that way, but that was exactly the truth. "I didn't have direction. Then I was sent to find you and I did."

Her slight smile grew. "So we had to come into our own before we could join forces and find what we deserved?"

"Love divine?" He resumed kissing her chest, up to her collarbone, then down to the top of her breast.

She threaded her fingers into his hair and whimpered. "Then this is the best love divine." She guided him, holding her to her boob.

He moved the dress out of the way. Soon, he'd get her an entire wardrobe of clothes so she could wear whatever she wanted. She wasn't bound by the curse of death any longer. She could have everything she deserved.

Sawyer sucked on her nipple, rolling the tight bud of skin in his teeth.

"Oh!" She tugged lightly on his hair and gasped. "Sawyer."

He'd never get tired of hearing her call his name. She made his heart light. He palmed her other breast, then tweaked her other nipple while continuing to lavish attention on the first one. The more he touched her, the more he fell in love with her.

She panted and rocked into him. "My Hero. My Sawyer." She clawed at his scalp. "Make love to me."

"Not yet," he whispered against her breast. He switched to her other nipple, giving it the same attention. He loved the taste of salt on her skin, the woodsy scent of her and the delight in her eyes. He scooted off the bed and yanked the dress along with him, revealing her completely. He'd seen her bare but wouldn't tire of the view.

She gasped. "Sawyer." A blush crept down her chest. She parted her legs, giving him a view of her pussy.

"Gorgeous." He nudged her thighs apart, her cream glistening on her cunt. His mouth watered. He needed a taste.

"Sawyer?" She grasped the blankets "What are you waiting for?"

"Nothing, but the view is fantastic." He dropped to his knees and slid his arms under her legs, dragging her to the edge of the bed.

"Why are you so kind to me?" The slight twinge of pain in her voice, despite her being turned on, bothered him.

"Because you haven't heard the truth in so long you've forgotten what it is, but I'm here to remind you. You deserve every kindness I can give you." Right now, he needed to taste her. He dragged his tongue along the inner swell of her thigh to her pussy lips, then across the top without stopping, to taste the other side.

When she cried out, he opted to spear his tongue in the slit of her pussy. The moment her cream exploded on his tongue, he was hooked. She tasted as sexy as she looked. The magic swirled again. Sparkles filled the air, but this time they were blue, green, and silver. He lapped at her, memorizing the taste of her, but also the things he'd done to make her cry out again. He could hear that sound over and over. Her delight made him happy.

"Sawyer!" She fisted his hair.

He wanted to tell her to enjoy and ride the wave, but he was too busy. He had to memorize every last moment of this. Not that he'd never have another time with her. He'd ensure he would. He lavished attention on her pussy, tracing the line of her labia, then sliding one finger into her cunt. He loved how she clamped around him.

She tugged on his hair again. Her cunt fluttered around his digit and the sparkles increased as she dug her heels into the mattress. “Fuck!”

He’d never heard her swear like this and rather appreciated it. She’d finally let go.

She tensed around him, then collapsed on the bed. She panted. “Sawyer.”

The whole moment had passed a bit too fast for him, but they had time to make more memories. He basked in the heat and sweetness of her climax.

“Sawyer.” She went limp. “You’re going to drive me crazy.”

“I’m supposed to do something else?” he asked. He lapped at her once more, then pulled his finger out. He sat back on his heels as he swept his gaze over her. The colors hadn’t faded, but she was more like a rainbow right now. Brilliant.

“No.” She didn’t move, but her chest did as she breathed. “You didn’t come.”

“Not yet.” He stood and stripped out of his jeans and boxers, then crawled onto the bed, over her again. “Hi.”

“Hi.” The lazy smile on her lips warmed his heart. She wrapped her arms around his shoulders again. “Funny seeing you here.”

“Oh?” He braced himself on one hand and arranged her legs around his hips with his free hand. “Want me to go somewhere else?”

“Never.” She kissed him. “I’m home.”

He’d never heard anything sweeter in his life. Yes, they’d fallen for each other fast, but they had time to make this work. Time to fall more in love. Time to realize this was where they were meant to be. He slid his dick over her wet pussy lips. “I’m home, too.” He’d never considered this old cabin home. It was a vacation place of sorts until now. But he hadn't felt he belonged anywhere until then. He hadn't belonged out in the greater world. Hadn't at his apartment or even at his parents' home. But now? He'd found the missing pieces. He was whole.

"Make love to me." She caressed his shoulders. "I can feel you. All of you. I don't want to miss a thing about this or have it ripped away. I want more. I want you."

"You've got me." He inched into her pussy, pushing in one smooth thrust. Once again, he'd come home. This wasn't a dream or a stolen moment. This was theirs. She snugged around him, holding him in as he moved. Like she was made for him. They were truly one body, soul and mind working together.

She bucked into him, coming alive and matching his rhythm in seconds. Thrust for thrust, she stayed with him. Not only frying his brain from making love, but the sheer weight of the moment. He'd never believed he'd be here, but with her, he belonged.

She dug her heels into his lower back, holding on. "I just came. Gonna again."

He slipped one hand between their bodies and caressed her clit. He had to make her fly.

Her eyes widened and she whimpered. "Sawyer."

"Good?" He continued to play with the tight bundle of nerves while he pumped into her. It didn't take long for the waves of orgasm to start crashing in him. He tried to hold back for as long as he could. His moves turned jerky and nothing would keep this contained.

"Very." She panted harder. "I..."

"Come with me." He tensed as long as he could.

"Come apart and come with me."

She shivered and her eyes rolled back in her head. Instead of words, a feral cry ripped from her and she trembled. More sparkles filled the room, but this time with little explosions like fireworks added to the mix.

He stopped trying to hold the tidal wave back and embraced the climax. The warmth of her body around him, the headiness of the moment and knowing he'd found his perfect person. He hadn't believed his person was out there, but he'd not only found her but made love to her as well. "Mine."

"Yours." She nodded. "Mine, too."

He came hard and surged to the hilt into her. When he looked into her eyes, he saw forever. Was it too fast? Who gave a damn. Not him. He knew this was right and had no doubts. He added a couple more thrusts, then stilled, remaining within her. "I claim you as my mate and perfect person. You're all I want."

She caressed his cheek and flexed around him. "I claim you, too. No one else."

He planted both hands on the bed and willed his strength to hold him up until he could pull out. He sank beside her on the bed and tucked her to his chest. Even if the world fell down around him, he had her and they'd be all right.

"Sawyer." She splayed her hand on his chest. "I never thought when I went into that water that I'd come back out. You showed me the biggest kindness and the most compassion. You weren't afraid of me."

"Can't be. You entranced but never scared me." He kissed her temple. "Now we can forge a path together for the future."

"We can."

"Will." He had no doubts.

She snuggled into him. "I love that you're so confident."

"I know this is lightning fast and new, but I will spend the rest of the time I have proving to you that I'm not him, and showing you how much you mean to me." He traced the line of her jaw. "You're the best thing to happen to me, and I'll do what it takes to restore your faith."

"Thank you." She sighed and toyed with his sparse chest hair.

He loved that she liked playing with his body and exploring.

"Do you realize you're turning blue?" she asked. She sat up. "Sawyer?"

He flexed his hand. Sure enough, there was a blue-green tinge to his hand. "Huh."

"You're not upset?" She shook her head. "You're blue. Something's wrong. There has to be something wrong."

"No." He didn't need to look at his skin again to know. "It's the magic of our pairing. Piper said our magic would increase and that you and I would meld." She hadn't actually said that last part, but it made sense.

"What?"

"Yeah. We declared each other as our mates or whatever. Because we did that, we're connected and our magic entwined like our fate lines, which means we boost each other's magic and we're one."

"So I'll never get rid of the blue?" she asked. Her voice broke. "I'll always be marked by the way I died."

"I know it bothers you that you might be, but it makes you unique to me. Makes you beautiful to me, too. It shows you survived and you're back to tell the tale," he said. "That's nothing to write off."

She sighed and reclined on the bed again. "I suppose you're right."

"Piper said we'd be stronger together and she did offer us a spot on the court. I know you're not wild about going back to the dead, but you wouldn't actually go. We'd find people who've died and never got closure. Our knowledge of the Fates and abilities to hear the dead will help people. We might be able to find and close cases," he said. "I even have a lead on someone."

"You do?" Her eyes widened and she rolled onto her side, then propped herself up on her elbow. "How?"

"I told you. When I was looking for you, I heard someone in the woods and I know it wasn't anyone of the living. I know they heard me, too, because I promised to come back."

She nodded slowly and toyed with his chest hair again. "We should find this person. Do you know where they were? Or where you heard them?"

"Do you want to be part of the court and solve cold cases together?" He couldn't imagine doing this by himself.

"I absolutely do."

Then they were so in business.

Chapter Eleven

Amanda dressed in one of Sawyer's shirts. She wasn't sure how he managed to get jeans that would fit her, but it didn't matter. He'd probably been able to conjure them and flats. She'd grown so used to her tattered sundress that wearing pants was almost foreign to her. She followed behind him through the cabin. "So we're finding this voice?"

"Yeah." He swept his gaze over her. "You know, you could make sack cloth sexy."

"Thank you." She grasped his hand. "We should get moving, though. I don't know how long it'll take to find the voice, but we only have a few hours before it starts getting dark and it gets darker in the woods much faster."

"I remember." He grabbed his keys and phone. "I don't know if we'll be able to contact Piper, but this will be my backup."

"Sure." She left the cabin with him and tucked her hands into her front pockets. She'd been given a second chance, and it was the biggest of her life. She had life again. It was almost unbelievable. A thought occurred to her. Could she die again? Or was she immortal? She'd never asked. She probably should.

"What's on your mind?" Sawyer asked. He held her hand as they ventured through the woods.

"I wondered if we're immortal now or if I can die again." She kept up with him but didn't want to discuss this in public. "Hush. I can't be sure someone's not listening."

"Who…" Sawyer nodded. "I get it."

"We should be listening to the voices or for them." She hoped they'd find the person they were looking for.

"Do you know of any cases of someone being dumped out here?" Sawyer asked.

"Could be. There're rumors people have been left among the trees for years, but I've been out of the loop," she said. "Do you hear anything?" Something felt off. Like they were being watched, but not by a spirit. She couldn't shake the uneasiness. She'd just been given her life back and wasn't ready to give it up again.

"The voice was over here." He directed her through the trees to a carved maple. "I left this to mark where I heard them."

"Good." She couldn't shake the strange feeling. "Someone's watching us."

"I heard you." He held up his free hand. He offered her a bubble. "I hear you. Where are you?"

She wanted to question him on the bubble. Should she? "What's this?" she blurted.

"I forget how much you've missed." He lowered his voice. "It's to contact the Princess. It's direct."

"Wow." For a moment, she forgot to be worried. The ability to contact each other through bubbles… It was almost unreal.

"Where are you?" Sawyer shook his head. "I swear I heard you."

She glanced up from the bubble and nearly screamed. Someone did look back at her, but they were most certainly not dead. She dug her elbow deep into Sawyer's ribs. "Oh Hera."

"What?" He froze. "Elijah."

She tried to hide her trembling. The way he waved the gun, she just didn't trust Elijah. "You don't want to do this."

"No?" Elijah held up the weapon and aimed in her general direction. "You took my father away and you were supposed to be dead."

She'd never stood up to Claude, but she wasn't backing down now. "You're right."

"Then die." Elijah's hand wobbled, but the steely hatred resonated in his eyes.

"Do you want to be in trouble with your father?" she asked. "You do realize the Princess still has guards all over these woods. She can see what you're doing. She'll know and you'll be right beside him. Is that what you want for your family? Don't you have kids?"

Elijah narrowed his eyes. "How do you know that?"

"How do you know that?" Sawyer muttered. He remained beside her and grasped her hand.

She shooed him away only in case she needed to defend herself. The gesture was kind on Sawyer's part, but right now she didn't need that.

"How do you know that?" Elijah asked again, through clenched teeth. "What do you know?"

"I used to see you when you'd bring your family to the lake. Remember, I couldn't leave the lake. He'd stoned me here and I could see you. I knew what you were doing. I had nothing but time to watch and you'd bring them to the lake for picnics. You proposed to your wife not feet from where I was." She didn't like dredging up this past, but it was true. "You came to the lake at least three or four times over the summer and fall. Birthdays for your son and daughter respectively and an anniversary with your wife. I believe you had tulips as the flowers. Your tenth, or was it fifteenth anniversary?"

Elijah paled and the gun wobbled again. "You don't know that."

"If I don't, then why are you upset?" She held up her hands. "Don't blame me for looking when I had no choice."

"You could've been somewhere else. Freak. You wanted to watch us because you were obsessed," Elijah said. "You wanted your magic back."

"He never had it." She didn't try to bridge the gap to him. There wasn't any point because he wasn't listening. "It wasn't in the locket. You heard him."

Sawyer put his hands up. "You can kill us, but it won't help your father. Won't help your kids. Won't get you out of trouble. It'll land you in more trouble."

"You shut up." Elijah waved the gun again. "Doesn't matter. You ruined my life and I'll finish yours."

"Please, don't." She flexed her fingers. "I can see your fate line and right now, you still have some control. You can change the course of your future."

"You don't know that." Elijah continued to wave the gun and his lips curled in a sneer. "You can't know that."

"That's the magic your father wasn't able to steal. It wasn't in the locket." She had to keep him talking. The more they conversed, the less chance she might get killed for real. "He couldn't take that magic."

"Your fate isn't sealed. You can change it," Sawyer said. "You could make the course go more toward the good of your children and potential grandchildren."

"You know I'll have grandchildren?" Elijah asked.

"You will." She could see them. "Three, but only if you put the gun down. The cycle can end with you."

Elijah narrowed his eyes, but his sneer softened. "Three?"

"Two by your son and one by your daughter," she said. "You'll miss that if you take the wrong line."

Piper and Diesel appeared in the woods. Diesel stood behind Elijah. Piper snapped her fingers and the world seemed to stop around them. "I know you had this in hand. You kept him talking a long time, but we can't have another murder in this woods and I won't have this guy's life and the lives of his family destroyed by one stupid decision." She stepped up to Elijah and waved her hand in front of his eyes. "You're going to go home, to hug and kiss your wife, to hold your kids and won't remember anything about this visit to the woods. You'll think of your father as a guy who made a mistake, but you can forgive him and you'll move forward."

"That'll work?" Amanda asked. "It's that simple?"

"No, but it's worth a shot." Piper blew dust into his eyes, then opened a portal. Once Diesel took the gun from Elijah, Piper sent him through the portal to his home.

"What about his car?" Sawyer asked. "He must've driven here."

"We'll take care of it." Diesel strode out of sight.

"He's on it." Piper said, then closed the portal.

Amanda sagged into Sawyer and her knees buckled. She and Sawyer had stared death in the face. She really needed to stop doing that. Stop being faced with her imminent demise.

"You had that in hand." Piper stood with them in the woods. "But he's not the reason you were out here. Who did you find?"

"We didn't get the chance to find out." Sawyer slipped his arm around Amanda's waist. "I heard the voice."

"I haven't had a chance to, but I trust him." Amanda scrubbed both hands over her face. "Before we do anything, you offered roles for us with the court, yes?"

"I did." Piper laced her fingers together. "And?"

"I'm in," Sawyer said. "I want to help people."

"And you?" Piper nodded to Amanda. "What do you think?"

"What's the status on our mortality?" Amanda asked. "I've come back from the dead, but can I be killed again?"

"Ah." Piper dipped her head and smiled. "Well, you've always had your immortality."

"What?" Sawyer held her a little tighter. "That's how she could come back."

Made sense to her.

"Not exactly," Piper said. "You've both always had your immortality."

"We have?" Amanda stared at her in disbelief. "He killed me."

"Sort of, but you were never really dead. You faded for a time, but when the right one came along, you came back to life. You came into your own."

She still didn't believe it. She'd been in the water. She'd had her last breath and had felt the cold sting of being murdered. "He strangled me."

"He did, but you weren't ever really going to die. You went into a kind of hibernation, but not actual death. He took the breath from you, but you weren't gone." Piper tipped her head. "And when you're with Sawyer, the pieces all fit… so to speak… and you're the way you were supposed to be. It simply took waiting those years and going through that ordeal to both understand and embrace your gift."

Piper was so full of bullshit. "So I had to wait for the right partner?"

"Pretty much." Piper sighed and nodded to

Sawyer. "Am I to understand you found someone?"

"We did." Sawyer held up his free hand. "I hear them now."

Amanda shook her head and didn't bother listening. She had too much to ponder at the moment. She'd been alive, but in a version of stasis for that time? So he hadn't really murdered her? But he'd lied. That wasn't right. Claude hadn't just lied to her, but he'd misrepresented himself to everyone. Then he'd abused her.

Sawyer let go and pointed to the leaves on the ground. "Under that heap. Her name is Marissa. She's a faerie, but she was left here twenty years ago. She's afraid to be found because she's all bones."

Amanda shook her head. She needed to focus. There was someone else here in the woods and her problems weren't all that big. This poor soul's issues were bigger. She massaged her forehead and listened. "She thinks she's guilty," she said, listening to the being speaking through her mind. "She'd cast a few spells that were wrong and someone took offense."

Piper folded her arms and shifted her stance. "Marissa Tucker. She was around twenty-seven, and a faerie who cast spells for the shifters. She could change them and could heal them when they needed it."

Sawyer shrugged. "I've never heard of the case, but she's sorry about helping the wrong person."

She'd heard that, too. "I don't detect dishonesty from her. She knows who she helped wasn't the best, but she didn't do it out of a bad place. She thought it was the right thing to do."

"Who killed her?" Piper asked. "According to what was reported, she ran away."

"Seems to be the popular thing to say." Amanda focused on the problem at hand and not her own. "She helped a wolf shifter by the name of Terry."

"Oh." Piper exhaled. "Shit."

"Do you know him?" Sawyer asked. "I've never heard of him."

"I do." Piper rubbed her hands on her thighs and nodded, then turned away from them. "Okay, I need some help. We have a recovery mission."

Amanda elbowed Sawyer. "Recovery?"

He shrugged. "She's buried right over here." He pointed to the heap of leaves. "Under this pile. They buried her deep."

She couldn't detect it, but she believed him. This was why they had to work together. If she couldn't make sense of it, then Sawyer could and vice versa.

"Yes, team, and bring the squad." Piper faced them again. "Okay, so I can't say I won't need you again soon, as you can talk to our friend here and probably understand this better than I can, since I don't have the ability to speak to her. But we're going to find her and get this sorted out. Even if it's only to help her move on, we'll do it."

"That's all I'd wanted when it was my turn," Amanda said. "If we can help her, then let's do it."

"Perfect." Piper stepped out of the way as a swarm of bees converged on the area. "The cavalry is here."

The insects shifted form into the recovery crew.

Sawyer helped Amanda out of the way as the various workers moved dirt, shifted through the leaves and eventually reached the remains.

Amanda's heart sank. She'd worried Marissa would be nothing but bones and now that she saw the evidence, the truth was hard to handle. "The poor thing." She reached out but didn't touch the remains. "This wasn't how she wanted to end. She thought she was helping a man she'd once been involved with and thought she could get him onto the right path, but he double-crossed her."

"We'll get you home, honey." Piper winced. "Why do we do this to each other? Cruel."

"Because small minds don't think or stretch." Sawyer hugged Amanda. "And jealousy is rampant."

He had no idea how close to the truth he was -- especially for her. She buried her face against his shoulder and a sob she'd held in couldn't be contained any longer. She cried for the woman they'd found, but also the woman she'd been before she'd died. Amanda sobbed for the woman she'd also been before Claude. The person who trusted and wasn't afraid. Such innocence quashed and for what?

She wasn't even sure.

"I need you to look into this shifter, Terry," Piper said, pointing to one of the crew members. "Go to the Hall. Sawyer? Amanda? I want you to head back to the cabin. I have no idea how much this has taken out of you, but you both look weary."

"I'll get her home." Sawyer slipped his arm back around Amanda and walked with her through the trails back to the cabin. "I'm sorry you had to be exposed to that, but if we take the job with the court, then we'll see a lot of things that will upset you."

"I know." She sagged into him. "It's not so much seeing the bones or knowing she was down there. It was the reason as to why she ended up in the earth. She wasn't trying to harm anyone."

"I know." He opened the door to the cabin.

After she stepped inside, he joined her and closed the door behind them.

"But it's a lot to handle."

"It is." She eased her arms around him again. "I

just need a moment."

"Or five?" He hugged her, brushing his fingers through her hair. "I get it."

"Just… hold me." She sank onto the couch in his embrace and rested her head on his shoulder. She'd forgotten the simple pleasure of being able to sit with someone, to be held and cared for. To be loved. "I don't want to talk for a while. I just want to exist."

"Then that's what we'll do."

* * *

Amanda walked with Sawyer to one of the back rooms of the police department. The moment she saw the oak box, she knew what they'd been summoned for. She sucked in a ragged breath, happy to be able to breathe again, but saddened by what she had to do. Yes, she could read the fate lines, but she and Sawyer also had the ability to communicate with the dead. What exactly did that make her in the paranormal world? Did it matter?

"We've got this." Sawyer caressed her back. "It's not my favorite thing to do, but we can do it. We'll get closure for her."

"We will." She exhaled and centered herself. "Marissa? Honey? Can we see you? We won't see bones, I promise."

A moment later, a ghostly form appeared. Marissa floated before them. Her red hair spilled around her shoulders in big curls. She had a sweet smile and wasn't very tall. She kept folding and unfolding her arms. "Sorry."

"You don't have to be sorry." She understood quite well. "It's odd, isn't it?"

"To be here? Yeah."

"To be sort of real," Amanda said. "You've been hiding all these years and here you are, even if only for a few moments."

"Can you help me move on?" Marissa asked.

"We can." Sawyer nodded. "Why don't you tell us what happened?"

Marissa seemed to tuck into herself, like Amanda had done the first time she'd seen Sawyer. Amanda wished she could hug Marissa and offer some reassurance.

"It's okay," Amanda said. "I've been in your shoes, so I know and we'll help you. It's time."

"It's time," Marissa whispered. She composed herself and stood a little taller, or at least as best she could. "I'd been learning my spells, but I wasn't very good at them. I'm terrible at remembering things, but I'd been practicing and had a few friends who were shifters who liked being able to be invisible. That was my best spell."

"Everyone has one," Sawyer said and smiled. "Keep going."

"You're doing fine," Amanda added.

"I could more or less get them invisible so they could do things like scare friends or sneak up on someone. But Terry, he wanted to be invisible to catch his girlfriend doing bad things. I guess she was assumed to be cheating on him. I don't know. I never checked, but I helped him get that invisibility spell going and he did catch her, but it wasn't with another man."

"No?" Sawyer sank onto the rolling stool. "What was she doing?"

Amanda reached out to Marissa, trying to caress her arm, despite more or less just grazing through the form of her arm. "It's okay."

"She had a girlfriend." Marissa shrugged. "I guess she was cheating with a woman and he didn't like it."

"What'd he do?" Amanda asked. She had a sinking feeling about it. "This didn't end well, did it?"

"Not for me. I don't know what he did to her, but if you ever find Charisma Morrison or Delia Snoak, and they're still alive, then they did better than me." Marissa's shoulders sank and she sighed. "He came back to my place and threatened me, then when I thought I had it all settled down, he attacked. I don't know if it shows in what's left of me, but he tore me to shreds." A tear slipped down her cheek.

"Honey." She wanted so much to hug her. "I'm sorry."

"He came to my cottage and I thought I'd explained that she loved him, but she was experimenting, or must've been, and he got upset. I thought I'd talked him down. He seemed calmer, but in hindsight, he'd made his decision. He tore into me and I barely knew what hit me. I saw my body in pieces and saw him stuff me into garbage bags, then felt him dump me in the woods. He tried to bury me -- he was a wolf shifter, so he could dig and he did -- then he abandoned me. I guess no one cared."

"They did." She couldn't be sure they did, but she'd assumed so.

"I know they did. There are posters up in some places with your face, trying to figure out what happened," Sawyer said. "Your cottage burned down and people assumed you were in there, but the police never found evidence of you, so they kept looking."

"What happened to Terry?" Marissa asked. "Did they catch him?"

Amanda wasn't sure. She glanced over at Sawyer.

"They didn't catch him," Sawyer said. "He was

involved in a car accident about ten years ago and died of his injuries."

Another tear slipped down Marissa's cheek. "So nothing ever happened to him? Figures."

"Oh, things happened to him," Sawyer said. "It wasn't sunshine and roses for him. I believe, but Piper could verify for me that Delia and Charisma stayed together. They had a sweet shop for years and I think they sold it to their son. Terry had to see them living their best life and knowing not only that he'd lost Charisma, but that he'd done something terrible. He wasn't right after you disappeared. Hell, I never saw him normal. He would go around town talking to himself and pulling a wagon. He never bathed and rarely ate."

Marissa didn't look convinced, but she nodded. "I see."

"You didn't die in vain. Yeah, you helped someone who wanted it, but it wasn't your fault he saw the truth," Amanda said. "Wouldn't surprise me if he already knew it but wasn't ready to face it."

"I don't know." Marissa bowed her head. "I still feel terrible."

"You're permitted to feel terrible, but you didn't deserve this." Sawyer knocked on the door. "I'll let the detectives know what's going on." He left the room and Marissa shook her head.

"I know it's a lot to think about, but you've told us what's going on. There are cameras watching what you've said and I'm guessing it's being recorded, so it's time for you to move on. You've paid for long enough and you deserve this," Amanda said. "We make choices, but it's not your choice to die. You can move on."

"It's time?" Marissa stared at her. "Finally?"

"Finally." Amanda dipped her head. "Move on."

Marissa stared at her another moment but began to fade. A soft smile curled on her lips. "Thank you," she said, her voice not much above a whisper.

Amanda sank onto the stool and a sense of peace washed over her. She might not have done the best things in life. Might not have been the best person, but she'd done something good. She'd helped someone and had redeemed herself.

Maybe she'd found her purpose and if she could do this with Sawyer, then all the better.

She bowed her head and her eyes watered. She'd finally come home.

Chapter Twelve

Sawyer finished speaking to the detective, happy the conversation with Marissa had been documented and that she'd be able to get closure. He ducked back into the room and paused. "Where is she?"

"She moved on." Amanda wiped her face. "She got peace and could go on to whatever's next."

"Funny how we don't know what that is." Sawyer trailed his fingers over the oak box. "At least she's at rest."

"She is." Amanda blew out a long breath, then stood. "So, what's going to happen to her?"

"We've got to talk to her family," Sawyer said. "They're upset, naturally, but think you and I had something to do with this."

"I was dead at the time, and you were seven." She shook her head. "That makes no sense."

"They don't believe you were dead and think I'm older than I let on." Sawyer waited for the detective to return before he left the cop alone with the wooden box.

"She's being respected and will be protected until final interment," the officer said.

"Thank you," Amanda said and cast a glance back, then left the room.

"Yes, thank you." Sawyer left with her, more than happy to be out of the suffocating space. "We meet with her family over in interrogation one."

"You're serious?" Amanda groaned but kept going. "I thought this would be over soon."

"It will soon." Sawyer directed her to the room in question. Piper was already there, along with Diesel and Chief Hornby. "It's a full house."

"I guess so." Amanda clasped her hands together

and stood beside Sawyer.

A woman with long white hair and another woman with red hair who resembled Marissa sat in the chairs alongside a man with little hair at all.

"This is Marissa's family, Clark, Nella and Mischka. Marissa was the youngest," Hornby said. "They'd like to know what you've learned. We've shown them the video feed from your conversation, but they need confirmation of your role."

"You killed her," Mischka shouted. "It's your fault."

Amanda knelt in front of the family and held her hands out to Nella and Mischka. "I know you're hurting. You've had twenty years to hurt over this and I understand. I shared that woods with her, buried in my own tomb, but she's at peace. She's happy and at peace."

Nella blew her nose and Clark said nothing. Mischka glared. "You know who killed her."

"And now you do, too," Amanda said, her voice soothing. "It's okay."

Sawyer marveled at Amanda's ability to be kind and level-headed. He'd have been a wreck trying to explain this.

"The man who committed this act wasn't arrested and can't be because he's deceased, but we're in the midst of contacting the other players in this situation," Hornby said. "Marissa has been lovingly placed in an oak casket and the department will cover the costs of burial as well as funeral arrangements."

"Thank you," Clark said. "We're grateful."

"I'm not," Mischka snapped. "She was killed and no one's paying for it. We have to accept that no one was jailed for it, and these two charlatans are here claiming it's all okay. It's not. I want a pound of flesh."

"You can't get one from a dead man," Clark said. "Or his family."

Sawyer wanted to say something, but what? He didn't have answers for them. He barely understood the depths of their grief. He'd thought life was terrible after his aunt's passing and he'd known it was coming. They hadn't known Marissa would be taken from them. Sometimes life was unfair.

"I know there isn't much good to come of this and it's not going to make up for your pain, but we've made it our mission from here on out to help the other Marissas around Eerie," Amanda said. "There are some parts of this town and stories going around that need to be sorted out."

"And it'll take our particular gift to unknot those stories," Sawyer said. "Because we want to help the other beings like Marissa. It's her memory that keeps us going."

"You knew her?" Nella asked. She blew her nose. "Did you meet her?"

"Just today," Amanda said.

"Unfortunately, Amanda was the victim of domestic violence years ago and I was only seven when Marissa disappeared," Sawyer said. "But we've met her today and know her. She was a lovely person and it's because of her that we want to help others."

"She would like knowing she was able to help others," Clark said. "That her death wasn't in a vacuum."

"It wasn't." Sawyer shook hands with Clark. "We're honored and humbled to have helped her."

"Thank you," Nella said. She blew her nose again, then stood. "We have to plan her arrangements. Come on, Misch."

"No. I don't like this and I'm not going until I get

an apology. This stupid department didn't do their job. They could've sifted through the remains of the fire. Could've investigated a little deeper and followed Terry more. They could've demanded answers. Could've done something else. They didn't do anything." A swirl of clouds and lightning formed above Mischka's head. She waved her arms and snarled. "They forgot about her."

"She was never forgotten," Hornby said. "Just like we never forgot about Miss Fortune's case, but we didn't have any leads. You can't go anywhere without new leads and we didn't have enough on the force who could handle these kinds of cases to investigate in the alternative methods needed."

"Which is why we're here," Sawyer said. "We're not going to let those cases go cold, if we can help it." He'd found a purpose in his life and wasn't about to squander it.

Mischka's face darkened, but she said nothing.

"My aunt knew Amanda when she was alive and she might have known your sister. But it was my aunt that got me to go looking for Amanda. She must've known I had the ability, but I needed the time to harness that ability. With Amanda's help, I have and we're determined to help as many people as we can to find closure, peace and answers."

"Which is all we can ask," Clark said. "Come along, Misch. You can be upset but can't direct it at them." He slipped his hand around Mischka's arm and helped her to her feet.

"You don't have to love these people, but you have to respect them," Nella said. "Let's go."

Once the family left the room, Piper, who hadn't spoken much, finally did. "Well, that was soul-crushing."

"It wasn't easy, no." Amanda sank onto one of the chairs. "They're upset and it's not fair, what happened, so it makes sense they'd be that way. Can't take that from them, but like Sawyer said, we're determined now to find others and help with the stories of those people."

"You're serious?" Piper asked. "I want you to think it over. Are you willing to join the court and the police to solve these cases? If possible?"

Amanda glanced up at Sawyer, then nodded. "I am, if you are."

"I so am." If he could be with her, then he was happy and home. He'd found his person in Amanda. "Very much so."

"Then welcome to the court and expect to hear from us soon. I'd imagine the force has other cases for you to handle in the meantime, but I'd like you to get some proper clothes and another car. You're part of the upper echelon and expected to look a certain way."

Amanda tensed and Sawyer understood her concern. "What about we ease into that?" Sawyer asked. "We give a little time to change our look or whatever? We're not excited by money or status. We'd like to do our job and have time to be together."

Diesel grunted and Sawyer finally realized he was still in the room. "You be you and do what you do best. Find your footing and if you're happy in your own clothes, then fine. You be you."

He might not have many words and might look scary as fuck behind those glasses as he hulked in the corner, but Diesel had a point. Sawyer shook hands with him. "Thanks."

"I forget I'm not always dealing with people who see my role as a means to give them whatever they want. I also forget there's something fun about wearing a leather jacket, boots and jeans. Something simple about it, too," Piper said. "Yes, please be yourselves, but you'll be getting a bit of a bonus from the court. Can't work for nothing."

"Understood," Sawyer said. He didn't care if they were paid a fortune. He had Amanda and he'd been given the best prize in her. He had his mate.

"Oh," Piper said and held up her hand. "I also detected the change in the electricity around here. Do I sense a pair of mates?"

Diesel grunted again. "You do."

"Not us," she said and elbowed him. "So you two have decided?"

"We did." Amanda managed to stand and grinned. "I wasn't convinced, but we've been through a few things and I know personally that life isn't guaranteed, so I, for one, jumped at the chance at this new future."

"I did, too." Sawyer couldn't imagine not having Amanda around. In the short time they'd been together, he'd grown fond of her. Not only fond. Who was he kidding? He'd fallen in love with her. Did he need more time to fall harder? Sure, but they had that now.

"Good." Piper beamed. "By the way, you've both got a long career ahead of you."

"We do?" Amanda asked and snorted. "Other than you're the Princess, how do you know that?"

"Because you both gained your immortality when you found your mates. You were told -- independently -- that *you will find love divine upon the right time*. Have you not?"

Sawyer met Amanda's gaze and he knew for sure. "We did."

"Sure did," Amanda said. "But that means we're

immortal?"

"Shared magic that's been strengthened. You're of the Fates, both of you, and you've got a mission. You're too important to not have here in town."

"Then that's where we're going to stay," Amanda said.

"Unless a case takes us outside for a bit," Sawyer added. "Then we go where the case leads so we can find closure."

"You will." Piper smiled and waved her hand. "It's time you took a few days to recuperate and relax. There will always be cases, but you're not expected to be on every day. Take a few and get to know each other more. Maybe take a stroll along the river or have a couple date nights. Spend the day in bed. It's up to you."

Sawyer swore his cheeks roasted. He definitely wanted to spend a few days in bed with Amanda, but he'd also like to not be discussing this in front of the Princess.

"We'll do something like that." Amanda grasped Sawyer's hand. "Once I get him to stop being so embarrassed. I get it. We're blue-green and strange. People will fear us."

"Only outside of Eerie. Here, you're pretty well normal." Piper opened a portal for them, straight to the cabin. "Claude's family won't bother you and I'll handle any extra fallout if it comes from Marissa's family. You're in the clear and should go home. Get outta here," she said with a wink.

"You don't have to tell us again." Amanda tugged Sawyer through the portal, then waved to the Princess. "We're ready when you need us."

"Just don't need us for a few days." Sawyer scrubbed his free hand over his face to stop from saying anything else. He didn't need more embarrassment.

"We won't." Piper closed the connection, leaving them alone in the cabin.

"So..." Amanda let go of his hand and hiked herself onto the kitchen counter. "What do we do with all this time?"

"I can think of a few ideas." He slid his arms around her and her legs around his waist. He rested his forehead on hers. "We've got a long time ahead of us and so much exploring to do. Immortal."

"I know." She draped her arms around his shoulders. "I hadn't put that on my dance card. I thought I'd still be languishing in the water right now."

"And I thought I'd be trying to figure out what I'd be doing with myself these days." He stared into her eyes and saw forever. No, he saw his forever. He saw his heart in her hands. "I had no direction."

"And I gave you some?" She brushed her nose along his.

"You gave me that and so much more. I know who I am now and what I want to do." He kissed her lightly, then breathed her in. He didn't give a shit if she was blue or that she had a few years on him. He didn't care if she'd gone through hell. He would if it meant getting to her.

"Let me guess. You want to do me?" She laughed. "Or am I totally off?"

"You're very on." He scooted her closer to him, ensuring she felt the heat of his desire for her. "Want to find out how much?"

"Yes." She kissed him and every synapse in his brain misfired.

He kept her close and his world righted. She

might have thought she was taken with him. He'd fallen in love with her. He'd found his heart with the one person he hadn't thought existed. But that was life. Just when he'd thought he had everything figured out, he realized being taken by and with The Lady of the Lake was the best thing to happen to him.

His. Forever.

Megan Slayer

Megan Slayer, aka Wendi Zwaduk, is a multi-published, award-winning author of more than one hundred short stories and novels. She's been writing since 2008 and published since 2009. Her stories range from the contemporary and paranormal to LGBTQ and white-hot themes. No matter what the length, her works are always hot but with a lot of heart. She enjoys giving her characters a second chance at love, no matter what the form. She's been nominated at the LRC for Best Author, Best Contemporary, Best Ménage, Best BDSM and Best Anthology. Her books have made it to the bestseller lists on various e-tailer sites.

When she's not writing, Megan enjoys art, music, and racing, but football is her sport of choice. She's an active member of the Friends of the Keystone-LaGrange Public library.

Megan at Changeling: changelingpress.com/megan-slayer-a-161

Changeling Press LLC

Contemporary Action Adventure, Sci-Fi, Steampunk, Dark Fantasy, Urban Fantasy, Paranormal, and BDSM Romance available in e-book, audio, and print format at ChangelingPress.com – MC Romance, Werewolves, Vampires, Dragons, Shapeshifters and Horror -- Tales from the edge of your imagination.

Where can I get Changeling Press Books?

Changeling Press e-books are available at ChangelingPress.com, Amazon, Apple Books, Barnes & Noble, Kobo, Smashwords, and other online retailers, including Everand Subscription and Kobo Subscription Services. Print books are available at Amazon, Barnes and Noble, and by ISBN special order through your local bookstores.

ChangelingPress.com

www.ingramcontent.com/pod-product-compliance
Lightning Source LLC
LaVergne TN
LVHW050617100826
845148LV00011B/1621

9781605219639